I0659634

Cloudburst Coffee & Spa

Cloudburst, Colorado series, Book 5

Siobhan Muir

ISBN: 1-947221-07-8
ISBN-13: 978-1-947221-07-9

DEDICATION

Dedicated to all the people who take a chance on love across the country or online and find their HEAs despite the demons encountered. Love wins in the end.

ACKNOWLEDGMENTS

There are many people who have helped me develop this story and I'm so grateful for their help. Emily Drew made sure I wasn't repeating myself, had run-on sentences, or typos. Silver James helped me fix the blurb. Great thanks to Kris Norris for adding her creative magic to make the best cover fitting the tale. Special thanks to Rose Sogioka who beta read this ancient tale to make sure it was up to my usual voice and skill.

CHAPTER ONE

Aiden Westmorland parked his old Chevy pickup behind Mazie's Five and Dime, and wondered for the millionth time what the hell he'd been thinking coming back to Cloudburst. *Too stupid to live, I guess.* He could give any excuse he wanted, but deep down the answer would always be the same. Moira Callahan. She represented true north on his compass star.

He'd hit the outskirts of town just ahead of the snowstorm bearing down on the little Rocky Mountain town. He didn't believe this would be a quick one, despite the town's name. The scent in the wind suggested the storm might last for quite a while. *Lady Cloudburst strikes again.* The nickname made him grin and he turned off the truck before shoving his hands into gloves. The windows immediately fogged up as his warm breath hit the cooling glass, obscuring the view of the frozen parking lot.

Aiden's mind returned to Moira as he got out and locked the truck. He swore he'd seen her standing at the front doors of her family's pub, the Cliffhanger, as he drove through town. The light from the overhang had gilded her hair and left her looking like an angel in the glow. He'd almost driven off the road, but caught himself at the last minute.

It couldn't have been her. He'd heard she'd gone to school at UC Denver for business administration. With that kind of schooling, why the hell would she come back to this little town in the middle of the Rocky Mountains? *Probably for the same reasons you are, moron.* Family, connection, memories.

But he'd really come back for her. Moira had been the only one to calm the incessant voices in his head and removed the desperation of his dark sexual needs. Only pain had the same capability. When he'd left eighteen years ago to protect her from the darkness he carried, he'd turned to tattoos to keep the needs in check. Now he had one full sleeve, a gauntlet on the opposite arm, a large sweeping tribal across his shoulders, and "tramp stamp" over his hips. His shoulders still pleasantly ached from the touch-ups he'd endured just a week earlier.

Pain was good. It kept him anchored and focused on being "normal", and quieted the dark sexual addictions driving him. At least for a little while.

Aiden zipped up his jacket as the cold Cloudburst wind stole all the heat from his body. Damn, he'd forgotten how bitter it could be in the mountains of Colorado. His strides lengthened and he found himself standing beneath the overhang of the Cliffhanger Bar. *Don't go inside. You're asking for trouble.*

But he pushed the door open and sighed in relief as heat flooded over his chilled body. He shouldn't be there, not with all the animosity he'd experienced with Moira's family, but tonight he couldn't stay away. He settled on a stool at the bar.

"What can I get you?"

Aiden glanced up to take in the bartender and recognition dawned as quickly as the man's stats. Kieran Callahan, Moira's younger brother. *Blood type AB positive, BMI twenty-two point four, life expectancy ninety-one point six years, ninety-four percent chance he will marry outside his profession.*

Aiden dragged his eyes away from Kieran and focused on the handwritten menu on the wall. "I'll take a Powder Keg Stout."

"Comin' up." Kieran moved away and Aiden breathed a sigh of relief. He hadn't been recognized yet, but he'd changed a great deal. Hopefully, it'd keep him safe. At least for tonight.

Kieran set a glass and a chilled bottle on the bar in front of Aiden and gave him a neutral smile. Aiden didn't meet his gaze, but focused on the beer.

"How long you in town for, Westmorland?"

Aw, hell, that didn't take long.

"Dunno. Just got back in tonight to visit with family." Aiden took a swig from the bottle. "You got a problem, Callahan?"

"That depends."

"On?"

The younger man scanned the rest of the bar. When no one waved him down for anything, he turned his attention back to Aiden.

"On whether or not you're here to break my sister's heart again." Kieran grabbed some dripping pint glasses and set to drying them with a towel. "See, if you're only here long enough to see the town again and visit with family before you take off to parts unknown, I just as soon you keep your distance from Moira." He stacked the glasses in a cupboard below the bar. "She pined over you for years after you took off in the dead of night."

The news made Aiden's heart twist, but he shrugged. "I got the impression I wasn't real welcome here."

"Yeah, I can see how that might be given the way my older brothers and parents treated you." Kieran nodded with a half-smile curling his lips. "My dad always said never trust a man who won't look you in the eye."

Aiden grunted. He couldn't look anyone in the eyes. He'd see too much and sometimes could even hear their inner thoughts, thoughts not meant to be shared with anyone. Moira had been the only one who'd offered him total silence and peace from the unrelenting statistics when he met her gaze. He could've fallen in love with her for that alone.

"But Moira never had a problem with you and I trust her instincts more than I trust my brothers'. I figure they all had it wrong about you."

"Thanks."

"Yeah, well, back to my earlier point. If you're only here for a two-week spell and then gone again, stay away from my sister."

"And if I'm staying longer?" Aiden had come back to Cloudburst for only one reason. He'd lost the one woman the inner statistician said had a ninety-seven percent chance of being his life partner. *She'd been too young and too naïve then.* But she'd grown up and he wanted to be with his heart.

"I might just let it slip where she lives now." Kieran winked and patted the bar. "You just let me know." He offered a sly grin as he headed over to serve another customer.

Aiden sat rooted to his stool and blinked a few times as the information settled over him. Kieran might help him as long as he remained in Cloudburst. Aiden would stay for as long as it took to convince Moira he loved and wanted her. Then they'd hightail it out of this elitist little town for good. Aiden didn't miss Cloudburst. He missed Moira.

Things might just be looking up for a change. Aiden sipped his beer and listened to the hubbub of the sports games on the TVs in the bar, a smile curling his lips. All he had to do now was find Moira.

CHAPTER TWO

Moira jerked in her chair as her waitress Tess came screaming into her office.

"Ohmygod ohmygod ohmygod."

"Calm down, Tess. What's going on?"

"I just accidentally dumped some coffee on someone and she fell and hit her head and now she's not breathing, and—"

"Whoa, whoa, whoa. What happened?" Moira rose and followed the agitated woman out the door into the Cloudburst Coffee & Spa, her pride and joy.

"It was an accident. She got up and turned right into me, and the coffee spilled." Tess's expression filled with tears. "It burned her, I think, and she tripped over her chair and hit her head on the table…Oh my God, I'm sorry, Moira."

"Take a deep breath, Tess. We'll figure it out." Moira grabbed the cordless phone on the way into the main floor of her coffee shop and headed for the small knot of people standing around a handsome man kneeling over someone on the floor.

"Oh no." Tess twisted her hands in her apron and bit her lip.

Moira felt the breath leave her body as she recognized Sabrina Foxglove out cold, blood staining the floor. "Holy Goddess!"

"I know. It was an accident, I swear." Tears slid down Tess's cheeks.

Before Moira could say anything, Sabrina gasped and opened her eyes. She scanned the crowd around her in startled recognition and some of Moira's tension eased. The man hunched over Sabrina spoke with her a few moments, reassuring her, and Moira wondered who he was. She wanted to ask, but Sabrina's recovery meant more at the moment.

"Is she going to be okay?"

"I think she will be fine, but she needs to go home and rest." The man nodded.

"I have to get to work…" Sabrina struggled to get up, but the handsome stranger gently pressed her down.

"Not today, you don't." Moira shook her head and waved the phone. "I'm calling Mazie and letting her know you won't be in for at least a week."

"Wise choice, madam." The man reached for Sabrina's head to brush aside her hair.

Irritation flitted across Sabrina's face and her shoulders tightened. "You did this on purpose…"

The man reared back as if he'd been slapped. "I did nothing of the sort, Lady Foxglove. It was an accident."

A prickle started behind Moira's eyes and the energy dancing around these two sparkled with attraction and what she'd learned to call "positive potential". Something brewed here between Sabrina and the teal-eyed stranger, and Moira wondered if they knew.

"You just want me to host the…dignitaries. Best way to do that is get me out of my job." Sabrina's voice held anger and the energy urged Moira to speak up.

"I doubt a concussion and a first-degree burn is the best way to get you to host anyone." Moira snorted. "And

Tess said it was an accident when you two bumped and the coffee spilled."

Sabrina narrowed her eyes at her companion, but she let whatever she suspected go.

"Come on, Sabrina. Let's get you home so you can rest." Moira shoved the phone in her pocket and offered her friend a hand.

The man moved in time to pick Sabrina up and Moira couldn't stop her eyebrows from rising to her hairline. *Rather familiar for a stranger, aren't you?* But though Sabrina blushed, she didn't protest as he carried her toward the front door. Moira grabbed Sabrina's purse and followed them.

"How'd you get here, Sabrina? Did you drive?" Moira handed the phone to Tess and stopped them before they left.

"Yes." She squirmed in the man's arms. "Did anyone grab my purse and coat?"

"You have your coat on, hon, and I have your purse." Moira lifted her bag. "You shouldn't be driving with your injury. I'll give you a ride to the hospital in my Jeep." She motioned toward the back entrance to the coffee shop. "Let me just get my keys and coat."

"No, no hospital. I'll be fine."

"Sabrina, concussions are serious."

Sabrina held up her hand. "I'll be fine at home."

Moira's gut contracted. She couldn't let her friend go home so badly hurt, even without the liability to the shop. "Are you sure you'll be all right alone with the girls?"

"Yes, I—"

"She won't be alone. I'll be there to help look after her." The man spoke with such smooth assurance and the positive potential shimmered again.

"No, you don't have to." Sabrina tried to take the reins again, but her companion shook his head.

"I *want* to, Ms. Foxglove. And it's no trouble. I'll be

happy to stay as long as you need."

Most of the female patrons around them sighed with "awwws" and "ohhhhs" at his assertion and Moira nearly laughed out loud at her friend's frustration. Normally she'd be suspicious of a stranger, but the energy around him felt right and she didn't want to upset the Goddess's designs.

"All right then, we'll get you home in a blink." She held out her hand to the man and gave him a smile. "I'm Moira Callahan, owner of the Cloudburst Coffee and Spa, and Sabrina's friend."

"Very nice to meet you, Ms. Callahan. Darius Winterbourne."

Moira led them through the kitchen to the back rooms of the bar and gathered her purse, coat, and keys. *Darius Winterbourne, eh?* She smothered a smile. Hell of a name for him. He smelled like magic, but not the kind she was used to. *Goddess, I know he's the right one for Sabrina.*

Moira hustled them out the door to her snow-dusted Jeep parked beneath a small overhang. Darius set Sabrina in the back seat and climbed in beside her while Moira stepped out to sweep the windshield. An old envy rippled through her as she watched Darius fuss over her friend. It had been a long time since Moira had gathered such attention. *And an even longer time since the one I wanted gave it to me.* Eighteen years, to be exact. She shook her head and picked up her phone.

"Talia, I have to drive Sabrina Foxglove home."

"So that's why Tess came in all panicked. What happened?"

"Just an accident, but Sabrina hit her head."

"Oh glory! Is she okay?"

"I think so. She has a pretty good bump on her head, but she has someone to look out for her so I won't be gone long." Moira eyed her passengers through the windshield and shoved her envy away. "On second thought, I don't know how long I'll be. The roads are pretty slick with the rain on ice, but I shouldn't be more than a couple of hours tops."

"Okay. I'll cover the shop. See you soon."

"Thanks, Talia. Bye." Moira hung up and settled behind the wheel of her Jeep. "All ready?"

"Yes." Darius sat back and nodded. Sabrina turned her face to the window as she slumped against the seat, nodding.

Moira backed out and made sure the fan pushed heat into the cabin as they drove through town. She tried to ignore the attention Darius gave Sabrina. *I want some.* She mentally shook her head. *These are dangerous thoughts. You know where they lead and it's never good.*

Despite the warning, her mind filled with memories. *Oh, knock it off. He's gone and he's not coming back.* The summer she'd been sixteen and never been kissed, at least not until he came around.

Aiden.

But he'd left that fall, two years older and college bound, and she never saw him again. *So why do I keep pining over him?* Moira smothered a growl and stopped her thoughts before they wandered into the Forbidden Zone. It was the place reserved for memories she never wanted to look at again. Too many dark things resided there for her to face today.

When they crossed the railroad tracks, Moira forced her attention back to the world around her. She'd get Sabrina home and settled with Darius to watch out for her.

Moira glanced in the rearview mirror. "I'm sure she has my phone number somewhere at home, but you can call me if you need anything. Or ask Matilda to call."

"Who is Matilda?" Darius focused his unnerving gaze on hers in the mirror.

"She's Sabrina's babysitter. I'm sure she'll help you when you get her inside."

"Very well."

When they pulled up in Sabrina's driveway, Moira scanned his expression and gave him a half smile. *Tenderness there already. Well well well.* "Need some help getting her inside?"

"No, I'm sure we'll be well. Thank you for your help getting her home."

"You're welcome. Call me if you need anything."

"I will. Thank you, Ms. Callahan."

He got out of the Jeep and walked around to help Sabrina. Moira watched them as he led Sabrina up the walk to the front door where Matilda greeted them. Moira couldn't hear the conversation, but given Matilda's hand motions, she suspected the woman neared hysterics. *Good luck, Darius. You're gonna need it with her.*

Moira shook her head and backed out of the driveway, turning her attention to her "to-do" list. It didn't include pining over a personal connection with someone, much less a man with that kind of magical energy swirling through him. The last time had been a near-fatal disaster. *Not going there. Not thinking about it.*

Moira took a deep breath and resettled her shoulders. She was fine. She was safe, had her business, her overprotective family, and her best friend. Life was good. She didn't need anything else. *Leave the heavy-duty romance to the likes of Sabrina Foxglove and Darius Winterbourne. I'm good the way I am.*

Rounding a corner, her heart jumped into her throat when she caught sight of an old, rusted Chevy pickup, nosing the barbed wire fence like a curious puppy. Moira skidded to a stop and gaped, her mind skipping like a broken record. *Oh my glory, oh my glory, oh my glory...*

Aiden's pickup.

No, no, it can't be his.

Easing her 4x4 Jeep to the side of the road, Moira squinted to see through the glass of the pickup's windshield reflecting sky. She turned off the engine and listened.

Silence greeted her as her windows fogged up with her warm exhalations. She debated getting out, arguing she shouldn't even be curious, but helpless to the lure of the old truck. *It just looks like his old truck.* She pushed her door open and got out. *Right down to the rusted heart we carved in the front fender.* Shit.

Moira scanned the quiet road and the trees barely starting to bud as spring tried to show its face. The snow had stopped and a thin layer of white blanketed the roof and bed of the truck. But the hood remained bare. *The truck's still warm. Where's the driver?* She let her senses drift, searching the energies for a human occupant, but only forest calm came back to her.

I should really get back to the shop and just forget about this. It's not Aiden.

But curiosity gripped her body and she took the time to look for footprints in the newly-fallen snow. She eased around the vehicle, noting one tire mired deep in the new spring mud under the snow. *Gotten stuck. Wonder where he went?*

The driver had probably walked back toward town, but Moira searched the snow for prints and found a fading trail heading into the woods. *Why wouldn't the driver go for help?* She checked the charge on her phone before locking her Jeep and following the prints into the trees. She knew these woods well enough to help anyone lost in them.

It might be April, but that doesn't mean spring's here yet. She shook her head. The weather changed on a dime and another snow storm could blow in. She'd have to find this person fast before they became stranded. *At least if it freezes we'll be able to get the truck out.*

Moira inhaled the scents of the slumbering forest. The air smelled fresh and clean with a hint of new life waiting for the shift toward warmth. She shoved her hands into her pockets and listened to the crunch of her feet in the snow. The soft sounds mixed with the rattle of the branches in the wind over her head and soothed some of her concerns. She'd find the driver, guide him back to his truck, tow him out of the mud, and send him on his way. Then she could get back to her coffee shop and leave all thoughts of Aiden where they belonged—in the past.

But as the trail of footprints continued higher up the mountain her curiosity turned to concern. *Where is this guy going?* She followed the tracks all the way to an old mine site against a wall of rhyolite rock. The pink stone was stained red under the wet snow and Oro Creek dropped in a spectacular fifteen foot waterfall beyond the old mine shed ruins. The water filled the small clearing with joyful sounds and spread in a rippling pond shimmering in the wan light. The sight always filled her with wonder, but today something else stopped her feet and her breath.

Beneath icy cascade of water stood a man, naked, scrubbing his body under the spray. A huge elaborate tattoo covered his back from the shoulders to waist, and a matching sleeve coated his right arm. Dark hair, nearly black in the wet morning light, slicked down to his muscular shoulders and more of the robust muscles framed his lithe body.

Holy Goddess of the Valley. Moira damn near swallowed her tongue. *I want one.*

The sentiment surprised her. She hadn't wanted a man in a couple years, not like this visceral reaction. The man in the water turned and showed her his chest. Ridged muscles marched all the way down his torso, following a line of dark hair from his belly button into the water. *Sweet Goddess, he has a happy trail.* He wiped the water from his face and opened his eyes, his brilliant blue gaze locking on her.

Aiden.

Shock radiated straight through Moira and she swore her jaw hit the snowy ground. The gangly uncomfortable teenager had been replaced by an athletic man with strength and confidence in all of his moves. A half-smile curled his lips as he strode from the water, his nipples standing taut on his chest.

Moira could no more stop her gaze from dropping to his groin than she could stop the water in the falls. Dark hair led from his belly straight to his balls and despite the cold, she appreciated the size of his package. *Hell, if that's him cold...*

Aiden sauntered to his clothes left on a boulder beside the creek and scrubbed his body down with a towel, giving her a lovely view of his taut ass and back. Moira swallowed hard as she took in the intricate back panel tattoo of a Celtic knotted raven. She wanted to trace the lines with her fingers. Hell, even with her tongue. *There's no revenge quite like a man showing off for you.*

She realized she'd been staring when the view disappeared under his shirt and she'd already missed him pulling on his pants. *Get a hold of yourself.* Moira shook her head and squared her shoulders just as he turned around, shrugging into his jacket.

He met her eyes boldly, shocking her again. "Hello, Moira."

"Aren't you cold?" Not her brightest comeback, but his reappearance, naked, combined with his confidence threw her off balance.

"It definitely gives a whole new meaning to chilling out." He chuckled. "What brings you out here to the old Durango Mine?"

"I found your truck." Moira waved back the way she'd come. "Are you okay?"

"I'm fine. Are you? You seem a little flustered."

Understatement of the year. "Uh, yeah, okay. Right. Okay."

He laughed, a sound remarkably lighthearted and rich, and excited joy filled her chest. She had the unreasoning need to hear that sound more often. "Are you sure? You sound undecided."

Moira shook her head. "What are you doing here?"

He raised his eyebrows as he sat to tie his boots. "Taking a bath. It's been a long road to get here."

Heat suffused her cheeks and she shrugged. "Sorry. That came out wrong. I'm just really surprised to see you. It's been a while and I haven't heard from you, and now you're here." She frowned. "Why is that?"

"That I'm here?"

"That I haven't heard from you in all this time."

He dropped his gaze to his laces. "I went to college."

Moira snorted. "Where? In a remote village in the Amazon where they don't have computers, cell phones, or telegraph machines?"

He huffed a laugh, but his shoulders tightened and he didn't look up. "I'd forgotten your sarcasm. You've gotten better at it."

"I have five brothers. It was self-defense." But hurt and anger roiled in her gut. "Seriously, Aiden. Why didn't you write or call or hell, even find me on some social media sites? It's not like I got married and my name changed."

She wanted a good explanation. He'd been Shanghaied to serve in a foreign military unit or joined a biker gang. Maybe he'd fallen into a religious cult or drafted into a secret assassin organization that didn't allow for outside contact. Anything but he just didn't think her worth the effort to connect.

Aiden sighed and stood, his expression fading into a stoic mask. "Your family made it pretty clear they didn't want me to have anything to do with you. I thought it would be better if I left."

"That's it? That's your explanation for never contacting me again? My *family*?" Moira scowled. "I understand why you didn't try while I was in high school, but not for the entire time. I moved away and lived on my own. Why didn't you try to contact me then?"

"Why didn't you?" He threw the question back at her as he crossed his arms over his chest.

"I did."

She'd searched every place she could think to look. All the online social networks yielded nothing and no one would tell her which college he'd attended. She'd considered paying a private investigator to find him, but in the end decided it wouldn't be worth the expense. It appeared he'd wanted nothing to do with her.

She'd cried on her brother Kieran's shoulder for months after Aiden left, and she continued to vent her frustration for the first few years after she moved away. Eventually, she let Aiden go. Now he stood before her in all his adult glory, and threw her world upside down.

"Did you?" His lips quirked into a sexy half smile. "I figured you wrote me off."

I did, you jackass, after six years. "Why are you here, Aiden?"

"I came back to see family."

Anger curled in her chest. Family. Not her. "Then I'll leave you to it. Sorry to interrupt your bath."

Moira spun and marched back the way she'd come. *It's your own damn fault, you know. If you'd just left his truck alone you wouldn't have run into him at all.* It wasn't strictly true—Cloudburst wasn't large enough to hide him long, but she wouldn't have seen him today. At least her anger kept her warm as her boots marked a new trail in the snow. She should have just left painful enough alone.

"Moira, wait!" Aiden's voice hit her ears before his running footsteps, but she ignored him. Stick a fork in her, 'cause she was done with him for good. She didn't need another eighteen years of pining to get a clue.

"Please, Moira. Stop." A gloved hand wrapped around her bicep and tugged at her. She swung toward Aiden, her lips peeling back from her teeth in a snarl.

"What for, Aiden?" She spat the words with all the

weight of her anger and hurt. "You're here to see family, which I'm not. Sorry to trouble you." She fought the tears of frustration. *Why the hell am I so upset over this? He left nearly two decades ago.* She jerked her arm to dislodge him, but he held fast. "Let me go."

"No, not until you hear me out."

"What's to hear? You said your piece. You didn't try to contact me and you used my family as an excuse. And now you're using yours." She shook her head. "Let me go."

Aiden tightened his lips and pulled her closer to him until they stood face to face. He'd never been as tall as her brothers, but he fit her just perfectly and she met his brilliant blue gaze wishing she could scratch his eyes out.

"I'm sorry, Moira." He squeezed her arms to emphasize his sentiment. "I'm not saying any of this right. I've never been great with words." He grimaced and shook his head. "Yes, I initially stayed away because your family made it clear I wasn't welcome. My mom really wanted me to get my degree and she kept me updated on what you were doing."

"How would she know? I don't even know your mother."

"Your mom does. The point is I knew you were doing fine without me and by the time I graduated, you'd left Cloudburst." He shrugged. "There was no reason to come back here."

"So, you'd only contact me if I was still in Cloudburst? What the hell?" Moira jerked out of his grip and stood back. "I looked for you everywhere I went. But no one had a record of you, not even Google. So I let it go. I let you go because it was pretty obvious you'd moved on."

Aiden said nothing for a few heartbeats and betrayal wormed its way through her mind. How could he? They'd had a connection, one she would've liked to explore and foster. *Guess he didn't feel the same and I'm like some infatuated teenager. So pathetic.* The truth hurt more than the abandonment.

"Good to see you again, Aiden. Have a nice time with your mom and I wish you all the luck in the world."

Moira shot him a plastic smile and continued her retreat. Pain ate at her from the inside, but she forced it back into the box where she'd stuffed all her feelings for Aiden Westmorland. *It's better this way. He can't break my heart if I don't give it to him.*

"Moira." Aiden's voice cracked like a whip and she froze, her heartbeat ratcheting up from sorrow to excitement. How the heck could he make her stop with just her name?

His boots crunched in the snow behind her, each step sending a shiver of delight up her spine. *I haven't seen him in two decades and he still makes me sweat. What is wrong with me?*

Aiden came around and stopped in front of her, reaching out to lift her chin until her gaze met his. Bright blue irises full of churning emotion hit her and stole her breath. He tilted his head and rubbed one thumb over her lower lip, sending cream flooding her panties. *Something's wrong with me.*

"I can't change the past, I can only start from now, and right now, I'm here. I'm not going anywhere." His lips quirked into a half smile. "While I did come back to see my mom, my main motivation was to see you. I want you, and I'm not going anywhere without you. You're my Lady Cloudburst. Give me the chance to show you I'm serious."

She snorted. "Those are pretty words, Aiden. I guess I'd believe them more if you'd made an effort sooner." She shook her head. "I grew up and I stopped believing liars and players when I was in my twenties. I'm too old for that shit."

Anger seared her from his gaze, his cheeks flushing. "You think I'm a player?"

She raised an eyebrow, not impressed with his fit of

temper. "Why else would you come back here after years away without a word and say, 'Hey babe. Missed ya. Let's get together now that I'm at loose ends and my most recent lover kicked me to the curb.' That's it, isn't it? Life got too hard so you came back here to your hometown and thought the girl you'd left behind would just take you in? Fuck you. I'm not that desperate."

That might not have been completely true, but she couldn't let him know her heart would crumble so easily.

"My lover didn't kick me to the curb and life didn't get too hard for me." Aiden actually growled, impressing her more than she wanted to admit. "I came back here to see you because I realized you were the one I'd wanted all along, and I finally have something to offer more than just my sparkling personality. I want you, and want to be with you, Moira."

She wanted to believe him. She wanted him to mean everything he said. But she didn't know him anymore, and he'd become a smooth talker for sure. *People change drastically in two decades. I've changed drastically.*

"Why?"

"Why what?"

"Why should I give you the chance? You've had plenty of time to make an effort."

"And I'm here now."

"Why now? What's so special about now?" A rancid thought arrowed through her mind and her gut sank as anger rose. "Oh my glory, this is because of my inheritance and my new business, isn't it? Holy shit, you've come back to court me because I now have something of value to give to you." A scowl pulled at the corners of her mouth. "That's sickening."

"What? No, I'm not here because you have money or a business." His scowl dwarfed hers in its ferocity. "I don't need your money. I'm here for you."

"Right, because you've made so much effort to contact

me before this." She lifted her chin out of his hand. "Give me a break. I may have been naïve when I was sixteen, but life has taught me a few things, Aiden. Not buying."

"And I'm not selling you a load of shit." His growl rattled through her chest. "I don't need money. I have my own."

"But you drive that beat up truck." She stepped back and scanned his clothes. "Those aren't exactly designer duds you got on."

His lips quirked into a small smile. "The truck is paid off and it runs like a bear. Tags and insurance are cheaper on it, too." He tugged at the hems of his jacket. "And clothes are clothes. Just because I've had them awhile doesn't mean they're garbage. My wardrobe doesn't dictate my financial status. No point in getting rid of perfectly good clothing."

"See, there. Right there. That tells me you're looking to save money."

"Everyone wants to save money, Moira. Social trappings don't equate to financial stability." Aiden met her gaze and she swore he saw deep down into her. *Oh, Goddess, please don't look there.* "I don't need your money. I'm not here to take anything from you. I just want to try again with you now that we're old enough to make our own decisions. No one can tell us how to be or who to love."

"Love?" Sadness made her heart clench. "We haven't known each other long enough to talk about love."

"We've known each other for eighteen and a half years."

"For most of which you've been gone and know nothing about me. That doesn't count."

"It does count. Give me the chance to learn about the woman you are now."

Moira clenched her teeth. "At risk of sounding like a three-year-old, why?"

Aiden grinned. "Because you're just as curious about me as I am about you. Don't you want to know how I've changed?"

Desperately. The curiosity ate at her like rabid weasels, but she wasn't willing to give him so much power over her. *He already has enough, dammit.*

"Tell you what, let's just start with friends and go from there. How long are you planning to stay?"

"To visit family, not too long. But to get to know you again?" He smacked her with a sultry smile full of naughty, sexy memories. "As long as it takes to show you I'm serious." He slid the backs of his fingers over her cheek as his gaze bored into hers. "I've missed you, Moira."

His last statement snapped her out of her romantic daze and she snorted. "Really? You're going with that line after all the years you didn't try to connect? Calling bullshit, Aiden." She shook her head and held up her hand to stop his next barrage of explanation. "Come on. I'll help you get your truck unstuck."

"How do you know I didn't just park it like that?"

"Because of the deep furrow the tire is buried in and the large mud spatter on the fender." She jabbed herself in the chest as she led the way back to their vehicles. "Hello. Local."

Amusement rumbled out of his chest and Moira tried not to enjoy it. *You're mad at him, remember?* She couldn't help her smile as they tromped through the snow toward the road and some of her tension lifted off her shoulders. *It's okay to just enjoy his company.* She could do a friendship with him without the attachment, right?

"So where are you staying while in town?"

"Last night I stayed at the Waterwheel Inn because I got in so late, but I was planning on staying with my mom if she has room." He spoke in a mild voice, but his expression said he'd rather chew broken glass.

"Not looking forward to that?"

Aiden grimaced. "I love my mom, but she'll mother-hen me to death. She'll worry I'm not eating enough or I'm not getting enough sleep." He sighed. "Eighteen years in her care was plenty for me. I don't really want to stay with her more now that I can choose something else."

Moira narrowed her eyes. She imagined it would be a pain in the ass to stay with his mom. *Hell, I'd move heaven and earth not to stay with mine.* And given the state of his truck, he might be short on cash. Despite her anger, she didn't mind sharing her place with him. As friends.

A spark of hope and irrational excitement bloomed in Moira's chest. "You know, I have an extra bedroom. You're welcome to stay there if it doesn't work out with your mom."

Aiden's brilliant blue gaze slammed into her and she stumbled a little as they walked. "I'd like that a lot, actually. Thanks."

"Anything for a friend." She waved her hand, downplaying her thrill. "I just need to clean up the guest room a little."

"Friends, right." A sultry smile curled his lips. "Let's get my truck unstuck then I can help you with anything you need, Moira."

Does that include relieving my sexual frustrations?

Moira sealed the words behind her teeth and marched on down the muddy road, following her footprints backwards. Aiden walked beside her, his presence both thrilling and unnerving. The scent of warm cedar filled the space between them and she tried not to be obvious about inhaling. *Stop it.*

They found his truck where he'd left it, covered with an inch of snow and the tire frozen in the mud. Moira snorted with rueful humor. Why had she offered to get him out of this again? "Forgot what spring's like around here, haven't you?"

Aiden gave her a rueful smile, warming her inside her

jacket. "Yeah. I expected it to be frozen still."

"Not this late in the year." Moira glanced around for something to use for purchase. "You got a shovel in that old thing?"

"Yep. Never leave home without it."

"And where's that?" She scrounged around for a large piece of Ponderosa bark still solid enough to stay together

"Where's what?" Aiden's muffled voice came from the cab, his body hidden except for his ass flexing against the worn denim of his jeans. Moira forgot to breathe for a moment.

"Moira, are you okay?" Aiden looked over his shoulder.

She blinked, swallowing hard. "Uh, yeah. Sorry. So, where's home?" She ducked her head and bent to look at how much they'd need to dig the tire out.

"Were you staring at my ass?"

Moira snorted and hoped her blush didn't translate. "You wish. You got that shovel yet?"

"Here." He handed it to her. "And home is any place I need it to be."

"This place is mine. Busybody family and all, it's still the place that holds my heart."

"The place holds your heart? Not a person?"

She met his gaze solemnly. "Not in a long time."

He nodded. "I'm sorry I left without a word all those years ago."

Moira shook her head. "Don't worry about it. It's in the past, like you said. Not worth holding on to. Why don't you dig and I'll get the bark under the tire?"

Aiden took the shovel and set to work. Moira stood back and watched, but her mind traveled far from their spot in the woods. Memories of searching through every city she visited filled her mind's eye and the hollow sensation returned to her chest.

Ugh, go away. She shook her head and tried to find

something else to think about.

"What about you? What have you been doing while away from Cloudburst?"

He nailed her with his intense gaze, the brilliant blue blazing against the white snow. "A little of this, and a little of that. But it wasn't enough. Couldn't live anywhere very long without my heart."

"Cloudburst has your heart?" Hope sparked inside Moira's chest. *Maybe he's here to stay.* She tried not to pay it any heed. *Don't set yourself up for a fall.*

Aiden grimaced as he tipped his head. "Yeah."

Something about the way he said it seemed off, but she refused to go down that road. *You promised yourself you wouldn't pine over him anymore.*

"I can understand that." She allowed her gaze to rest on his ass again as he turned back to digging. "There are days I hate this town with everybody knowing everybody, and my family always butting in. But I left and I liked the other places I lived even less." The hollow feeling returned as she remembered living in Chicago, Salt Lake City, and Denver. "Everyone was so busy and lost and scared and uncomfortable. Reading them all the time made me sick to my stomach, and in the end I had to come back here. Even though my family gets into my business more often than not, the energy here is..." Moira waved her hands in little circles. "Quieter. More settled. Does that make sense?"

Aiden coughed a laugh filled with unspoken pain. "More than you know." He straightened. "I think it's ready for the bark."

"Oh, right. Here." She trudged around him and helped him fit the drier piece of wood under the tire. "That should do it."

"Let me start 'er up and see if it worked."

Moira raised her chin. "It'll work."

He winked and pulled out his keys as he strode to the cab. *Why can he stride and I trudge in this stuff?* The truck

23

rumbled to life, the exhaust steaming in the snowy air.

"Ready?" Aiden said.

"Yeah. Let 'er rip."

He threw it into gear and the wheels shifted into motion. The tire spun in short jerky movements, twisting the bark, but Moira shoved it back with her foot, and the truck lurched. She jumped out of the way as the metal beast shot backwards.

"Keep going! It's still soft for another twenty feet." Moira waved him past her and he kept the truck moving until he'd reached solid ground. Too bad her heart couldn't find such comfort.

Aiden waved her closer and she shoved her melancholy thoughts away as she skirted the mud to his truck.

"Can I give you a ride to your Jeep?" Those blue eyes still stole her breath.

"No, it's right there over the fence. Can you find your way back to the road from here?"

Aiden dipped his head. "Yeah, not a problem. Is that invitation to stay in your guest room still valid?"

"Yeah, why wouldn't it be?"

"Sometimes they die too soon after they're offered. I just wanted to be sure." He grimaced. "I know I let you down by going off the grid for so long, but I intend to make it up to you."

"Let's just start with friends and go from there. Stop by the Cloudburst around five or so. We don't close until eight, but you can help me clean out the guest room."

"Sounds good." He paused and scanned her face once more. "It really is great to see you again, Moira."

She ignored the happy-dancing her heart executed at his words. "A free place to stay will do that, yeah."

He laughed. "That must be it. See you around five."

She patted his door and headed for her own Jeep as he backed down the snowy dirt road. *Friends are good.* Less heartache, less attachment, and she could learn about him as the man he was now, not what she thought she remembered. *It's been a long time and we've both changed.*

Moira climbed through the wire of the fence and unlocked her Jeep. She didn't know what had kept Aiden from meeting people's eyes, but she'd recognized his defense mechanism. She'd had to shut down her own abilities when in the bigger cities, drowning them out with alcohol first, then too much food, and eventually hard-core sex. She didn't go for pain, but she liked bondage and the power exchange of BDSM.

Yeah, until my Dom got off on spanking me so hard it left bruises and he couldn't hear the safeword. It was her hard-limit and she'd broken up with Lenny Corsica the next day.

Black panic rose in her chest at the thought of him. She clamped her hands to the steering wheel and shut her eyes in an effort to hold it off. *He has no power over me. He has no power over me.*

The mantra helped push back the dark hole ready to suck her down into the depths of despair. Lenny had scoffed at her reasons for walking away and told her she'd be back in a few days when she needed her fix.

Moira swallowed against angry tears. He'd almost been right. But she'd gotten her shit together, quit her job, and moved back to the quiet mountain atmosphere of Cloudburst.

Yeah, ran home to mama, so to speak.

She took deep breaths, calming her racing heart and the swelling shame. "I'm happier here. Stronger. Safer."

Thank the Goddess Aiden had left before she followed the old line of thought. *Aiden doesn't have your kinks and doesn't need to know your issues.* She hated admitting she'd run from Lenny rather than standing her ground, but she hadn't trusted him not to hurt her again. And she'd feared the overwhelming press of negative emotions from the city would drive her back to him.

Moira had been home for two years now, but the idea of seeing Lenny again still froze her blood and sank her stomach. She liked her loving rough, but he'd liked it painful and she didn't go for that. *He doesn't live here and he didn't want me enough to come after me. I'm safe. He has no power over me.*

She'd repeated it hundreds of times, but the fear never really left.

Her breath fogged the windows of her Jeep as she searched for calm. In. Out. In. Out. Every exhalation took some of her anxiousness with it. Eventually she found a measure of calm to allow her to drive home. *Yeah, but you can't see out your windows.* Moira cranked the defrost and waited for the glass to clear.

She took the time to check her phone for messages, but the screen showed nothing more than a few new emails and she left them for later. When the windows cleared, she pulled back onto the road and headed into town. Her mind returned to Aiden and she hoped he made it to the blacktop again.

He said he'd come back for her and her inheritance hadn't mattered. Time would tell if he meant it. *But you're gonna give him that time, aren't you?* She would. She was curious about him and what had changed. He'd certainly become more bold and sure of himself.

Moira made it back to the coffee shop and parked in her spot. She'd see Aiden later and let him stay a few nights. *It's okay to start over as friends, right? I don't have to give him my heart.* She had the sneaking suspicion she'd never really gotten it back, but she shoved the idea aside and focused on work.

"Hey, there you are. Is Sabrina Foxglove okay?" Talia greeted Moira as she hung up her jacket.

"I think so, yeah. Mr. Winterbourne is watching over her."

"Mr. Winterbourne?"

"The guy who was with her. You know, tall, teal eyes, smelling of magic?"

Talia raised her eyebrows.

"Oh, right, you didn't see him." Moira laughed to hide her envy. "She'll be okay. I'm fairly certain he'll make sure she's fine. I told him to call me if he needs any help."

"Good." Talia sighed. "You don't think she'll file charges against us or Tess, do you?"

"What?" Moira blinked. She hadn't even thought of the legal ramifications. "No, no, Sabrina isn't that kind of person. She knows accidents happen. In fact, I think she'd blame Mr. Winterbourne first."

"Why?"

"There's something going on between them, but I have the gut feeling it's going to work out well for them."

"I hope so." Talia shook her head and laughed. "Your gift is freaky sometimes. Oh, hey, I wanted to let you know some guy dropped by with a bouquet of flowers for you."

"What?" Moira scanned the coffee shop. "Where?"

"He came in just a bit ago with them." Talia led Moira over to the front counter. "Aren't they pretty?"

A large vase held a glorious mixture of pink roses, white carnations, burgundy Gerbera daisies, and purple grape hyacinth. The floral scents mingled with the usual coffee and cinnamon smells of her shop and Moira gaped at the lovely display. A small white envelope lay nestled between the blooms.

"Wow. Who did you say brought these?" She picked up the card and opened it. The thing resonated in her hands with an odd vibration.

"Slender guy, dark hair, not too tall." Talia tilted her head. "What does the card say?"

"Making up for lost time." No signature, just the statement. *Weird.*

"Oooh, romantic."

Could Aiden have beaten me here to deliver the flowers? If so, he'd picked all her favorites. But something didn't ring true about it, and the whole vase felt off. Moira didn't recognize the writing, but it had been years since she'd seen anything he'd written.

"Wow. These are amazing. Did the guy leave his name?"

"No. He just said they were for you and he'd be back later."

Aiden had agreed to show up that evening. Maybe he'd had them stashed in his truck. *Then why didn't he give them to me then?* She hadn't seen them in the cab when they dug it out of the mud. The flowers had to be from someone else.

"They sure are pretty." Moira shoved the vase aside and tried to refocus on work, but the vibrations coming off the vase rattled her.

"So, do you have any sexy plans tonight I should know about?" Talia winked as she shoved some of the used coffee litter into the trash.

"No." Moira laughed. "Don't be fooled by the flowers. I don't know who they're from."

"Do you want to catch movie, then? I heard the new Thor is awesome."

"I can't go with you tonight. I have a friend coming over."

"Oh, a *friend*, huh?"

"Not like that." Moira grimaced. Talia already knew the story. "Aiden showed up today."

"What?" All the humor left Talia's face. "Oh no. No, no, no. You can't do this to yourself, Moira. What is he doing back in town?"

"He said he's here to reclaim his heart and visit family."

"What the hell does that mean?"

Moira shrugged, unwilling to share and endure her friend's derision. "He didn't say. But he wants to spend some time getting to know me better."

Talia's eyes narrowed. "You don't think the flowers are from him, do you?"

"I don't know. Did the guy who came in have any tattoos?"

"No. He was smartly dressed. You know, like a businessman with suit and tie sort of clothes."

"That's definitely not Aiden, then."

"Oooh, a *secret* admirer." Talia winked. "How exciting."

Moira laughed, but didn't touch the flowers again. They smelled wonderful and looked great, but something about them unsettled her. She closed the door of the office and shoved the eerie feeling aside. *They're just flowers.* But she couldn't ignore the itching unease between her shoulder blades.

CHAPTER THREE

Aiden parked his truck behind Mazie's Five and Dime for the second time in two days and cracked his neck before he got out. Visiting Mazie was an exercise in patience. Each year he made a resolution to spend more time with her, but life would get in the way and phone calls seemed enough. *At least for me.* He suspected Mazie had a different perspective.

Mothers always do.

He stepped through the door out of the snowy wind and smiled at the joyful tinkle of the bell above his head. Scents of cardboard and floor wax filled his nose as he spotted Mazie behind the counter.

"Aiden?"

"Hi, Mom."

Her smile lightened her face and made her appear several years younger. "When did you get into town? I didn't know you were coming back." *Ever again* hung in the air, but neither of them would say it aloud as she came around the counter for a hug.

Despite his misgivings about seeing her, her hug settled some of his trepidation and he relaxed for the first time since he'd driven into town. *Feels like home.* He ignored the tiny voice saying it was the first time he'd felt this way in decades.

"I got in late last night. I didn't call because I didn't want to wake you."

She snorted as she pulled back. "No matter. I'm just glad you're here now. How long are you in town?"

Aiden scanned the store, looking for inspiration—or absolution—in the shelves full of candy boxes and cigarette cartons. *No help for it. Gotta tell her the truth.*

"For a little while. I don't have any immediate plans to leave."

Mazie tipped her head. "Just going to see how it goes, right?"

He grinned. "Something like that."

She nodded. "You got a place to stay?"

"Yeah. Moira Callahan offered me her guest room."

Mazie blinked and a curious smile curled her lips. "The same Moira Callahan you were sweet on all those years ago?"

"That's right."

"I thought her family wanted you to steer clear of her." Some of the same hurt Aiden experienced filtered into his mother's expression. "They were pretty adamant as I recall."

Aiden nodded. "They were, but we're in our thirties now, Mom. Moira and I can make our own decisions. Besides, it's only as friends."

Mazie snorted. "Is that your choice or hers?"

"Hers." He grimaced as his mother gave him a knowing look. "She's still pretty mad at me for not calling or connecting with her."

"Ya think?" Mazie shook her head. "I can't imagine why she'd be upset when you didn't bother to contact her. I mean, it's not as if she liked you all that much, is it?"

Aiden sighed. "I know, I know. She reminded me I've been a moron and a jackass. You don't have to add your condemnation."

"But she's letting you stay with her?"

"As a friend."

"That's quite a transformation from furious." Mazie eyed him over carefully, taking in the wet ends of hair. "Did you fall into the creek or something? Let me get you a towel and a warm cup of coffee." She paused and tipped her head. "Although the best coffee in Cloudburst is at the Cloudburst Coffee & Spa, Moira's new place."

"I'll try there next."

He followed her into the back and up the stairs to her apartment. She kept it cleaner than he remembered from when he lived with her. But the same scents of lavender and furniture polish floated in the small, neat rooms.

When she returned with a fluffy hunter-green towel, her expression had clouded.

"What's wrong, Mom?"

"Just be careful of Moira, Aiden. Her family is a very powerful influence in this town."

Aiden's initial reaction to her warning was to laugh, but his mother had lived in this town longer than he and had seen the Callahans' machinations. She'd bore the brunt of it a few times. It shouldn't surprise him she'd go all mama-Bengal-tiger to protect him. She'd done that a few times, too.

Aiden nodded. "I remember the Callahans' influence. But here's the thing—it's been almost two decades and Moira's a woman now. We can make our own decisions about who we want to be with."

Mazie snorted and raised an eyebrow. "This is their only 'little girl', and they don't take a lack of control over said girl very well. You should've been here when she demanded her inheritance and said she wanted to start her own business. Her family just about lost it entirely. They even went so far as to see if they could legally keep her from building any business that remotely resembled the

Cliffhanger Bar."

Mazie shook her head as Aiden scrubbed the towel over his hair and shoulders. "It was sad how controlling they wanted to be." A smile curled her lips. "But that woman has guts and she stuck with it. Now she has the most popular coffee shop in Cloudburst, and she's only been open six months."

"And her family's still complaining?" Could they really be that blind to Moira's abilities?

"No, they were mollified when she didn't choose to serve alcohol." Mazie shrugged. "I think they worried both that they'd lose business to her, affecting her brothers' livelihoods, and she wouldn't do well, affecting hers. It's an odd way of doing things, but parents are rather particular about their kids."

Aiden dropped the towel on the back of a chair and laughed. "Yeah, Mom, I've noticed *that* trait, for sure."

"The point I'm trying to make is the Callahans might still have something to say about you dating their daughter." Mazie paused, raising an eyebrow. "Have you seen any of them yet?"

"Yeah, I stopped at the Cliffhanger when I got into town. Talked to Kieran."

"And?"

"And he was the one who told me where I could find Moira." Aiden gave her a tight smile. "He won't stand in my way if I mean to stick with her. It's good to have his blessing, but it's not required. To be honest, it's not really up to any of them."

"Don't just write them off, Aiden." Mazie headed back down the stairs into the store and set an electric kettle on to boil. "You need to be aware of their influence when it comes to her."

"And they need to be aware of her autonomy." Anger simmered in his chest from the idiocy of the Callahans dictating who Moira could see.

Mazie barked a laugh as she handed him a mug with a bag of peppermint draped in it. "These are her parents. They don't see her as autonomous. They see her as their little girl—their only girl."

"What does being a girl have to do with it?" Aiden hated gender stereotypes. "She's strong, beautiful, smart, and a businesswoman with her own shop. Having breasts doesn't negate her skills."

Mazie studied him for a few moments, a small smile curling her lips. "Well, haven't you just grown up?"

Aiden snorted as the kettle pinged its readiness. "Society likes to judge based on appearances, not capabilities, even after they've been proven."

"Yes, but you need to focus on what you can do about it. You won't change them. You can only change how you deal with their views."

"They can go fuck themselves." Aiden poured hot water in to his mother's mug before his.

"While you want to fuck Moira."

"Mom!"

"Well, it's true, isn't it? Listen, I might be older, but I'm not dead. I remember what it's like to burn for someone." She gave him a reproving look. "So here's what I recommend. Treat everyone here as if they're on the Callahans' side. They most likely are. But you treat Moira like she's your sole focus and that will win you more points with the Callahan groupies. Moira has stood her ground and made her mark. The community likes her."

"Good. I like her, too." Aiden snorted.

"I wish you luck." Mazie settled herself behind the counter. "At least you're staying with her. That's a step in the right direction."

You have no idea. Getting into her home had been the first step in winning her back. He'd fucked up by staying away so long, but he had the present and that was where the magic happened, anyway. *You have to have the right tool for the job.*

"Yeah, it is." He paused and eyed his mother, debating before he said more. "She's the one worth all my time, Mom. She always has been."

Mazie's face creased into a compassionate smile. "Then make her, and the town, believe it. It's gonna take work."

"She's worth it."

"Okay, then." Mazie nodded. "So how you gonna start winning her over?"

"Uh-uh. I'm not giving you my plans. I don't need a mama-matchmaker." He smiled at her scowl. "Don't worry. It'll be fine. Do you need any help around the shop while I'm here?"

Mazie gasped and threw her hand over her chest in theatrical amazement. "Are you *offering* to help around the store?" She narrowed her eyes and pointed at him in suspicion. "Who are you and what have you done with my son?"

Aiden laughed. "Maybe he just decided to grow up a little. What do you need done?"

Mazie had him help her move around the stock and fix a couple of the shelves in the back room. He enjoyed feeling useful again and spending the afternoon with his mother became an enjoyable experience rather than a drudgery.

Despite his work with his mom, he found his mind drifting to Moira and the way her eyes flashed. He agreed she had a right to be angry with him, but he'd show her he'd made changes. *I'm not going anywhere unless she's with me.* That would be the trick, to get her to leave Cloudburst. He ignored the voice warning she wouldn't leave her business or her family.

****

Moira rolled her shoulders to release some of her tension as she wiped down the counter. Talia locked up her massage room and collected any stray cups and dishes left out in the main room of the coffee shop.

"You sure you're going to be okay with Aiden tonight?" Talia gave Moira a hard look as she scrubbed her hands in the sink.

"Yes, I'll be fine." She set the flower vase to the side, swept up some of the fallen leaves and petals, and tried to ignore the misgivings about them. *Calm down, they're just flowers.* From someone she didn't know. Or worse, from someone she did.

The only new person in town is Aiden and he doesn't wear a suit and tie. At least, I don't think he does. She doubted he'd changed in a telephone booth after they split just to bring in flowers.

"Do you want me to hang around until he gets here?" Talia crossed her arms over her chest. "I don't mind and I don't have any big plans tonight. I got time."

"Don't be silly. You don't have to stay. I'll be fine with him. We're just going to be friends."

"Uh-huh."

"What?"

"Moira, don't forget what he did to you."

She leveled Talia with a flat look. "I was sixteen, Talia. Melodramatic as all hell and at the capricious mercy of my family." She filled the last of the dishwasher with cups and soap, and slammed it closed a little harder than she meant. "I've grown a lot since then, and they don't get to make my decisions for me anymore. I'm capable of learning the real him, and the real me. We probably don't have anything in common now."

"Then why are you letting him stay with you?"

"Because we were friends once and I'm curious what has happened to him since he left."

Talia shook her head. "That sounds like dangerous

ground, Moira."

"You worry too much." She softened her rebuke with a smile. "Besides, you should call up my brother Kieran and see what he's up to tonight instead of babysitting me."

Talia's expression took on a decidedly innocent air. "Why would I want to call Kieran?"

Moira snorted as she switched off some of the lights. "Really? You're going to go with that response?"

"What? I don't have anything going on with your brother."

"No, not at all. That's why you have a special ring tone in your phone for his number and keep tagging him in all your pictures on Facebook."

"I tag *you* in them, too, you know." But a blush worked its way over her freckled nose.

"I know. That's why I know Kieran is in all of them." Moira laughed as Talia stuck her tongue out. "Look, I'll be fine. Just head on home and text me when you get there. The weather has been crazy today and I'm sure black ice is developing on the roads now that the sun has gone down."

"If you're sure..." Talia paused as she slung her coat over her shoulders.

"I'm sure. Go. I'll be fine."

"All right, but call me if you need anything." Talia headed for the back door.

"I will. Good night." Moira followed her and waved from the threshold.

"'Night."

She waited until Talia had gotten into her car and started the engine before waving and closing the door. The heat from the Cloudburst chased away the chill of the April evening and she shivered a little with the cold. *Aiden could warm me up just fine.* She growled and shook her head. *Stop those thoughts right now, missy.* They'd work on friendship. *Because Goddess knows he hasn't been much of one for years.*

CHAPTER FOUR

Moira dropped her keys and shrugged out of her jacket as she stepped inside her apartment door. She plugged in the string of old Christmas lights and they brought a warm, cheery feeling to the dark space as they twinkled around the windows. Her brothers teased her about keeping them up for so long after the holidays, but the lights brought her too much joy to take down.

She toed off her boots and shuffled up the stairs to check on the rooms. One guest bedroom had stuff piled everywhere, stuff she'd always meant to put away, but just couldn't seem to find the time. *Better find time now that Aiden will be staying.*

Aiden.

She flicked on the light and scanned the boxes stacked on the bed. So many memories buried in the cardboard containers. But none of Aiden himself. She grimaced and shook her head. *Probably for the best after what I went through.* She hadn't kept much from her time in Denver. Too many scars permanently etched in her psyche to need physical items. Moira rested a hand on one of the boxes, inhaling the scent of old cardboard. It had seen a lot of miles. Most of them had, though she couldn't really remember what all sat in them.

I should just get rid of them without checking.

It was a noble idea, but she couldn't quite bring herself to throw them in the trash. Instead, she rolled up her sleeves and set to moving them to the side so Aiden could at least sleep in the bed. *This bed, not mine.* She put her mind and back into shifting the boxes to the outer edges of the room. *Won't think about Aiden sleeping.*

The doorbell made Moira jump and she glanced at her watch. The hands pointed to quarter after nine and she wiped her dusty palms on her jeans as she headed for the front door. Her heartbeat pounded harder the closer she came and she had to take a few deep breaths before she could answer.

Aiden stood on the other side, his duffel bag slung over one leather-encased shoulder. Even dressed for the cold weather, his masculine beauty made her heart flutter.

"Hi, Moira. Can I come in?"

She gaped at him, still not certain he was real. How many years had she hoped he'd show up at her door only to find it a fantasy?

"I can't believe you really showed up."

He quirked an eyebrow. "Did you think I'd find somewhere else to stay after what I said at my truck this morning?"

"No, not really. It's just..." She gestured helplessly and stood back. "Please, come in."

He strode past her and scanned her apartment. She'd converted the top two floors of the building into a three-bedroom apartment with three full baths and a luxurious kitchen and living area. Her brother Kallen had helped her remodel. Now the space seemed small with Aiden's presence.

Moira took a deep breath and opened her senses, testing the energies of her home with Aiden in it. Hot, sensual pleasure mixed with a sense of belonging swamped her and she staggered against the door.

Aiden materialized at her side, his eyes blazing and his grip warm. "Are you all right?"

"I think so."

She met his gaze and before she could stop herself, she'd leaned forward. She brushed her lips across his, desperate to taste the energy for herself, but something stopped her from doing more and she pulled back. His expression hadn't changed, but his energy had cooled. She searched his gaze, hoping for...something. Anything. But nothing came to her.

Well, that hadn't worked like she'd hoped.

"Sorry." She blushed and shifted away from him, her gut churning.

"Moira—"

"No, don't worry about it. I think I've been wondering what it was like to kiss you since I was sixteen, so I took a chance." She gave him a rueful smile that didn't begin to cover her chagrin. "I guess I have my answer. Sorry for being so in-your-face. Quite literally."

She turned her back and headed for the stairs. "The bedrooms are up here. Let me show you the room that's yours."

Aiden muttered something that sounded like, "Dammit", but Moira focused on getting up to the room. She didn't want to push any other boundaries while he stayed with her. *Hey, at least I know he was all talk and no follow-through.* She forced her disappointment down deep and tried to find some relief at discovering the lesson now.

She paused at the door to the guest room and gave him a distant smile. "Here it is. It still needs a little work. You caught me in the middle of rearranging when you rang the bell."

"Thanks." Aiden dropped his bag and tried to catch her gaze. For the first time, Moira refused to meet his eyes. "The room is great."

"I'm glad you like it." She studied the walls. "It's pretty nice when not full of boxes." She cleared her throat and stepped out in the hall. "I hope you've eaten already because there's nothing prepared for dinner here. You can always order from Nicola's Greek Bistro down the way if you really need something."

"Moira, wait."

"Look, Aiden. I'm sorry I overstepped. I told you we'd be friends and offered a place to stay. I shouldn't have thrown that kiss at you." *I should've known better, even when he said he wanted a chance.* She gave him a tight smile.

"Don't apologize. I should be apologizing to you." He took a deep breath to let her down easy.

Here it comes—the truth after all his pretty words this morning.

"I don't want to screw up this time." His brilliant blue gaze zinged her when he locked it with her own. "I want to make sure you know I love you and don't just want to take advantage of your hospitality. I'm here for the long haul, Moira, but I want to make sure our love is based on respect and friendship, not just sex."

Okay, now I feel like a horny strumpet.

"Right. Okay. Anyway, the kitchen and extra bath is downstairs." She waved toward the staircase as she headed for it. "I'll be down there if you need me."

"Moira—"

But she wasn't waiting to hear all the ways she could screw this up more. *I need to find my backbone. He left and never said a word. I can't trust him.* Her heart screamed in protest, but she clenched her jaw and forced herself downstairs. *It's better this way.*

****

Aiden swore and ran his hand through his hair. *I don't*

think I could've screwed that up any worse. Moira's move had surprised him, especially since he knew she hadn't forgiven him for his stupidity of years past. So, he froze and she got the wrong message.

He had to come up with a plan to make it very clear how he felt. *And not just the guy feelings of 'empty my balls for me, baby.'* Not that his dick was listening. It throbbed behind the fly of his jeans with just her scent.

He swung his gaze around the room for inspiration, but only old boxes with labels like 'memories' and 'VHS Movies' greeted him. *VHS, really?* He thought they'd gone the way of 8-track tapes. He was tempted to see what movies she'd collected, but he shook his head. *Focus or you'll lose her for good.*

Aiden turned off the light and headed back down the stairs in search of Moira. His interaction skills had suffered in the time he'd been alone and he needed to recall how to communicate again. His mother had asked him about how he'd win Moira over, but in truth, he had nothing planned. He'd thought winging it would work, but he hadn't reacted well when she changed the program. *So what's plan B, genius?*

How had he wooed women before? Movies and food.

"Hey, are those really old VHS tapes in that box up there?"

"What?" Moira looked up from wiping down her spotless kitchen counters. Granted, black granite surfaces hid dirt pretty well, but the whole kitchen gleamed.

"I found a box up in the room labeled VHS movies. Do you really still have the old tapes?" He settled on one of the tall stools placed in front of her bar counter behind her sink.

Moira frowned, then laughed. "Oh, no. That's just an old box. All my VHS tapes were traded in for DVDs a while ago. I think that box has things like old class notes in it or something."

"Class notes? From college?" She nodded. "Why are

you keeping those?"

She swiped at the counter again and shrugged. "In case I ever need the information in them, I guess."

"Have you ever thought of scanning them into your computer? They'd take up far less space that way, and you could catalog them better for future reference."

"That's a good idea." She gave him a brief smile before biting her lip and looking away. "So, do you want something to eat or drink? As I said, nothing is prepared, but we can order from Nicola's or scrounge something from the fridge."

He sighed as he settled on one of the kitchen stools. "Anything is fine. But can we talk? I feel like we got off on the wrong foot tonight."

"Sure. Talk." She turned to him and gave him a polite, but distant stare.

"Dammit, I'm not saying or doing anything right by you today." Aiden grimaced and shook his head. "Hell, this decade."

"Two decades." She narrowed her eyes. "I'm sorry I kissed you. I should've left well enough alone and kept to my word we'd just be friends. Too much time has passed for us to be anything more."

Aiden's gut sank to a level somewhere around the Earth's molten mantle. "Not for me. I never stopped thinking about you."

Anger flashed in her eyes. "Really? And silence proves that?"

Chagrin wormed its way through his gut. "No, my return to Cloudburst does. I want the chance, now that we're adults, to see if we can be what we hoped as teenagers. I want us to work so bad it hurts. But I don't want you for your money, or looks, or the prestige it would bring me in this town. I'm interested in the whole person. That's who I'm in love with."

"In love?" She shot him a dry look, her mouth tight.

"How the hell can you know what 'in love' means when you've spent the whole time we've known each other avoiding me?" He opened his mouth, but she shook her head and held up her hand. "No, don't. I don't want to talk about it anymore. We're done for now. Focus on food. Takeout or fridge?"

Aiden sighed and shrugged. "Takeout works for me. Do you have a menu?"

"Yes. Why?"

"I'd like to see what I'm buying." He waited for her to dig one out from her catch-all drawer in the kitchen. "I'm kinda particular about food from take-out places. Are there any good ones still around here?"

Moira nodded as she handed him the menu. "I like Linn's Noodle House. They serve different kinds of a pasta from all over the world. Over the years, Madelinn has hired different chefs from Italy, India, China, Vietnam, Greece, and France to cook for her little restaurant. That's how she learned all the recipes. There's a nice variety."

"Sounds good." Aiden pretended to look over the menu, but his attention wandered after he'd seen the vegetable chow mein. "What are you going to order?"

"I usually get some chicken alfredo, but tonight I'm feeling more like some paneer and nan."

"I didn't know you liked Indian food."

Moira snorted. "Now there's a surprise. You've been gone how long? Oh, that's right, forever."

He gritted his teeth against saying something stupid. *She has a right to be angry. I just wish it would mellow sooner.*

"Yeah, I know. I'm sorry, Moira. I thought you didn't want to talk about it."

"I don't." She scowled.

"Then let's move on from me being gone and start with here I am to get to know you again. And to order food."

"Fine." She gestured to the menu. "Do you know what you want?"

"Yeah." He stood directly in front of her. "I want you and I want to be friends and more." He held her gaze. "I want to make amends for being a scared jackass, and I want to be sure you know I'm not going to give you up this time."

Moira met his gaze, the green of her eyes filled with both hope and hopelessness. His Lady Cloudburst had been hurt, by him and others, and he'd have to work hard to get back into her good graces.

"What if I've given up on you?"

The question damn near froze him to death, but he rallied gamely with a determined smile. "I'll just have to convince you otherwise."

She searched his expression for something, but nodded sharply before he saw what it was.

"Good luck with that." She shook her head. "What do you want to order?"

"Vegetable chow mein."

She called the Noodle House and made their order while Aiden poked around her home. Despite being an older building, Aiden admired how Moira had remodeled and furnished her living space. It held the right combination of sophistication and cozy homeyness. *Not that it's surprising given her gift.* Snow fell outside the arched windows looking down on the street and he settled into the cozy feeling of her home.

I could live here.

The thought stopped him short. Live here? In Cloudburst? He'd done everything but ride a rocket to get out of this little backwards town. How the hell could he be thinking of staying? But deep down, his soul craved to be with the piece Moira had stolen and suddenly the outer location didn't matter. *It's said home is where the heart is and Moira definitely has my heart.*

His thoughts drifted and he didn't come back to the present until Moira thanked the delivery person and closed the door.

"Dinner here already?" Aiden rose to help her carry the bags to the kitchen.

"Yeah. Please take the food to the table. I'll bring the plates and silverware."

He followed her directions, trying to think of a way he could break through her perception of him. *Actions speak louder than words.* But what action could he perform to show her he meant everything he'd said?

Despite wracking his brain for several minutes, he couldn't come up with anything useful to say. Perhaps he had been gone too long. They ate dinner in an awkward silence until Aiden's frustration grumbled right along with his stomach.

Talk to her, you jackass.

"Since I haven't been around much, tell me what you've been doing. Where did you go after you graduated high school?"

CHAPTER FIVE

Moira tried to rein in her conflicting emotions. Resignation warred with hope as Aiden sat quietly beside her. Some part of her enjoyed his company, but the silence wasn't comfortable and she hated having such unsettled energy in her sanctuary.

"Since I haven't been around much, tell me what you've been doing. Where did you go after you graduated high school?" Aiden tried to sound so casual, but tension and frustration bloomed around him like an aura.

Moira shivered, old memories crowding more of her mind, and cleared her throat. "I toured around the country for a little while, visiting Chicago and Salt Lake City. But in the end, I went to Denver for college. It was good for school, but I'm really not much of a city girl." She waved her hand to dispel the rancid memories. "I stayed as long as I needed to, then came back here." She'd hoped to make a miraculous recovery in the bosom of her family, but she hadn't been able to tell them what had been so wrong with Denver. Kieran suspected, but he'd never pushed for more than she'd been willing to tell.

Aiden tipped his head, his brilliant blue eyes seeing through her deflections. "I can see Denver hit you pretty hard. I wish I'd been there to help you through."

Old anger flared and she bit back a snarky remark. *Yeah, I wished you'd been there too.* But that wouldn't change the present, so she only nodded. "I looked for you there, but of course, didn't find you."

He nodded and sadness filtered across his expression. "I ran from you. Hell, I ran from myself. There was so much wrong with me when I was eighteen, I don't even know where to start."

Moira's heart sped up with hope. "Why don't you start with why you left that night. What happened and where did you go?"

Aiden dropped his gaze and pushed the chow mein around his plate for a few moments. "I left because..." He looked like something strangled him and his fist tightened on his fork. "Because I have really messed up sexual needs and you were too young for them."

Sexual needs? Moira blinked. She hadn't expected that.

"My sex drive is over-developed. At least that's what the therapist said." He grimaced and shook his head. "Of course, it could be she was just an old prude afraid of sex in general, but for years before I talked to her, I knew something wasn't the same as everyone else."

"And that's why you left without saying anything?"

"What could I have said, Moira?" He grimaced. "We hadn't even kissed, and I needed sex a lot more often than just once every couple of days. You weren't ready for that and I didn't want to lose you by taking things too far, too fast."

"So you hit back first by getting lost rather than losing me." She narrowed her eyes. "Nice."

"Yeah, not my brightest moment."

Understatement of the decade. "How do you know I wouldn't have been ready?"

He gave a short unhappy laugh. "Even if you'd been

ready, your family wouldn't have been, and I didn't really want to fight off all your brothers."

She groaned and rubbed her face with her hands.

"Yeah, they have old-fashioned ideas of a woman's sexuality and ability to choose. Even if they could screw as soon as they got hair between their legs."

Aiden laughed in surprise.

"What? The sexual revolution may have happened, but men still get the lion's share of allowances for sex before commitment." Moira shook her head. "Women are still expected to save this hideous thing called virginity for 'someone special' because men still can't tell who's the father of any children she produces. Stupid."

"I'll have to revise my perspective on this."

"Damn straight." She nodded sharply. "But fighting off several backwards-thinking men would be exhausting so I understand that. Why didn't you come back when I was older?"

Aiden sipped his soda as Moira waited, eating her paneer with restrained impatience.

"At first it was because of the sex issue. I needed a lot of it and I didn't want to show you how much."

"How many partners have you had?" Goddess, was he a gigolo?

"More than I'm comfortable relating, but always with protection."

"Really?" Moira raised a dubious eyebrow.

"Yes, really. I needed sex, not a host of diseases, so it was either with protection or not at all." He shrugged. "It was during one of those times when the woman didn't have protection and I was out that I remembered pain took the edge off."

"Wait, you need pain for sex?" It didn't sound good.

"No, pain made my sex drive come back to 'normal' levels." He straightened his shoulders and glanced toward the window. "Pain made the drive settle enough that I could jack off and I'd be good for a while. When I realized that, I started turning to tattoos."

She nodded with understanding. "Tattoos are painful, so they'd calm you down."

"Right."

"Wow." She recalled the large back panel across his shoulders. "Wow. You've needed it a lot."

He shrugged again. "There's only one other thing that mellowed me out better than pain."

"What?"

"You and your energy."

She blinked, her meal forgotten. "What? How would you know? You've been away for almost two decades."

"I knew the moment I left." Aiden sat back in his chair, his hands fisting on the tabletop. "You kept the urges down to a minimum even though I couldn't do anything about them with you. But the moment I left, they came back like a raging flood. It was all I could do to find a woman to take the edge off. I didn't have much money at the time, so I traded some computer work at a tattoo parlor for some ink. They had a new artist who needed practice, so that's when I got my first tattoo."

She dropped her gaze to the ink peeking out from his sleeve. "Why did you stay away after I'd gotten old enough to make my own decisions?"

He barked an unhappy laugh. "You're not going to let this go, are you?"

"Would you?" She tilted her head in challenge.

"No, I guess not." He shook his head, regret tightening his features. "I stayed away from habit and cowardice, I guess." He met her gaze and grimaced. "And the old-fashioned idea of you being a "good girl" who shouldn't be sullied by my deviant needs for sex."

Moira scowled. "But you said my energy calmed that, even if it's true about me being a "good girl". Good girls can make decisions about their bodies and their sexual needs better than men can, anyway."

"Yeah, I know."

"Do you? Because I'm telling you right now, regardless of what my father or brothers think, if I want to fuck someone and we're both consenting adults, I will damn well fuck them." She raised her chin. "And I'm still a good woman, because my value has nothing to do with my sexual promiscuity." She narrowed her eyes. "Would it surprise or appall you to know I've slept with more than one man in my life and have my own deviations?"

Aiden looked at her a moment before he grimaced. "No, but I'm sure you're not as sexually messed up."

"How would you know?" She snorted. "You think you have the monopoly on deviance?"

"What was I supposed to say, Moira? That I needed it more than twice a day? You were sixteen and we hadn't even kissed."

"Maybe not then, but what kept you from talking to me when I was twenty-five?" She gave him a hard stare. "Is this the male belief that women are pure as the driven snow until some man ruins her, in which case it's her fault for tempting him, and then she's irredeemable? Or is it that we never have sexual thoughts or kinky ideas until men introduce them?"

Aiden gaped at her, but she wasn't finished.

"Here's the thing, Aiden. You say you've loved me since that summer we spent time together, but you didn't have enough respect for me to find out if I liked sex as much as you, or if I had similar needs. That's not love. That's cowardice and misogynistic arrogance. I'm not a person to you if you can't talk to me about sex. It's sounds like I'm something either too precious to take down off the shelf you hide it on or too valueless to bother with the effort. Either way, fuck you and your lack of effort."

"You think I didn't want to talk to you?"

She threw her hands out and raised her eyebrows.

"How would I know, Aiden? Two decades is a long time to avoid a conversation about needs. You're here now because you think you can handle your sexuality, but you didn't respect me enough to ask how I felt about it. Were you afraid to ask?"

"Hell yeah! I didn't want to lose you until I understood them." He frowned.

"So you lost me in a way you could control, by choosing to walk away and never come back."

"I'm back now." His frown turned petulant.

"Yeah, you are. What's changed, Aiden? What's the big deal about now that you can finally see me as a person, not just someone to benefit you? Or is that it? I can benefit you now that I'm 'old enough' to understand your needs." She shook her head with a scowl. "Again, I say, fuck you. What about *my* needs? What about what I wanted?"

Moira rose and leaned over the table toward him, fury pushing at her chest. "I looked for you everywhere. Everywhere. And you effectively hid from me because of your 'sexual needs.' I call it cowardice. I have no use for cowards or men who can't see me as anything other than a release valve. Been there, done that, got the T-shirt. I'm not going to be your plaything, your trinket, your precious possession. I'm a person regardless of my gender, and I want to be loved, needed, and respected as a person, not as a female. You can either treat me as a person you respect and like, or you can pack your shit and hit the road again. Got it?"

She gathered her dishes and hauled them to the sink before she said anything more. She hadn't been this angry or able to let it all out since before she'd met Lenny in Denver. He'd squashed her ability to let out her emotions.

But Aiden's arrival had brought all her hurt and frustration back to the surface. *I guess I wasn't so over him.* At least he'd given her an explanation for his disappearance.

Without a look back, she marched her ass upstairs to run a shower. The hot water would help her release some of her anger and she might be able to face her houseguest again without killing him. Moira closed her eyes as she tested the water temperature, waiting for the heat to catch up to her fury.

****

"Fuck."

That hadn't gone well. He'd known he'd been stupid to come back here and think it would be easy, but Moira's anger had been greater than he'd reckoned. And her accusations of his view on her sexual innocence hit too close to home. He'd always thought her more sexually 'pure' than him because he'd known his own appetites. But now he realized he didn't know Moira at all, or what turned her on. *And what the fuck does "pure" even mean?*

He heard the shower come on upstairs and ran his hands over his face, considering his next move. He wanted Moira, and he wanted her to understand his needs, but he wondered if understanding her might make it easier. While his mother had kept him in the loop on Moira's life during his time away, there were bound to be things he'd missed.

He snorted. *You think, jackass?*

Misogynistic arrogance. Moira's words echoed in his head and he had to agree. She deserved better than a man who made assumptions. Now the question became, how did he fix this problem?

Aiden rose, carrying his dishes into the kitchen then filled the kettle and set it on the stove to boil. He leaned back against the opposite counter and rubbed his chin as he tried to come up with ideas of how to remedy the situation. He had to prove to her he wouldn't leave again, wouldn't run, and could face hardship with her.

Yeah, like she'll believe that. He'd walked away when

things got tough. He didn't know what she'd endured in the years he was gone. Hell, he hadn't bothered to check on her more than through his mother. The thought soured his stomach, but he couldn't change the past.

The only thing so constant is change. The present consisted of shifting perceptions and conclusions. If he could show Moira he'd learned from his mistakes, and they were huge ones, he could win her to his side. Hopefully her anger stemmed from her interest in him. *Please Goddess may that be true.*

The kettle whistled and he lifted it from the stove just as the water upstairs shut off. Part of him wished he had some rum or brandy to add to the tea to ease the coming conversation. He shook his head as he found a spicy tea bag and dropped it in a mug. He wasn't sure he could get drunk enough. To deal with it in such a fashion would only confirm Moira's assertion of his cowardice and he'd given up such drinking anyway.

Pouring a second cup of tea, Aiden took a deep breath and girded his loins for the metaphorical crotch kick he was likely to get. At least he had the courage to talk to her again. *Can't call me a coward for that.* He took his time, careful not to spill the full mugs as he mounted the stairs. The scents of hot water and a fruity shampoo hit his nose as he reached the landing and he paused to savor them.

Or to still his galloping heart as he faced the firing squad. *Goddess, let her be willing to be soothed.*

"Moira?" He shouldered the bedroom door open. "Would you like some tea? I wanted to—"

His words stuck in his throat as his breath reversed direction. Moira stood with her back to him in nothing but a towel. And the terrycloth only covered her front from breasts to thighs. Her back remained gloriously exposed in lovely, smooth curves. A small watercolor tattoo in the shape of a dripping heart decorated the skin on her spine between her shoulder blades.

Aiden damn near swallowed his tongue and all the blood in his body headed south to stiffen his dick. She'd been lovely as a sixteen-year-old girl, but her body had filled out into this magnificent woman, and he was struck dumb. *Want. Mine. Need.* The staccato thoughts punctuated a flex of his dick.

Moira looked over her shoulder at him without a trace of embarrassment. "Something you wanted, Aiden?"

"Uh-huh." Damn, what was wrong with him? No one had ever done this to him before.

She turned and set the towel aside before walking to him for the mug he held. "Tea? Thanks. Smells good. What did you want?"

He'd lost all his cool. She stood before him "sky-clad" like an ancient priestess and sipped her tea, waiting for him with raised eyebrows. "Uh..."

"What?" She sipped her tea and tilted her head. "I thought a man with your 'needs' would've seen a naked woman before."

Oh, he'd seen naked women, just not his heart's desire. Not this woman. And the others hadn't compared to this golden skinned goddess. *Mine.* He tried to rein in his baser, Dominant side before it pushed her farther away. *That's probably not her kink. Ease back, jackass.*

"Your beauty is beyond compare." He had no idea where the poetic words came from, but he meant every one of them. "I want to worship you and show you your beauty, Moira."

She snorted and rolled her eyes. "Thanks, but I'm not as pure as you're painting me."

"I disagree." He took the mug back and set both on her bureau before grasping her hands. "Purity is subjective, and you're pure goddess, beauty, and goodness. Not in some archaic, religious hoo-hah, but in a way that makes me aspire to be a better man and revel in your regard."

"Aiden—"

"Moira, hear me out." He shook his head. "I know words mean next to nothing when it comes to reality and action, but right now they're all I have, and I mean every one of them." He squeezed her hands and tried to put all his sincerity into his eyes. "You asked me about my needs, and I fear they'll be too extreme for you, but because I want you and want to please you, I'll tell you what drives my fantasies. Is that what you wanted to know?"

She sighed and closed her mouth with a nod.

He gritted his teeth and swallowed hard. *Holy shit, this is the scariest thing I've ever done.* He needed her to understand and not fear him, but to keep this hidden from her would cost him in ways fear couldn't override.

"Let's sit on the bed." *So I don't fucking collapse when she runs away from me.* He drew her to the bed and let her sit while he retrieved their tea. "Okay, here goes." He rubbed his thumbs over the sweating mug, trying to find the courage to spit out the words he had to say. *Hell, maybe I am a coward.*

"It's okay, Aiden. I understand."

"No, no you don't. My sexual needs are rather unconventional."

"Yes, I know, just like last time, when you told me you needed pain to control them."

"No, that's not what I meant." He shook his head and tried to spit the words out. "The pain controls the desire, but when it comes to actual release, I need something more intense. Have you heard of BDSM?"

Moira blinked slowly, her expression going so still she could've turned to flesh-colored stone. *Dear Goddess, I've lost her already.*

"Why do you ask, Aiden?"

"Do you know what it is?" He didn't relish the idea of explaining it to her, but he'd do what he could. *If I don't explain, we can't be together anyway.*

She nodded slowly. "I know what it is."

His shoulders relaxed as relief filtered through him. "Good. So you know there's different flavors of it. Some are into pain, some are into Dominance and submission, some are into bondage, and there are all levels of all of those." He sipped his tea to gather his thoughts. And more of his courage. "I'm what's considered a fringe player. I don't need D/s all the time, I prefer it only in the bedroom, and the only rule I follow is safe, sane, and consensual."

She blinked and cleared her throat as color suffused her cheeks. "And which are you? D or s?"

Aiden tried to make his smile compassionate. "D. Definitely Dominant."

"That's Double D."

He blinked then laughed. "I guess it is." But he sobered when she didn't match his smile. "Is this a problem?"

"N-no." Moira straightened her shoulders and met his gaze steadily. "After I left home, I moved around a lot. I learned about the lifestyle, but didn't get involved with it until I moved to Denver. When I did get involved, it was as a submissive. It was the best way for me to relax and retreat from the overwhelmingly negative energy in the city." She grimaced and shook her head. "I was so lost and lonely without my family or you." She shrugged as his guilt surged. "The nights seemed to drag on forever, and the lifestyle took me away from that. It was good for a while, but eventually I found it became too demanding for me. Turned out it wasn't something I wanted."

Aiden's gut sank. *Damn, I am too kinky for her.* "You can understand why I didn't want to tell you."

Her brows lowered. "Why, because you think you're too kinky for me?"

He clenched his teeth to keep his jaw from dropping. *Damn, does she read minds?*

"The lifestyle in Denver, with the people there and the sickness I couldn't avoid, wasn't what I wanted. Yes, I'm still submissive, but only to the right person. A competent Dom. Those I met in Denver...weren't."

Hope expanded in microbursts in his chest, but he reined them in. *Walk softly here.* "So, the lifestyle doesn't bother you?"

She shook her head, but her expression remained stoic. "No, but it takes a lot to earn my trust, and my submission now. I prefer to live without BDSM than put myself in the position of mistreated submissive."

Anger flared. "Someone hurt you in the lifestyle?"

She dipped her chin and looked up at him from under her brows. "Yes, genius, and you don't have any cause to get angry. You took a hiatus, remember? If you wanted to initiate me into the lifestyle, you shouldn't have done your Houdini act. As it was, I figured it out on my own and learned exactly what I do and don't want."

"And what do you want, Moira?"

"For starters, I need my partner to understand who I am and what I'm worth, rather than what I can be for him." She rose and headed for the closet. He swallowed hard at the glorious expanse of skin and her beautifully rounded ass. "Second, I want someone who will be around for me when I need him, not when he needs me." She threw a long t-shirt over her head and blocked his view. "And third, he has to understand I'm me, as I am, not as he'd like me to be on his pedestal."

She retrieved her mug and handed it to him while drawing him upright. "So that's my deal. But I'm too tired tonight to negotiate, so off you go to your room and I'll see you in the morning."

"Moira—"

"Good night, Aiden." She pushed him out the door and closed it behind him.

He stared at the oak surface and some of his uncertainty faded. He'd win her submission by learning the woman she'd become.

CHAPTER SIX

Moira woke to her alarm and groaned as she rolled out of bed. *Why did I agree to open on a Saturday?* Especially now with Aiden visiting. She scrubbed her face. Aiden, who was a Dominant to her submissive. She snorted. Former submissive. She'd given up the lifestyle when the rules weren't followed and she'd ended up subbing for a sadist who ignored safewords.

She shook her head and took herself into the bathroom to shower and get ready for the day. She'd damn near done a frickin' happy dance when she realized Aiden was Dominant and interested in BDSM. *Not just interested, but practicing.* But she had the wits to remember she knew very little about him and certainly not enough to just jump into a D/s relationship with him. Part of her wanted to bow at his feet and submit to him, to let him take care of her emotional and sexual needs. But the hard-won independent woman insisted she be sure of him. *I thought Lenny would do that and all he wanted was my pain.*

She scrubbed her body harder as if to rid herself of the memories along with the dirt. *I'm not that person anymore. I'm stronger and I know what I like.* He'd tried to break her, to make her think she liked it. He even gaslighted her, swearing she'd never said her safeword to make him stop. If it hadn't been for the Playroom Master, she would've been traumatized beyond healing. *Hell, I would've been broken.* Lenny had been thrown out and she'd managed to move within the next week.

Never again. I'm in control.

That was something Lenny never learned. The subs had the control, but he'd ignored her warnings and her safeword. She wouldn't allow anyone to do that again.

What about Aiden?

She turned off the shower and dried her body, letting the question simmer in her awareness. Aiden claimed to be Dominant, but she didn't know him well enough to trust him with her sexual pleasure or submission yet. Being restrained was an act of trust so profound for her, especially after Lenny's betrayal, she couldn't let just anyone do it, not even Aiden.

I laid out the rules. We'll see if he rises to the occasion.

Dressing in comfortable, casual clothing, she slipped out of her room and trotted down the stairs. She let her body go through the motions of setting up the coffee makers and fresh pastries for the early morning customers as her mind focused on Aiden's declaration. Part of her wanted to try out his paces, but her commonsense warned her to require his proof. *Actions speak louder than words.*

The bells on the doors jingled and Mazie Westmorland stepped into the warm interior of the Cloudburst Coffee & Spa. Moira smiled at Aiden's mother, not at all surprised to see her.

"Good morning, Mazie. You're out early." Moira rested her elbows on the top of the pastry display counter. "What can I get for you this morning?" A high-pitched whine shot past her ear, but she ignored it.

"I came to see how you're doing and to check up on my son. Is Aiden up yet?" Despite her pleasant words, the tension rolled off the older woman.

"No, not yet. Oh!" Moira slapped her arm as the first of the spring mosquitos died an inelegant death on her arm. "Little bastard."

"Sorry?" Mazie shot her a wide-eyed stare.

"Oh, no, not Aiden." Moira shook her head. "The mosquito I just killed."

"Oh." Mazie chuckled, but sobered fast. "A man stopped by my store yesterday, looking for you, Moira."

Uneasiness skittered up her spine, but she only raised her eyebrows. "Oh?"

"Yes, he said he was an old friend and wanted to know if I knew you."

Moira turned her back to pour some coffee into a to-go cup for Mazie while she gathered her thoughts. "That's weird. Did he leave his name or say why he wanted to know?"

"No." Mazie shook her head as she accepted the coffee. "He seemed to know a lot about you already, but he was sussing out how well-known you are here."

"Huh. What did you tell him?" Part of her wished Mazie would say no.

Mazie shrugged. "I didn't say much of anything. He gave me a bad feeling. Is Aiden staying with you?"

"Yes, for now."

"Good. I don't want you to be alone when this man comes calling. And I have the feeling he will." Mazie looked troubled. "Seriously, Moira, I don't like this man. He's carrying dark energy with him and he smelled like mildew. I'm going to mention him to Lt. Fitzroy when I see him today."

Despite the disturbing news, Moira smirked. "Are you sweet on Fitzroy, Mazie?"

The older woman gave her a dreamy smile. "Who wouldn't be? But no, he was my first friend in this town after I got pregnant with Aiden. We've maintained that relationship. Besides, his energy isn't right for me. I'm happier being single."

"Good for you, Mazie. Say hello to Fitzroy for me when you see him, and I'll keep an eye out for this mysterious 'old friend' of mine."

Mazie paused as she laid cash on the counter for the coffee. "Will do. Just be careful, Moira. This man scared me. You take care of yourself." She patted the counter and left, the bells jingling over her head.

Moira swallowed hard and continued to set up for the day, but her gut roiled. She didn't like the sound of this stranger. *Who the hell would come looking for me?*

She retreated to her office to open up her computer and check over the orders she'd made for more coffee beans and the various creamers, and her eyes rested on the large bouquet of flowers she'd neglected to take up to her apartment. Were they from the man asking about her? She picked up the card again. *Making up for lost time.* It sounded romantic, like thinking of old loves and wedding gowns when the world is cold and dark. But something about it gave her the heebie jeebies, especially after Mazie's warning.

"Are you okay, Moira?"

Aiden's voice made her jump and she pressed a hand to her chest as she tried to catch her breath.

"Good glory, don't sneak up on me like that." She tried to still her thundering heart by taking deep breaths. "I didn't hear you come in."

"You weren't in the apartment, so I figured you had to open. Who are these from?" He gestured to the flowers, his expression neutral, but his eyes narrowed. "A secret admirer?"

She really looked at him, scanning his body language and facial cues. He appeared nonchalant, but tension stretched across his shoulders and his jaw clenched. Despite the current of emotion, he looked damn good in her office with a long-sleeved black T-shirt hugging the taut muscles of his chest and arms over a set of soft, worn gray jeans. It took her a moment to recognize her own unease had lifted with him in the same room.

"Yeah, kinda." She frowned as she handed him the card. "I originally thought they were from you. But I guess you answered that question. To be honest, I don't know who they're from and it's unnerving."

"You don't recognize the handwriting or the message?" Aiden raised his eyebrows.

"No. And other than you, I can't think of anyone who needed to make anything up to me."

He grimaced and handed the card back. She dropped it on the desk and repressed a shiver as she rubbed her arms with her hands. Aiden's gaze caught on her motions and his brows lowered.

"Are you all right?" When she shook her head, he came around the desk and knelt beside her chair. "What's wrong?"

"Your mom stopped by today."

"My mom?" He raised his chin. "What did she say?"

"She wanted to see how you were doing and to make sure I was okay." Moira bit her bottom lip as her gut clenched. "She said a guy stopped by her store yesterday asking about me. He wouldn't leave his name and it's got me a little freaked out." She gestured at the flowers again. "Talia said someone dropped these off for me here yesterday, too. Since they're not from you, I can only assume they're from him. He shares your description, which is why I thought of you first. But Talia mentioned he wore a suit and that doesn't seem like your style."

Aiden snorted. "Not anymore."

Before she could ask, he grasped her hand. "Why does this unnerve you so much?"

"Because I don't have any admirers I'm unaware of and the energy surrounding those flowers is all wrong." She scowled at the offending blooms. "I should take them out to the trash before the poison the energy of the Cloudburst."

"I'll help you." He backed away so she could get up and held her office door open as she grasped the vase. She damn near dropped it as the wrongness of it hit her awareness, this time much stronger, and she shuddered as she held it as far from herself as possible.

What's wrong with these flowers? They're my favorites.

Aiden settled his hands below hers on the cool glass vase. "Let me take them."

That felt even more wrong than her touching them and she shook her head. "No, I have to do this. If I let you take them, the energy will transfer to you and..." She looked into his light blue eyes. "Poison you."

He raised an eyebrow. "Poison me?"

"Yeah. Trust me on this. I'll take them out."

"I do trust you. More than you know."

Despite the itching and biting energy suffusing the flowers, his statement warmed her all the way to her heart and she gave him a grateful smile. He opened the office door and held it wide for her to pass. The energy hurt worse when he kept his distance, but brushing his chest with her arm helped mitigate it.

They took the bouquet out to the back Dumpster where she parked her Jeep and she remembered Sabrina. The energy in the flowers flared with agitation and she hissed in pain, almost dropping the vase.

"What's wrong?" Aiden rested his hands on her shoulders when she halted.

"Please open the Dumpster for me."

He ducked past her, his feet leaving new prints in the sloppy snow as he threw the lid open. She upturned the vase in the gaping maw and ignored the sorrow of losing such beauty to the stinky interior. The energy went with the flowers, but the vase still held some of it and she threw the glass into the nearby recycle bin as Aiden closed the lid.

Relief hit her so hard, she staggered against the bin. "Oh, thank the Goddess."

"It was that bad?" Aiden grasped her elbows and lifted her upright.

She nodded. "I don't know who sent the flowers, but his energy is poisonous. Maybe your mom was right to tell Lt. Fitzroy about him."

"She's going to the cops?" Aiden blinked as he helped her back inside the Cloudburst. "Wow. Mom doesn't trust law enforcement that much. She must really be weirded out by this guy."

Moira frowned. "Really? She seemed to be very enamored of Fitzroy. But yeah, if the flowers were from the same guy, she was smart to let the police know."

"Enamored of Fitzroy? Mazie?" Aiden followed her back into the main portion of the coffee shop. "I think you have the wrong woman. She lives to be single."

Moira snorted. "Just because she's single doesn't mean she doesn't want a physical relationship with someone. She's not dead."

"Okay, you have to stop. I can't think of my mom like that." Aiden shuddered as he leaned on the counter.

"Stop being such a baby. Are you going to stop having erotic thoughts just because you're sixty-five years old?" Moira made sure the door locked behind them.

"No, but this is different."

"How is it different, Aiden? She was having sex long before you were born, and I bet she has it now when the mood strikes her."

"It's different because I don't want to think of my mother being sexually active."

"She had you, didn't she?" Moira shook her head and wished there was more items to set out. She didn't look forward to being in the back office all day. "Ugh. I don't want to go do what I have to. Especially after those flowers being in my office."

Aiden's tension released at the change in subject. "What do you have to do?"

"Balance the books, take a look a payroll, and make sure the schedules are clear for the next few days." She rubbed her face with her hands. "Beltane is on Thursday and the town takes it off to celebrate, but that means I have to be open for at least the afternoon while everyone comes in for a pick-me-up."

"Don't you have people to work for you?"

"Yes, but I usually give them the day off, so it's just me and Talia here that day."

"For the busiest coffee shop in Cloudburst?" Aiden shook his head in disbelief.

"How do you know I'm the busiest?" Moira stepped up behind the counter just as the door jingled and Saturday customers filed in along with her two weekend servers. She waved and sighed with relief. *Thank the Goddess none of them called in sick.*

"Do I really need to answer that?" She didn't have to look to know Aiden smirked.

"Good morning, Moira." Talia called as she bustled through the doors. "Looks like the weather is clearing a little and we might get some sun. Sorry, I'm late. I got to talking with my roommate Matilda. She went on and on about the guy staying with Sabrina."

"Oh?" Moira followed her toward the massage room. "Everything okay?"

"Yeah, good. Can you help me carry my hot rocks? I'm out of hands." Talia juggled her massage table linen basket as well as her bag of towels and oils.

"Aiden, would you be willing? I can't leave the front now that we're open."

"Aiden?" Talia stopped, her eyebrows raising. "Wow, you really are here. Planning to stay long?"

"Talia." Moira shot her a warning look.

"Oh, all right. If you could take this, that would help." Talia handed Aiden her linen basket and strode for the massage room.

Aiden winked at Moira before he followed. Talia knew about all her pining over his disappearance, but it wasn't her problem to fix. *Or to hold Aiden accountable. That job's mine.* So far he'd insisted on making it up to her. *We'll see.*

More customers came in and she focused on serving them, their festive mood brightening hers. It got so busy, she didn't notice Aiden helping behind the counter until she ran into him.

"Oh glory, I'm sorry."

He caught her against his chest with a warm smile. A frisson of awareness shot up her spine and his scent filled her nose under the sultry fragrances of baked goods and coffee. She froze and met his cerulean blue gaze, the moment pushing away the world around her.

"Careful. You don't want to spill that."

Aiden's voice held a note of arousal as well as humor. The urge to throw her arms around him and taste his mouth screamed into her awareness. *What the hell is wrong with me?*

She cleared her throat. "I didn't know you were helping behind the counter."

"Until you suggest something else I can do for you, I figured I should pitch in." The undercurrent in his words matched his sly grin as he set her back from him and moved around her.

I could suggest something he could do for me. She mentally slapped herself and delivered the coffee order to the person waiting. The rush lasted for another fifteen minutes and she found herself more energized while working with Aiden. Despite his lack of knowledge toward coffees, he fit in behind the counter more easily than she expected.

"Wow, that was intense." He gave her a tight smile, tension bracing his shoulders. "Is it always like this?"

"It comes and goes. Are you okay?"

"Yeah, yeah, I'm good." Aiden nodded, but Moira didn't need her extra abilities to know when he lied.

"Hey." She pulled him aside, not liking the glazed look to his eyes. "Come with me for a moment." She waved at one of her servers. "Ashley, please watch the counter for me for a bit. I'll be right back."

As the shorter woman filled in behind her, Moira shoved Aiden into the back office once more. He went, not even protesting. She sat him in one of the chairs in front of the desk and handed him a glass of water, watching him until he'd taken a few sips. He leaned his head back and closed his eyes, his chest rising and falling as if he needed to catch his breath.

"All right, what gives, Aiden?"

He didn't bother to open his eyes. "What do you mean?"

"Come on." She crossed her arms over her chest. "You were tense enough to break if I tapped you on the shoulder out there. What happened?" She crouched in front of him, resting her hands on his knees. "What's going on?"

He didn't answer for a long time as he took deep, calming breaths. The tension slowly released from his body, but he didn't open his eyes. She tried to sense his emotional state, but he'd shut down and she had to wait.

"I told you about my odd sexual needs and how pain keeps them in check."

She frowned. "Yeah. What does that have to do with this?"

"Do you remember how I wouldn't meet anyone's gaze while talking to people when I was a kid?" He still hadn't opened his eyes now, either.

"Yes, I remember. I just thought it was a defense mechanism."

"It was—is. But not because of anxiety or fear of connecting." He sighed and finally met her gaze. "Your family isn't the only one with special talents."

Moira blinked. The stories of the Callahan family had been passed down through the generations, of how their people were the only survivors of the old Roanoke settlement in Virginia. They'd made it across the wild, untamed country back in the late seventeenth century and settled in what would be Cloudburst, Colorado. The Goddess had bestowed great abilities and blessings on the three founding families of the town. The Callahans were the most prominent and had become discriminating about who their children married because of it. *Mated is a more accurate term.*

"I have abilities, too, but they're more of a curse than a blessing." Aiden's voice sounded raw and he drank more water. "I learn things about people, things I shouldn't, just by looking them in the eyes. I know their BMI, weight, height, probable lifespan and date of death. I know how much they exercise per week, how many cigarettes they smoke, and what's afflicting them at the moment I see them." He grimaced and slid his gaze around her office. "I can't shut it off. Not meeting their gaze helps and protects me from the overwhelming statistics, things I don't want to know."

"You meet my gaze all the time." She dipped her head to recapture his gaze. "Do you see my statistics?"

"No." He drank again. "You're the only one from whom I didn't get a list. Around you, the energy is calm and the numbers don't run." His gaze turned intense. "In fact, the only thing I get from you is you're my one and only, the woman who holds the other half of my soul."

Moira waited for him to crack a smile or make a joke of it, but Aiden kept his gaze steady. *Wait, what?*

She set her hands on her hips. "You say I'm your 'one and only' because I don't make the statistics run in your head. Is that why you've come back to Cloudburst?"

He dipped his chin in agreement. "Yes."

She narrowed her eyes. "How long did it take you to come to this conclusion?"

He dropped his gaze again with a grimace. "Almost immediately after I left."

Anger kindled again. "Okay, stop. I can't do this. You left me wondering what the hell happened to you, for damn near two decades, but you *knew* I was that important to you the moment you left? What the fuck, Aiden?"

"I know—"

"No, stop. I don't want to hear any more."

"Please, let me explain."

"No." She held up her hand and shook her head. "You're back here now, in my place, so you get to live by my rules. But now you're telling me that being around people overwhelms you." She shot him a flat look. "I own and operate a coffee shop, a public venue full of people every day."

"Yes, I know."

"Then why the hell are you here, Aiden?" She stopped, her breath failing and her stomach dropping. "Did you come here to take me away from Cloudburst?"

He sighed and set the glass down on her desk. "Yes, originally that was the plan."

Dismay and betrayal ricocheted through her chest. *He doesn't know me at all.* "Wow. You selfish lowlife. What I want doesn't matter at all to you, does it?"

"What?" His eyebrows rose at the venom in her voice. "No, that's not it at all."

"Isn't it? You came here for you, to get what you wanted, whether I felt the same or not." She scowled and shook her head. "I don't need another selfish lover. Maybe you should pack up and head back to where you came from." She turned away, her heart breaking. She'd never told anyone to leave before, but it felt both painful and empowering. This was her choice and her place. He didn't have to stay, but she didn't really want him to leave.

"Moira." He rose and took a few steps toward her before she put her hand up. "Please, hear me out. You're right. I thought I'd be able to return to Cloudburst and sweep you off your feet. But now I see you have a business and a good life here, and it means a lot to you. I could never take you away from that."

"How generous of you." Sarcasm became a living thing in those four words.

"I hadn't planned to stay, it's true. There are a lot of old memories for me in this town, but not necessarily good ones." He rubbed the back of his neck as she shot him a triumphant look. "That's part of the reason I stayed away for so long. But I need you, Moira."

She snorted. "You need me?"

"Yeah, more than I realized. You're my Lady Cloudburst, and you're established here with a business and family. I'll just have to find my place here with you."

"Whoa back there, Hoss." She held up both hands and he sat back in his chair. "We're just working on friendship last I checked. You don't have to stay. I'm not requiring it, especially if you don't want to be here."

He shook his head. "You don't understand. I need to be here, Moira. I came back because I acknowledged it. I'm not going anywhere."

"But I don't want you here if you hate it. That's the quickest way to resentment, and I've had enough of that." She retreated behind the desk, to give them both perspective, and him some safety. Her temper threatened to boil over with violence. "And what about my needs? What if I don't need you?"

It wasn't true, not really, but so far Aiden's visit had been all about Aiden. He'd returned because he needed her, on his time, when he was ready. Not once had he asked her what she needed or wanted. *Beyond my sexual kinks. Why is it always about sex for men?*

"What?" His eyes widened as his eyebrows rose.

"Look, Aiden, I appreciate the realization of your needs and your interest in me now that I'm old enough for you, but I'm not convinced you really want to be here." She held up a hand to stop him from interrupting. "I promised friendship, but if you're hoping I'll fall down on my knees and thank my lucky stars you've deigned to notice me now, you need to rethink things. I don't need a man in my life to be happy."

****

Aiden's heart stuttered in his chest and panic welled up from his gut. *She doesn't need me?* He'd never considered Moira wouldn't need him as much as he needed her. He suspected she'd be angry with him for having avoided her for so long, but he never thought she'd move on without him. Not when he sat in front of her baring his heart.

Think, jackass. What does she need beyond someone taking up space?

He had to find something to connect them while he worked on rebuilding the relationship they'd once had. He'd thrown away the last opportunity, but he wasn't so arrogant as to believe it would come again.

"What about your books?"

Moira raised her eyebrows. "What?"

"Your accounting books for the Cloudburst, for taxes, payroll, orders, et cetera." Aiden waved at the desk, hoping his expression looked reasonable enough. "I'm sure that's not your favorite activity of running your business. I'm a wiz at those sorts of things. Let me keep your books for two weeks and see if things go well. If not, you can kick me to the curb. Please, Moira."

As a sexual Dominant, he wasn't used to begging, but he had to convince her to let him stay. He couldn't think of another way to show her he meant what he'd said. The thought of leaving, of walking away from the very woman who held the foundation of his sanity scared him more than death. What more could he say to sway her?

"Why, Aiden? What's the point?"

He rose and skirted the desk to kneel in front of her. "The point is to be and stay with you." *Cards on the table.* "I've squandered too many years being too far away to act on how I've felt. Now that I'm here, I refuse to lose the one chance I've been given."

"You mean the chance you've taken." She crossed her arms over her chest and he grimaced.

"Yes, the only chance left." He wanted to reach for her hands, but his gut said it would diminish his chances. "I need you, Moira, and I want to show you I can and will be what you want in your life. You might not need a man, but everyone needs someone to have their back. Please, give me the chance to be that person."

She tilted her head and regarded him in stoic silence. Aiden swore his heart slowed down until it almost stopped. In all his travels, he'd never considered she'd tell him to leave her alone. *Shows what I know about her.* He sent one last prayer up to the Goddess before his hope shriveled and died.

"All right. I could use the help with the books, and I definitely can always use a good friend." She nodded, but her expression remained enigmatic. "I can't teach you how I do everything today, so you'll have to work the front with me for short periods so you can see how we do things here. But tonight, we'll go over the way I like my books done and see if you got the job. Deal?"

Unmitigated joy ricocheted through him and he nearly threw himself into her arms in jubilation. But a voice cautioned restraint and he contented himself with a nod and a relieved smile. His mother had taught him when it came to matters of the heart and soul, the choice belonged to the woman, and he'd fought too hard to screw it up now.

"Deal. While I'm not good with people for long periods, I can stock items just as well as I can keep books."

"Very good. Now, I've been in here long enough and have to get back out front. Do you need more time to recuperate?" She stood and he scrambled back out of her way.

"No, thank you. I'm good." And later when he had more time alone with her, he'd work on the other half of his plan. Staying with her was the first step. Winning her heart was the ultimate goal, especially when she already had his.

"All right. Let's go check to see what all is needed and we'll go from there."

"Moira, wait."

She paused at the office door, looking back at him with a polite expression.

"Thank you for trusting me."

"Oh, I don't trust you yet, Aiden. But I'm willing to give you a chance. Don't screw it up."

CHAPTER SEVEN

The rest of the day progressed pretty well with Aiden helping stock the items on which they'd run low. When he served a few customers, he interacted fairly well. Moira cautiously admitted she liked having him in the coffee shop and some of her tension retreated.

But everything shifted at Happy Hour.

One of the sinks in the men's room had plugged and Aiden retreated with a wrench and bucket to fix it. Talia had her last massage of the day and Moira had her back to the front door, selecting a new playlist for the PA system. The front door opened and closed, allowing a blast of cold air to dance around the interior. Moira shivered and hit play before she turned around to see who'd arrived.

Sweet Goddess help me.

Her body froze and cold seeped into her chest as her gaze met that of the man who'd arrived. He wore a light gray suit under his wool overcoat and white scarf. Pale blue eyes crinkled at the edges as they looked out over a beaked nose and his thin lips creased into a smile. Her hands tightened on a dish towel below the counter as he sauntered toward her.

Why the hell is he here now?

She swallowed against bile, clenching her jaw to hold it down as her stomach rebelled in panic and fury.

You can't fight the pain, gosling. You know you love it. He'd called her his silly goose, his little gosling, and at one time she believed he loved her. But those times had passed, and she knew the truth. He only loved pain, and the infliction of it on someone else. He got drunk on it, and she'd left him to his addiction.

Get down! With the thought fresh in her head, she dropped behind the display case as if picking something off the floor. *It's been two years. He shouldn't be here.* She swiped at the floor with the towel and rose, wishing she had more time to figure out a response.

"Hello, Moira."

She almost pretended not to recognize him, but refused to take the coward's way out.

"Lenny. What brings you to Cloudburst?"

"That should be obvious. Didn't you get my flowers?" He gave her his patented slick smile.

The flowers she'd tossed that morning. *No wonder they'd seemed poisonous.*

"Oh, those were from you? The note didn't say." She didn't match his smile. "What do you want?"

"Just what my note said. I want to make up for lost time." His pale eyes flared with lust and desire, but it only turned her stomach.

"I said no, Lenny. We broke up two years ago and I meant it. There was no time lost."

"Aw, come on, gosling. You know we had a great thing going there." He tilted his head with a half-smile. "I know you've missed me."

A tight smile quirked her mouth. "If I promise to miss you, will you go away?"

The half-smile never slipped, but anger kindled in his eyes. *Good, now he's getting the message.*

"To be absolutely honest, I haven't missed you." She

dropped her smile. "When you ignored my needs, treated me like your personal plaything without regard for my well-being, I made it very clear we were done. Hell, I even moved away. I'm pretty sure that's a good sign I'm finished with you. So no, we didn't have a good thing going, and I don't want to start up again." She patted the counter. "But thanks for stopping in."

Her heart thundered as she moved away from him, but he followed along like a dog on a tether, and his scent made her stomach curdle. *Why won't he take the hint and leave?* She heartily hoped Talia or Aiden would come out and rescue her from her tormentor, but the only person she could expect to save her was herself. She didn't want to turn her back on him, but she wanted him to go.

"Come now, Moira. You can't mean that." His voice settled into coaxing tones.

"There's something you need to know. I'm no longer in the lifestyle. I was done the moment you ignored my..." She glanced around to make sure no one listened too closely. "Safeword. You threw away my trust and my submission, Lenny. For that there is no forgiveness, and no going back. Leave me alone."

Lenny scoffed, his half smile still in place. "No one leaves the lifestyle, Moira. It's not something you can ignore. It's part of you like the size of your breasts or the color of your hair. But I understand." His gaze shifted past her toward Talia's massage room as the door opened. "It's been two years and seeing me might be a bit of a shock. I'll give you some time to think about it and get used to me. But don't worry. I'm not going anywhere. We'll be together again."

His full smile bloomed before he waved and headed back out into the street. Moira gaped after him, fury and amazement flashing through her like fireworks. *What the fuck just happened? How can he think I just need to get used to him?*

Moira shot a look at the big fancy clock over the back counter and swallowed a groan. She usually kept the coffee shop open for another two and a half hours. Talia appeared with her last client, drying her hand on a soft towel she accompanied the woman out. She took one look at Moira's face and hurried to her side.

"Are you okay? You look like you've seen a ghost." She touched Moira's shoulder. "Damn, the energy coming off of you could power the town for a whole week. C'mere." Talia drew Moira into her massage room and sat her in the rolling chair beside the massage bed.

The moment Talia closed the door, Moira's shoulders relaxed and the tightness constricting her chest loosened. She let her eyes slide closed and took a deep breath.

"Wuff. That's better. Take a few more of those." Talia folded herself into a cross-legged position on the floor at Moira's feet.

Moira breathed for a few minutes, trying to calm her anger and fear. *Why did Lenny come now?* She'd never mentioned her hometown to him. Something had warned her from doing so. But it hadn't been enough.

"All right. Tell me what happened."

Moira straightened her shoulders and raised her head. "Lenny found me."

"What?" Talia's jaw clenched and her eyes widened. "He's here?"

"Yeah." Moira shivered, the fear returning despite the calm energy in the room. "He left just before you came out."

"What is it with the long lost men in your life showing back up?"

Moira shook her head. "I don't know. But I didn't ask them to come back. Particularly not Lenny. He says we'll be together again. Talia, I can't. He's messed up and sick. But he says I'll get used to him."

Talia patted her knee and squeezed. "Breathe for just a

bit. That's it." She waited for Moira to calm a little more. "So, here's the deal. There's no way your brothers or me will let him get anywhere near you. Hell, I bet Aiden will help in that department." She snapped her fingers. "There's an idea. Why don't you tell Lenny that you have a new boyfriend now? That should give him pause, right?"

Moira bit her bottom lip, her mind going back to Aiden's plea to stay near her and help her. Maybe he could be more helpful than she originally thought.

"I don't know." She bit her lip. "Lenny gave me the crazy vibe when he came in. You know, the obsessive type who won't take no for an answer? What if I tell him I'm with Aiden and he comes after him? I don't want to put anyone in danger."

Talia grimaced. "But if you don't, *you* could be hurt. At least give Aiden the choice. Please, Moira. I got a bad feeling off you before I brought you in here."

"I don't know..." Could she trust Aiden to step up? The last time he'd been confronted with conflict, he'd disappeared.

"At least let me tell Kieran and Lt. Fitzroy."

"The police?"

"He's more than just an ordinary cop, Moira. Didn't you notice his energy signature?" Talia sighed dreamily. "I just like sitting next to him at the library or bus stop. He could calm a hurricane."

Moira snorted. "What is it with women and Fitzroy? It sounds like you have a thing for him. You know he's old enough to be your dad, right?"

"Eww! No, I don't have a 'thing' for him. I just like his energy. The next time you see him, tell me you don't calm down. Sheesh." Talia shook her head. "But you need to tell him about Lenny. You're not safe if that asshole is in town. From what you told me he did before, he's a monster."

Moira gave a one-shouldered shrug. "Yeah, but I gave

him permission then. Now there's no way I will. What can he do to me now?"

"Are you serious?" Talia gaped. "His behavior screams 'stalker', and that's just in the first few minutes. And just a bit ago you were worried about telling Aiden to keep him safe."

"Who needs to keep me safe?"

Aiden stood at the door of the massage room, his broad shoulders filling the space as his brilliant blue gaze took in Moira and Talia.

"No one."

"You need to keep Moira safe." Talia rose to her feet and pulled Aiden into the room before closing the door again. "Lenny's back."

"Who's Lenny?" Aiden's gaze zeroed in on Moira as she shook her head.

"What do you mean, 'who's Lenny?'" Talia shot Moira a startled look. "You didn't tell him?"

"He's only been here a day, Talia. We have eighteen years to work through. Lenny...didn't come up."

"Oh, glory, Moira. You know the slow reveal doesn't work, right? Jeez, how could you be so...so..."

"So, what, Talia?" Moira rose to her feet, her fists clenched. "So private? Aiden's essentially a stranger and my past is mine. I tell who I choose."

"I'm also standing right here, ladies." Aiden waved a hand. "Moira's right. Her past is hers to share or not as she chooses." He swung his gaze to her. "But if there's something from your past that's posing danger right now, I need to know about it."

"Why?" Moira knew she sounded belligerent, but she didn't care. "Who made you a caretaker for me? I gave you the chance to be here and work with me, but I didn't ask you to defend me." *Even if I want it.*

"No, you didn't ask, but that's what friends do, and no matter how long I've been gone, I'm still a friend." He crossed his arms over his chest. "So who's Lenny?"

"And that's my cue to leave." Talia headed for the door. "I'll hold down the fort out there while you folks catch up." She leveled Moira a hard stare. "Tell him everything. He needs to know. And I'm gonna get the phone so you can call Lt. Fitzroy and have him stop by."

"Talia—"

"Just tell him, Moira." The door closed behind Talia's back.

"Want to fill me in now?" Aiden settled on the massage bench and fixed her with his intense gaze.

CHAPTER EIGHT

Moira wrapped her arms around her chest and Aiden wished he could be the one to do that. But she also wore a prickly vibe screaming 'stay-away,' and he forced himself to sit still, his shoulders relaxed.

"Who's Lenny, Moira?"

"I heard you the first time." She grimaced so strongly, she looked like she'd taken a bite out of a lemon. Her lips pressed tightly together and she turned her gaze toward the black hot rocks Talia used for massage. They looked like smooth skipping stones and they felt wonderful when applied to sore muscles. But no amount of skipping would save them this conversation.

"Who is he?"

"He's an ex-boyfriend. From Denver."

The words scored his chest. Ex-boyfriend. Someone who'd cared for her while he took his sabbatical. Aiden curbed his jealousy. "How long have you been split up?"

"Two years now."

He took a deep breath and let it out slow. "Why did you break up?"

Her hands tightened into fists again. "He was the Dom I played with in the lifestyle, and he ignored my safeword.

He's a sadist, but I'm not into pain. But he got off on hurting me and pushed me too far. The Playroom Monitor had to stop him."

Fury roared through Aiden and he had to count to twenty before he hit something. No one was allowed to touch Moira but him. *Oh yeah? Where were you, jackass?* Unfortunately, he couldn't change the past, but he could definitely influence the future.

"How long before you broke it off with him?"

"You mean from the night he went too far?" Moira raised her chin and glared. "The next day. I also packed my shit up and ran home to mama like a scared little girl. I might be a wimp, but I'm not stupid enough to stay near the asshole who gets off on my pain."

"I'm sorry, Moira." Aiden gentled his voice. "I didn't mean to imply you'd let him continue. Why do you think he's back here now? I mean, you made it clear you were done, right?"

"Yes, very clear. No uncertain terms." She wrapped her arms around herself again. "And I moved. Changed my cell phone number, blocked him on Facebook and Twitter, and forwarded none of my mail. We were done. He betrayed my trust and I didn't want him near me. I thought it was over." She shook her head. "I don't know why he's here. I never told him about my home town. All he said was making up for lost time."

Aiden blinked and something registered. "Wait. The flowers were from him?"

She nodded. "Yeah."

"Did he come back?"

She nodded again. "Yes, he was just here before you came out of the bathroom."

He bit back a curse. If he could handle being around people more, he would've been there when the asshole came in. But the sink had needed unclogging and he'd been grateful for the escape. *Gotta get better with that to protect*

Moira.

"I'm sorry I wasn't here, Moira." He didn't say anything about it being a repeated pattern. "If I was watching, maybe he wouldn't have approached."

Moira shook her head. "No, he isn't like that. He might've been furtive at first, but eventually he'd view you as competition to be removed." She grimaced. "I didn't recognize it when I lived in Denver, but I've seen him do that with others. With anyone who'd become my friend. He'd slowly separate me from them and make it seem as if they didn't want to see me. I believed him at the time, but now with the gift of distance, I can see what he did."

Anger made her eyes sparkle as she lifted her chin. "This is my home town and my family. These are my friends. He's going to try to take me away from you all, and when that doesn't work, he'll see you as threats." She rubbed her hands over her face. "I don't want him here, I don't want him in my life. When he is, love winds up being lost."

Aiden's anger kindled as he crouched in front of her. "No love is going to be lost. You have too many people here who know you."

"You don't know him, Aiden. He's a master manipulator, and so smooth. He makes everyone believe he's this good, kind, generous man, but he's selfish. He only does 'nice' things to get what he wants. And right now, that's me."

"But we're one step ahead of him." Talia waved the phone as she returned to the massage room. "Here's the phone to call Lt. Fitzroy. There's something special about him and he's wiser than your average cop. And he knows you, Moira. Lenny will never convince him you're the one at fault." She snapped her fingers. "I bet the bastard's been caught by our security cameras. Now we'll know what he looks like."

"You already do, Talia. He delivered the flowers

yesterday."

Talia blinked. "That was him? The guy in the nice suit and overcoat with the scarf?"

"Yeah."

"Damn, he was slick. All pleasant and friendly." Talia shook her head. "If he wasn't on the cameras today than he definitely was on them yesterday."

Moira nodded with a grimace. "Yeah, he's good at making people believe he's not a sociopath."

"We need to tell Fitzroy. If you don't do it, I will." Aiden crossed his arms over his chest, knowing he'd ignite her fire.

Her eyes narrowed and anger tightened the skin over her cheek bones. "Who gave you that right, Aiden? I can take care of myself. It's my life."

"Yeah, so you say, but you're not taking care of it. You're going to let this guy run over you while you hide in hopes he'll go away." He shook his head. "So if it's your life, get it done. And if you don't, I'm going to, because I'm your friend, and I've missed out on doing so for too long."

"Whose fault is that?"

"Mine, and I'm changing things." He scowled. "This guy has been gone for two years and he's still messing with you, with your body...er...chemistry."

"My body chemistry?"

Aiden nodded. "When you get a dose of fear-driven adrenaline, it sends your body into fight or flight mode, unsettles everything. Yet, two years later, he shows back up and messes with you."

"And what do you think you're doing, eighteen years later?"

"Trying to put right what I've done wrong." He dropped his hands to her shoulders and met her angry gaze. "Call Fitzroy, Moira. Protect yourself."

Talia held out the office phone. "I dialed already. All

you have to do is talk to him."

Moira gaped, but Talia waved the handset at her and she took it out of self-defense. "Hello?"

She turned away as the person on the other end began talking and Aiden pulled Talia toward the front of the office. Talia raised her eyebrows, but said nothing until he was sure Moira wouldn't hear them.

"Can you close the shop?"

Talia nodded slowly. "Yes. Why?"

"Because Moira needs to resettle. This guy has totally jacked up her energy."

"How do you know that?"

Aiden shot her a dry look. "The same way you know where someone needs the most attention during their massages. I'm from this town, too, Talia. My family goes back almost as long as the Callahans and yours."

"You mean—" She stopped herself and shot a look at Moira still on the phone. "Do the Callahans know?"

He shrugged. "Don't know, don't care. But I do care about Moira, and she needs to reset and recuperate. Can you close tonight?"

"In my sleep, underwater, with the lights off." Talia nodded and gave him a smile. "Are you going to take care of her?"

He heaved a sigh. "If she'll let me. Do you know anything about what happened in Denver?"

She hunched her shoulder in an uncomfortable shrug. "A little. I know about Lenny Corsica and how he badly betrayed her trust. She never said how until today, but it was like deal-breaker bad."

If he ignored her safeword, it makes sense. He shook his head. "If he's as bad as she's said, he could lose all control if she doesn't give into him. I'm glad you called Fitzroy. I hope he can stop by tonight. I have a bad feeling about this Lenny guy."

"You and me, both, Aiden." But she shifted her jaw to

the side and tipped her head. "But then, I've had the same sort of feeling about you before you showed up again." She narrowed her eyes. "How do I know you're not going to do the same sort of harm to her? She mourned you a long time and now you show up out of the blue. What's to say I shouldn't let Fitzroy keep an eye on you, too?"

Anger flared, but he beat it back behind his eyes. The questions were fair from those who didn't know him. *And after two decades away, they don't know me.*

He shook his head with a grimace. "I can't tell you that. In this case, actions will have to speak louder than words."

"Yes, they will." Talia's eyes remained narrowed, but she said nothing else as Moira hung up the phone. "What did Fitzroy have to say?"

"He said he'd drop by tonight or tomorrow morning to get a picture of Lenny so he'd know what to look for." Moira rose and headed toward the door of the massage room. "I need to get a picture off the security system in the office."

"He's going to keep an eye out?" Aiden let some of his tension go as he and Talia followed.

"Yeah. I just hope it's not like a watched pot that never boils." She hunched her shoulders and sighed. "I just hope this'll work. I don't trust Lenny. I can't ever trust him again."

Aiden scanned the coffee shop before he continued toward the office. Moira's body language screamed emotional exhaustion. He closed the office door behind everyone as she settled into the chair behind the desk.

"You need some rest, Moira. Let's go up to your apartment and I'll run you a bath."

She shook her head. "That's probably a good idea, but I need to make sure the files from yesterday's security records are up." She shot a look at Talia. "Are you okay with closing up and showing Fitzroy the images of our intruder?"

"Yes, I can do that." Talia smiled as she stopped beside the door. "I'm sure Fitzroy knows exactly how to take care of people like this. But don't be surprised if he comes up to ask a few questions from you directly."

Moira sighed and nodded again. "Yeah, I figured he would. I don't plan on going anywhere."

She sounded so defeated, Aiden drew her to her feet and wrapped an arm around her.

"Come on. Up you go. I'll text you my cell number, Talia, so you can keep us in the loop."

"Sounds good. Feel better, Moira."

Aiden led her out of the coffee shop and up the stairs to her apartment, his concern rising at the lack of fire in Moira's compliance. Lenny Corsica's appearance had shaken her and her docile responses infuriated Aiden. *Something has to be done about this guy.* Fortunately, they'd called the police and Talia trusted Fitzroy. *I'll meet with him when he comes.* Better to be on the offensive than merely defensive.

He led Moira upstairs to her room. "You get into your robe and I'll run the bath. Do you want me to make some tea?"

"Yes, please, but I don't want any until I'm out of the bath. No point of falling asleep and drowning." Her dry smirk encouraged him.

"Good plan." He chuckled as he retreated to the bathroom.

The pale stone tile squeaked beneath the soles of his shoes as he leaned over the bathtub to adjust the water temperature. As much as he'd like to watch her bathe— *hell, I'd be happy to help her*—he wanted to make sure she felt protected. The last thing she needed was another man intruding on her personal space.

Even if that's exactly where I want to be.

****

True to his word, Aiden ran the bath then left so fast to make her some tea, Moira questioned whether she'd started to stink. She discreetly sniffed her armpits, but she didn't smell any worse than usual. *Maybe he doesn't like my scent.* The thought left her feeling worse than when Lenny stopped by. *Great, the creepy one wants me and won't leave me alone, and the sexy one leaves me alone and doesn't want me.*

Except, he'd said something different earlier.

Oh, shut up, and get in the bath.

She settled herself into the hot water and let it take away some of her tension. She leaned back against the tub and closed her eyes. She forced herself to breath slow and deep, ignoring the thoughts yammering about Lenny and Aiden and Lt. Fitzroy. It was hard with all that racket, but she focused on the heat of the water and the sounds of Aiden moving around downstairs.

What the hell is he really doing here?

She sighed and opened her eyes. At the moment, it didn't matter. He said he wanted another chance and she'd allowed him one. But was she doing it because he'd help her stand up to Lenny or for some other reason?

"I have your tea. May I come in?" Aiden's voice came from behind the door.

"Yes, thanks." She cleared her throat when her voice came out as a croak.

He stepped into the bathroom and set the tea on the edge of the recessed tub. "How are you doing?"

"I'm fine."

"Don't bullshit me, Moira. How are you really doing?"

Her gaze locked with his as her anger kindled. "Where do you get off telling me what I do or don't feel, Aiden? You're not my keeper."

"No, not yet, but I'd like to be."

She gaped at him for a moment. "Not yet? Why? Why should I allow you or anyone near me? I've already been hurt bad enough by Lenny and by you. It's like a sickness with me or something. I don't need any more of that."

"Maybe we have the remedy for each other's sickness." He tilted his head without a smile. "Maybe the cure for our ailments is actually each other."

When she narrowed her eyes, he sighed. "You still don't trust me, do you?"

"Look, Aiden. Trust isn't something that shows up just because you've been nice to me. You have to earn it, and in your case, it could take years." When his face blanked, she grimaced. "Or at least weeks. You've been here two days. That's not enough time."

"Can we try to make the time, then?" He looked so hopeful. "Give me a chance, Moira. Give me the opportunity to prove I can be what you need."

She dropped her chin. "And how do you propose to do that?"

"Let's have a playdate."

"What?" She blinked.

"A playdate. Time to get to know each other in a more intimate way." Some of the erotic heat returned to his gaze. "Not tonight. Too much has happened at the coffee shop. But let's set up a date and time to play together, to learn each other. Let me earn your submission. Let me be the cure for your needs."

"You're assuming my needs require a cure."

"Touché." He inclined his head. "A balance, then. I already said I need you. I wasn't kidding. What do you say to exploring the possibility that we need each other?"

"Are you suggesting we try BDSM together?" Why did her heart hammer with hope around that idea?

He nodded. "Yes."

That was all he said. No embellishment, no entreaties. Just a simple affirmative.

She pushed herself up in the bath until her breasts appeared over the water. She knew he'd look, but she wanted to know if he meant what he said or just wanted to see her naked. To his credit, his eyes never dipped from hers.

"Aiden, it's about trust."

"I know—"

"No, that's not what I mean. I'm sure you know the rules of BDSM. But because you know them, how can I trust you?"

Sorrow and pain tightened his features. "I don't think I understand where your question is from. I'd always respect your safeword. You know that about me."

She sighed. "My trouble is not in believing what you say. My trouble is your past actions make it hard to believe things are different. What guarantees do I have?"

He shook his head. "None of us ever have guarantees. But I can't say I've changed, I can only show you I have. And you're who I want in my life. You always have been."

"What about the perspective of your kinks being too much for my 'driven snow' purity?" She cupped one breast and squeezed the nipple. His gaze dropped to watch a moment, but he returned his gaze to her face.

"I've come to the conclusion that I'm an unmitigated jackass and someone definitely needs to teach me to be smarter." A smile quirked his lips. "Would you be willing to take the job?"

Despite the seriousness of their conversation, his words sparked a laugh. "Do I get paid?"

"In pleasure? You bet." He winked, but sobered. "In all seriousness, Moira, I can't change the past, but I can make efforts in the present. I want to be different than I was. I *am* different, but I can only prove it to you if you let me. One chance. One playdate. If I don't live up to your needs and expectations, we'll call it quits."

One night in play with Aiden? Moira didn't know she

could stop at one. But what if he hurt her more than Lenny had? *Then I'd only need one night to know.* She could be a chickenshit and run from Aiden because she feared getting hurt. Or she could woman-up and see if the past was truly past.

"All right, Aiden. We'll have one playdate and give it a try. One question, though."

"Yes?" His gaze turned intense at his anticipation.

"What happens if I scare you with my needs or interest? What if it's too much for you? Will you run again?" She raised her chin in challenge.

He took a breath, but held it as he considered her words. "I don't believe anything will scare me away. But if I do find something unnerving, I promise to at least talk to you about it before taking off."

I suppose that's fair. She nodded as she set her tea aside. "Shake on it."

He grasped her hand and shook solemnly, some of the tension leaving his shoulders.

"You've got yourself a deal, Aiden."

"Hot damn." He grinned, but it faded as the doorbell rang. "I bet that's Fitzroy. I'll go check."

Moira nodded and gathered herself to get out of the bath. Some of her tension had disappeared with the deal she'd struck. She'd give Aiden a chance, see where it took them, and cross any crazy bridges when the time came. The water sluiced off her body as she rose. Win or lose, at least she'd made the effort to get what she wanted.

CHAPTER NINE

Aiden shot a look through the peephole and recognized the older balding man on the other side. Lt. Henry Fitzroy had released some weight since Aiden had last seen him, but otherwise the man looked the same. Aiden took a deep breath then opened the door.

"Thanks for coming, Lieutenant. Come on in."

"Aiden Westmorland. Long time no see." Fitzroy nodded with a thoughtful smile as he stepped across the threshold. "How have you been?"

"Good."

When Fitzroy raised an eyebrow, Aiden shrugged. "Mostly good. Busy."

"I see you've reconnected with Moira Callahan. You're not the reason I'm here to talk to her, are you?"

Not this time. Of course, Fitzroy might disagree if he knew the deal Aiden had just made with Moira about their playdate, but he didn't need to know that.

"No, sir. This is someone else from her past." Aiden kept his gaze on Fitzroy's lips. He really didn't want to know the man's stats or anything else his abilities could discern.

"Have you met this person?"

"No, sir. He left before I came back into the coffee shop today, but he really shook Moira up."

"Yes, that's what Ms. Williams said." Fitzroy paused and eyed Aiden frankly. "And why are you here after all this time, Aiden? As I recall, the Callahans weren't all that keen about you sniffin' around their daughter."

"Number one, Lt. Fitzroy, Aiden's not a dog, so that reference is pretty damn disgusting." Moira appeared in a robe beside Aiden with her arms over her chest. "Number two, my family doesn't get to make the choices about who I see or what I do. That would be all me. Number three, it's none of your business who I allow in my home or why. Just take it on faith that I've made a sober and lucid decision and keep your disdain to yourself." She nodded sharply and waved toward the door. "Thank you for stopping by tonight. You can head on out the way you came if you're not going to be civil."

Fitzroy had the grace to blush and clear his throat. "Yes, ma'am. I'm sorry, ma'am. I understand you had a bad visitor today?"

"Bad doesn't even begin to cover it."

His blush cleared up fast. "Why don't you tell me about it and we'll see what all we can do."

Moira sighed and retreated to her living room. Aiden followed, concerned about the slump in her shoulders. He hated her having to relive the incident, but Fitzroy for all his patriarchal responses would be able to protect her better than if no one knew.

"You know I left Cloudburst for several years."

Fitzroy nodded as he pulled out his phone to take notes. "Yes. You moved to Denver, is that correct?"

"Among other places, but I met someone in Denver, someone in an alternative lifestyle."

Aiden watched Fitzroy carefully, waiting for the sneer of disdain as she described the BDSM lifestyle. But Fitzroy nodded, his intensity never changing as she described the events leading up to that afternoon. Surprise flooded through Aiden. *He's not put off by this kind of love?* The lieutenant took notes and asked pertinent questions about Lenny Corsica, including appearance and demeanor.

"There's something wrong with him."

Fitzroy raised an eyebrow. "How do you mean, Moira?"

"I don't know how to explain it." She shook her head with a frown. "He was intense when I met him and had this magnetism that attracts people. There was always an undercurrent of something dangerous underneath, but he kept it in check. When I saw him yesterday, the reins had been thrown off and the intensity had taken over. I don't know if he's stable or in control. He had an addictive personality, but the addictions seemed harmless at the time. Now, I'm not so sure."

Fitzroy narrowed his eyes. "And you say he wants to get back together with you?"

"Yes, but I told him no, hell no, and fuck no."

"But that didn't deter him?"

"I don't think so. He said he'd come back to the coffee shop. I don't want to see him again. I don't even want to be in the same town with him, but this is my home and my shop. I can't just up and leave."

"No, and it'll be easier to catch him here than if you went somewhere else. It's probably for the best if you try not to go anywhere alone, though." Fitzroy made a few more notes before putting up his phone. "I'll get my best man on this and see what can be done."

"A cop? I'm not sure a regular cop would be up to this, Lieutenant." Aiden crossed his arms over his chest. "This guy sounds worse than the usual creeper."

Fitzroy nodded. "Yeah. My guy is a local and a sort of PI slash Jack-of-all-trades kind of contractor with the department. He's done several jobs for the Cloudburst PD. You might know him, Moira. Alex MacLaren? He has that big house on the river?"

"Oh, yes, I know Alex. He comes in for coffee every Thursday."

"Yeah, he's got a knack for this kind of surveillance so I'll ask him to watch for this guy."

"Thank you, Lieutenant." Moira stood, tacitly suggesting the policeman leave.

"Yeah, all right. I'll let you know if we find anything and we'll definitely keep an eye out for him." He paused and shot Moira a sideways look. "I noticed some major energy changes around town lately and wondered what was going on. How's your friend Sabrina Foxglove doing?"

Moira paused and eyed the Lieutenant critically. "She's fine and has a friend visiting. He's taking care of her after she hit her head. You know it's almost Beltane, right?"

Fitzroy nodded. "Yep. Things always get a little wonky, but it seems wilder this time. Just keep me in the loop if anything changes and I'll do the same."

"All right. Thanks, Lieutenant."

He nodded and Aiden followed him to the door while Moira remained in the living room. Fitzroy chewed on his lip for a moment before pausing in the doorway and meeting Aiden's gaze.

"I'll get Alex on this as soon as possible, but something about it doesn't sit right." He took a deep breath before he came to some decision. "Without trying to be patronizing, please keep an eye on Moira, Aiden. She's tough and strong, but something stinks to the peaks. I'm glad you're here to help her out." He paused again. "You planning on staying?"

Aiden opened his mouth, but hesitated. How much was he willing to share with Fitzroy? The man knew his mother, but he'd never really gotten along with the officer. *And I haven't squared it with Moira, either.*

"I have no immediate plans to leave. And I'm not

going anywhere until this problem has been taken care of."

Fitzroy eyed him a bit longer before nodding. "Fair enough. You both have a good night. I'll call with any developments."

"Thanks, Lieutenant." Aiden closed the door and returned to the living room.

Moira sat with her arms cross and her chin tucked against her chest. It was an inherently defensive position and he ached to ease the tension out of her. *There's always our playdate.* But tonight wasn't the right time to insist on it. He told himself a good Dom knew when to push and when to let go. Tonight, she needed to rest, regain her own strength, but damn if he didn't want to protect her with his.

"Come on. Let's get you into bed."

Moira snorted, but she didn't smile. "Somehow I'm not surprised to hear you say that."

He grimaced. "Yeah, that didn't come out right. I thought I'd get you into bed and come back down here to make you something to eat."

She raised an eyebrow. "Is this the prelude to the playdate?"

"Nope." He took her hand and pulled her to her feet. "This is just taking care of you so you can get some rest. Tonight's not a good night for playing, but food and rest are always good restoratives."

"Are you saying you don't want to have sex with me?"

Aiden barked a laugh as he led her up the stairs. "I'd never say anything so ridiculous. But what I'm proposing goes well beyond sex and orgasm. Neither of us have the proper preparation for such intimacy, and emotions are running high. Rest is what's needed."

"What about your kinky needs?" She raised her chin. "I thought you couldn't go long without satisfying them."

He paused and met her gaze, raising his own eyebrows at her. She had the grace to blush with chagrin and drop her eyes.

"Sorry, I'm don't need to be ill-tempered or foul to you. I'm feeling cornered and that makes me react badly, striking out at anyone close enough." She rubbed her hands over her face and his heart melted a little more. "I'm going to get into bed. I would like something to eat, but if I don't before I go to sleep, I don't really care."

She pushed past him into her room and headed for the bed. He stood there, anchored to the floor as she dropped her robe and climbed into it naked. *What I wouldn't give to be in there with her, keeping her warm.* But it was too soon and he'd botch everything if he made that choice.

"I'll put something together for you. Get some rest."

Moira nodded and waved as she settled into the pillows, turning her head away and closing her eyes. Aiden reminded himself she needed food more than she needed his arms around her, but it almost hurt to walk back down the stairs.

CHAPTER TEN

The playdate Aiden had proposed settled onto the back burner for various reasons. The next morning Sabrina called and asked Moira if she could return her minivan to her. Moira asked after her health and her guest, but Sabrina didn't share much more than she was feeling better. The tension in Sabrina's voice suggested she had doubts about Mr. Winterbourne, but everything inside of Moira said he needed to be there.

When Moira arrived at Sabrina's house, Darius answered the door like he lived there full time. *What's that all about?* She nodded to him and stepped across the threshold to hand the car keys to Sabrina.

"Feeling better?"

"Yes, much. Thank you for bringing my van. I really appreciate it." Sabrina gave her a warm smile. She didn't look like she suffered any ill effects from her impact with the coffee table.

"It's no problem. Talia says we could close for a week and we'd still be able to offer everyone a Christmas bonus this year." Moira winked. "I told her I'd only be gone an hour or so."

Sabrina laughed. "How were the roads?"

"Good. The sun came out and melted them."

"I hope it stays out long enough to dry them or we'll have black ice." Sabrina glanced around at her children. "Come on, ladies. Let's get our butts in the car if you wanna go skating."

They herded the girls into the van and Darius came after, his expression wary. She suspected he thought she'd made some remarks about his continued company in Sabrina's home, but it really wasn't her business. *And Goddess knows this town takes that to an art form.*

"Are you going to do anything for Beltane this year?"

Sabrina stiffened like she'd been poked with a stick, but she shook her head. "Not that I've planned. The rituals are exhausting." Her gaze flicked toward Darius in the back seat and Moira wondered if there was more than just friendly concern going on between them.

When they arrived back at the Cloudburst, Moira climbed out of the van, but stopped to level a thoughtful look at Mr. Winterbourne. Something about him seemed right despite his strangeness. Moira had learned long ago to trust her instincts, and everything said he'd help Sabrina when she needed it.

"Right. Thanks for the ride back home. Have a good weekend."

"Thanks, Moira." Sabrina waved and drove away.

Moira watched the van slide through the afternoon traffic until a creepy feeling zinged up her back. She scanned the street and buildings around the Cloudburst for signs of something untoward, but nothing stood out. Rubbing her arms with her hands, she retreated into the coffee shop to resume her life.

Between the business of the weekend and Beltane on Tuesday, Moira's worries about her life settled into the background. Aiden helped out keeping the books and managing the orders better than she ever could. When Sabrina called her to ask if she'd take her kids for the night,

Moira suppressed a laugh.

"I thought you weren't doing the Beltane rituals because they were exhausting."

"Yeah, me too." Sabrina sounded like she chewed on broken glass to admit that. "But this is something that needs to be done and I can't have the kids with me. Can you take them?"

"Sure. I'll try to make a mini May pole and May boughs out of mountain ash to burn in the fire."

"Are you going to extinguish the hearth fire and restart it from the bonfire?"

"Yes." Moira laughed. "I'm not sure Aiden will be thrilled with the idea of leaving the woodstove cold until after we celebrate, but I'll make it up to him."

"Wait. Aiden will be there tonight?" Sabrina sounded wary.

Moira cleared her throat. "Yeah, he just returned to town a few days ago and has nowhere else to stay. Is that okay?"

"Well, I don't really know him."

Yeah, neither do I. But she could sense energy, and Aiden had always been good with kids, even when he was one himself.

"He's really good with kids. He always has been. He says their minds are the least cluttered with junk and judgment." Moira paused, trying to think of something else she could say to reassure her friend. "And I'll be there all night. I can vouch for him."

"All right. I trust you, Moira. Thank you for taking the girls. I really appreciate it."

"It's no problem. Thanks for trusting me, and Aiden. You're one of the only ones." She closed her mouth. She hadn't meant to say the last.

"Your folks still giving you grief over him?"

Moira grimaced even if Sabrina couldn't see it. *They would if they knew he was here.* "They always have." She sighed. "Comes with the territory. I promise your kids will be safe with us."

"Thank you. Have fun tonight." Something in Sabrina's voice suggested she hoped the same for herself.

"I will. You, too, Sabrina. It'll be great. I can feel it."

"Thanks. I'll drop the kids by the Cloudburst around four today, okay?"

"Sounds good. See you then."

Moira set the phone aside and shot a look at Aiden in the office, his head down over the books. *It's now or never.*

She strode back into the office and closed the door before perching on the edge of her desk. Aiden looked up and smiled, but it faded into a frown as he took in her tentative body language.

"What's going on, Moira? Has Corsica come back to the shop?"

"No, no, nothing like that. I need to ask you something is all, and it's a big favor."

"Oh? What kind of favor?" He wore wariness similar to what she'd heard on the phone.

"Sabrina Foxglove had her plans for Beltane change and she needs someone to watch her kids for the night."

"When's Beltane?"

Moira bit her lip. "Tonight."

He raised his chin and inhaled sharply. "Tonight? Whoa. Uh, all right. Is there anything special we need to do to prepare for them?"

For a moment, Moira's mind went blank. What the hell did she know about kids or their needs? Shit, it's not like she did a lot of babysitting even before she moved out of Cloudburst.

"Uh…"

Aiden laughed. "Let me call my mom and see what she suggests. She's pretty good with kids."

"Oh, right. Good." Moira supposed she could call her own mother, but she didn't want to deal with the inevitable disdain from her parents over Aiden's proximity. "I thought we'd do a May Pole and May Boughs, but I remember those from when I was a kid, so that won't be bad."

"Good thing. We didn't do that. Mazie always had to work."

Sorrow hit Moira's gut as Aiden whipped out his phone to call his mom. She'd forgotten his family hadn't had the luxuries hers did, nor the social standing. In fact, she recalled her father mentioning something to the effect of one of his granduncles slumming it with Mazie's grandmother. The ugliness of the words struck her in that moment and she wondered if some of her family's animosity toward Aiden came from inbred disdain.

So why am I immune to it?

"Thanks, Mazie. I'll be by in ten." He poked his cell phone to end the call. "All right. I'm gonna head over to Mazie's to get the foods that might be interesting to kids and maybe a bottle of wine for us oldsters." He winked. "See you in a bit."

He made to leave, but she grabbed his arm. "Wait, Aiden. I'm...I'm sorry."

His brows lowered. "For what?"

For my great granduncle sleeping around. But was she really sorry? Without that action, Aiden wouldn't have been born. Did she really regret his birth?

"For...accepting Sabrina's children without checking with you first. You're my primary guest and I should've been more considerate." That sounded plausible.

His frown faded. "Oh, not a problem. Where would single moms be without the kindness of their friends? I don't mind, really. I'll see you in a few."

She watched him leave and thought about his rhetorical question. Who'd been the friend to help out Mazie back in the day?

****

Aiden hoofed it down the street to Mazie's, enjoying the warm sun on his shoulders. It had snowed when he arrived, but the summer was on its way. Still, he kept his eyes open for any sign of Lenny Corsica. He hadn't come back to the coffee shop yet, but that didn't mean the bastard wasn't lurking around.

"Mazie? I'm here." Aiden closed the door behind him.

"Yeah, I'm in the back. Be right there."

A few minutes later she came bustling out with two plastic laundry baskets under her arms. Both held food, beverages in bottles, goodies, and candles. She hauled them up to the counter and set them down with a big sigh.

"Good to see you. How's it going with Moira?"

"It's going good. Getting her books up to date." He shrugged, not willing to give his mother matchmaking fodder. "I see you've been gathering a few things."

Mazie laughed. "Just a little." She shoved a laundry basket to him. "There are candles and a few fragrant boughs to burn in the Beltane fires. And some treats and ribbons for your May pole." She pointed to the other basket. "I also included some hair ribbons and some plastic tiaras for the girls to wear. Something to make them dressed up for the holiday."

He had the oddest thought of Moira dressed in nothing but a lacy thong and leather wrist cuffs, but focused his gaze on tiaras in the plastic basket before his body reacted. Instead he looked around for anything else he needed. *Condoms, definitely need condoms.* Though Moira hadn't given him the go-ahead for sex, he didn't want to be caught unprepared.

"Do you have any good wines I can take with me? I want to celebrate Beltane right."

Mazie snorted. "If you were planning to celebrate it right with Moira, you better take condoms as well."

"Mom!" He gaped at her. "That's a hell of an

assumption." *Even if she's right.*

"Is it? The original Beltane rituals required fire and sex. Where did you think you came from?"

"I—what?" He frowned as he thought about his February birthday. "Wait, I was a Beltane baby?"

Mazie laughed. "Of course you were."

"You never mentioned that before." He followed her through the aisles of the store, possibilities filling his head. "Why didn't you tell me I was a product of Beltane?"

Mazie grimaced as she handed him some condoms. "It didn't seem to matter when your father didn't bother to stick around. You know this town is full of witches and Beltane is a time of fertility." She shrugged. "Not really so much of a surprise that I got pregnant that night."

Aiden didn't know what unnerved him more, that his mother had gotten pregnant during the rituals of Beltane or that she'd just dropped condoms in his basket. He glanced down at the box resting on top of the ribbons for the holiday and wondered what Moira would say. *Maybe best not to show her the condoms.*

"Yeah, I guess not. I don't think I want to take the chance with Moira." He held up the condoms box. "I'd rather not have to deal with that quite yet."

Mazie nodded. "Yeah, babies don't always bring people together."

"No." He shrugged. "And I don't want to force the issue. I just convinced her to let me stay."

She raised her eyebrows. "And what did her family have to say about that?"

He scowled. "Her family doesn't get a voice in this decision."

Mazie snorted. "Right, and I'm likely to sprout wings and a halo."

"What the hell are you talking about, Mom?"

"Look, I know you really liked her back in the day, and I can tell you still do, but whatever scared you off better not rear its ugly head again. If it does, you're going to lose a lot more than Moira."

He narrowed his eyes. "What does that mean?"

"You know, at the time, I didn't know you left because of teenaged angst or threats from her brothers, or just plain 'free-bird' syndrome. But you ran like a dog with its tail between its legs." She narrowed her own eyes. "I don't like the Callahans and their manipulations, but if you run this time, you'll lose a part of yourself that isn't replaceable."

Aiden coughed a laugh. "Free-bird syndrome?"

"I read it, among other things I found, on the internet." She shrugged. "It happens to young men more often than you think, although most of the time it's really their excuse to have sex with more people. They need to be 'free to fuck as many people without consequences' as they choose." She scowled. "Yeah, as if the consequences don't arrive. Usually in nine months."

"Is that what happened with you and my sperm donor?"

"He wasn't a sperm donor, he was my partner during the High Beltane rituals. There was never any commitment between him and me."

"But he surely knew who you were."

Mazie shook her head. "We wore masks for the whole ritual. I had no idea who he was afterwards." She waved her hand dismissively. "It's not really important in the long run. You and I are a pretty good family, and he wasn't really needed. I don't even know if he's still in Cloudburst. But the point is, I'm glad you're with Moira, especially around Beltane. You're a good man, even if you don't believe it, and she's as lucky to have you as you are to have her."

"Mom, we aren't really that way together."

"That's why you're buying condoms?" Mazie winked and headed toward the front counter as the bell over the door rang with someone's entrance.

Aiden felt the heat suffuse his cheeks as he finished his shopping while Mazie helped someone else. He wanted to be with Moira, but he understood her reserve. She'd laid it out plainly that he wouldn't be able to have time with her if he didn't see her as more than a prize or pedestal dweller. The problem was he knew his own foibles and faults, and he couldn't see hers at all.

"Find everything you need?" Mazie grinned as she rang up the tiaras for the kids along with the condoms for him.

"Yeah, thanks." Aiden nodded. "What are you going to do for Beltane?"

Mazie smiled. "I'm going to hang the boughs and light a fire, and sip hot tea. I'm going to honor the Crone rather than the Maiden this year."

"Mom, you're not a crone." He shook his head.

"I'm approaching crone age, don't fool yourself." She shook her head. "But that's not a bad thing. The Crone is known for her wisdom and experience, and those are two things I value. You will too, in time." She made shooing motions. "Now off with you. Go woo that fantastic woman you're staying with. I'm not adverse to grandchildren, you know."

"Mom!"

"Well, it's true. Can't have any if I don't ask, now can I?"

Aiden snorted as he waved the condoms. "It won't be happening tonight." He smiled. "Thanks for the help getting this stuff together, Mom. Have a blessed Beltane."

"You, too, darling." She winked again. "I'll say a prayer to the Crone to give you a little push in the right direction."

He laughed. "I don't need it, but thanks anyway." He waved as he headed out the door, but his mind kept going over the idea of intimacy with Moira.

He'd come back to Cloudburst to be with her and he

wouldn't leave unless she came with him. The breeze sliding down Main Street cackled at him just like an old wise crone, and he had the distinct feeling he might not be leaving Cloudburst at all.

CHAPTER ELEVEN

The coffee shop remained busy right up until closing on the Eve of Beltane and Moira didn't have time to worry about Aiden or Lenny during the work day. Aiden returned from his shopping trip with enough groceries to feed an army, but he headed up to her apartment before slipping into the office. He'd worn a thoughtful expression, but she had no time to ask him about it as business picked up.

Just before closing, Sabrina showed up with her daughters and the mysterious Darius Winterbourne. Tansy and Holly chattered away about the decorations they'd put up for Beltane with Darius's help. Sabrina hugged and kissed her girls, reminding them to listen to Moira and she would see them the next day. She stood back and an odd expression slid over her face as the girls said goodbye to Darius, saying they were glad he'd been there. Darius blinked a few times, a curious smile curling his lips as the girls fluttered away.

"Thank you again for taking them tonight." Sabrina squeezed Moira's hands. "I really appreciate it."

"It's not a problem. We'll make tea and a fire in the fireplace. It'll be fine." Moira nodded to Darius. "Have a good time tonight, and don't worry about anything."

Sabrina snorted. "Yeah, I won't worry about the kids, how about that?"

"Close enough." Moira grinned and waved as Sabrina returned to the vehicle. "Have a good night."

"Bye, Mommy! Bye, Darius!" The girls waved as they drove off.

"All right, ladies. Shall we go upstairs and get the Beltane fire started?"

"Can we build a May Pole?" The youngest girl gave Moira a hopeful look.

"We already have one at home, Holly." Tansy rolled her eyes at her younger sister.

"I'm sorry, I didn't have time to make a May Pole, but we have other great things tonight. We still need to tie the pine boughs with ribbons and set the fire." Moira took a small feminine hand in each of her own. "Let's get started. I haven't had all day to prepare."

"Darius helped Mommy and us make our house ready, so we can help you." Tansy gave her a wide smile as they marched up the stairs to her apartment. "But it looks like you made at least one wreath."

"What?"

A freshly cut and strung wreath with a central quartz crystal hung on her front door, fresh crocus blooms stuffed between the evergreen. *Where did that come from?* Moira ran her fingers gently over the wreath, inhaling the scent of pine. *It reminds me of Yule.*

"Now, where did this come from?" She gave the girls a wide-eyed stare. "It must be magic, from the Goddess Herself."

"Let's see what else She's done." Holly dropped her hand and pushed into Moira's apartment with joy.

"Oh, sweet Goddess of all."

Her ordinary apartment had been transformed into a Beltane wonderland. Pine boughs tied with more ribbons lined the shelves and end tables around her furniture. Pillar candles burned in groups of three in strategic spots on the kitchen counters and tables. The wood stove held logs ready to be lit for the Beltane fire with boughs of mountain ash and ponderosa pine set aside to offer for blessings. And a small May Pole stood beside the window.

"Wow, Moira. Your house is so pretty. You're all ready."

"Yes, we sure are…" She gazed in wonder at the house. When the hell had all this gotten done?

"There you are. Welcome, ladies. You must be Moira's special guests for Beltane. My name is Aiden." He appeared at the foot of the stairs with a wide smile and two golden gift bags with iridescent pink ribbons stuck to them. "These are for you. Let's get you settled and you can open them."

The girls cheered and took off with their things up the stairs to the guest bedroom. Moira blinked, wondering when life had taken a distinct left turn. Then she remembered she only had one guest bedroom open for people to sleep in. *Where are they sleeping?*

She took a few steps down the hallway at the top of the stairs listening to the chattering of happy kids when Aiden returned and gave her a warm smile.

"Isn't that your room?" She pointed at the doorway behind him.

"Yep."

"So where are you sleeping?"

He tilted his head and winked. "With you." As she took a breath to refuse, he held up one hand. "I set some blankets and a pillow on the floor. I'm not intruding more than I have to, Moira." He shrugged. "And if that's too close, I can always take the couch once the festivities are done."

She thought about the tradition of extinguishing the fire at the end of the night. *He's gonna freeze his balls off.*

"No, that's fine. It'll be warmer in my room."

He raised his eyebrows. "Warmer?"

"Yeah. Because we extinguish the hearth fire, and restart it with the light for the holiday fire."

"Oh." He nodded, but shrugged. "Still, I can bundle up on the couch and stay warm enough as long as I'm not on the floor out here."

"You could, it's true. Is that what you'd prefer?"

He tilted his head. "Isn't it what you'd prefer?

"I'd like you in my room with me."

The words came out of her mouth before she'd thought them through and they both stared at each other for a few moments. Her mind listed all the excuses as to why she'd want him in her room, but none of them sounded plausible.

The reality was she'd lusted after him for years and for this one night filled with magic and promise, she wanted him close. Maybe not close enough for her to get pregnant, but closer than down on the couch.

"Are you sure? I don't mind."

"I'm sure." She nodded. "Now we better make something for supper or these little hooligans are going to eat us alive."

Aiden laughed and followed her downstairs as the kids came barreling out of their room. They lit five candles representing the bonfire of the elements and made toasted cheese sandwiches for supper. The girls dressed up in the tiaras Aiden had bought for them, and they all sang songs of blessing and renewal as the clock ticked toward midnight.

Holly and Tansy began to fade closer to ten and they compromised by lighting the hearth fire with the mountain ash and ponderosa boughs from their "bonfire" of candles. The girls cheered before their yawns took over their faces and Moira proclaimed it bedtime. She and Aiden escorted them upstairs, tucked them in, and promised to make sure there were still a few sweets to eat in the morning.

Aiden led the way back downstairs and set the kettle

on to boil while Moira returned to sitting before the fire. *Guess it won't be warmer in my room.* She rubbed her arms as a wave of energy flooded through the apartment. It tasted of sweet wine and smelled of new grass and pine fronds. She closed her eyes and let the flavors fill her up until the heady mixture made her shiver.

"Whoa. What was that?" Aiden shivered as well as he held two mugs of tea.

"That, I suspect, was from the start of the High Beltane rituals." Moira sighed and relaxed into her couch. "Sabrina and her partner must be bringing it tonight, for sure."

"She's participating in the High Beltane rituals?" He whistled as he settled beside Moira. "Oh boy. I've heard that's a wild ride."

"You know about the High Beltane rituals?" She raised her eyebrows.

He nodded. "I'm the result of them."

"What?"

He nodded again. "Yeah, my mom told me there's a reason my birthday is on Groundhog's Day." He shrugged. "And why she never knew who my father was. I'm a High Beltane baby."

She snorted. "That must have been an awkward conversation."

"You have no idea." He chuckled. "I can't believe she didn't know who my father was, and still doesn't."

She bit her bottom lip. "Does that bother you?"

He shrugged. "It used to. But now it's more of a curiosity than anything. Not having a father around didn't make me less of a man, but I would've liked to know what traits we shared."

Moira sipped her tea. "I suppose that's true. I sometimes envied you not having any siblings or an overbearing father. Being from the richest family in town had its advantages, but it also had major drawbacks."

"Like what?"

"Like there's a certain expectation of how you behave, and my family members started believe their own PR. They acted like they were as awesome as some folks said, and developed major attitudes about it." She scowled. "That also means if a daughter wanted to do something out of character or tradition, no one would support her if she went against the family's wishes when they disapproved."

"Are you telling me they threatened others in this town to sabotage your business here?" Aiden's eyes narrowed.

She nodded. "Yeah, they did. They don't see it that way, of course. They considered it protecting the family and their holdings. But it was about control and profits, and they didn't like that I might be competing with already successful businesses by doing my own thing."

"That's sick."

"That's my family and their influence." She held up a hand to forestall him saying anything. "I'm not a poor little rich girl, but parents think they know everything and want to keep control. At least my parents and brothers are like that."

"Oh, I definitely remember that."

She sighed. "Yeah. I wasn't old enough or independent enough to say anything to them about how they treated you. Not that they would've listened anyway. My dad taught us all to believe girls need to be watched and defended rather than seen as equals. My brothers took to it very well."

Another wave of energy shimmered through the house and she inhaled as her nipples hardened and her pussy tightened. *Damn, the rituals are off the charts this year.* She resisted the urge to set her tea aside and rub her body against Aiden. *That's not the right message to give him.* She shivered and sat back, holding her cup in front of her like a shield.

"Damn, it's potent tonight, isn't it?" Aiden rubbed his arms and swallowed hard.

"Yeah." She shot a look at the clock in the kitchen.

"Almost midnight. The local coven must be really revving it up this year."

He took a deep breath and nodded. "If you're tired, why don't you head on up to bed? I can shut the house down and sack out here on the couch."

"Nice try." She shook her head and stood, holding out her hand to him. "I told you, I want you in my room with me." She tilted her head. "To be honest, I simply want you. No games. No posturing. No family expectations or intrusions. I want you, Aiden. Come to bed with me."

He met her gaze, his vivid blue eyes solemn. "Are you sure? I'm fine sleeping on the floor."

She tilted her head, her hand still hanging in the air. "Did I miscalculate? Aren't you interested in me?"

He surged to his feet and cupped her face, laying a butterfly's kiss on her lips before pulling back. "I'm interested in you, Moira. I want you so much, my body aches. But I don't want this to be because of the Beltane energies or an itch-scratching. I want this to be you and me, connecting for real."

She nodded, holding his gaze. "That's what I want, too."

He moaned and leaned in for a much deeper kiss. She opened her mouth to welcome him and pleasure stole through her with the slide of his tongue against hers. She wrapped her arms around him and fell into his kiss, tilting her head to get closer. When he sucked on her tongue, she whimpered and rubbed her hips against his growing erection.

He pulled back, his pupils blown with arousal. "Sweet Goddess, Moira. I need to make love with you."

She gave him a shaky laugh. "Okay."

She slowly released him, the ache in her pussy growing as they moved apart. He banked the fire while she blew out the candles and checked the front door. They exchanged glances and her heart sped up with arousal as they headed for the stairs. *I'm finally getting the chance to make love with him.* The heat from his body warmed her back as they headed for her room. She resisted the urge to shiver from excitement.

She paused at her bed and he closed the door behind them, the soft click of the latch making her tremble. She expected his expression to be predatory, but when he turned, something resembling yearning and tenderness filled his face. A ripple of sexual energy slid across the room and her nipples hardened against her shirt. She stifled a moan as her pussy flexed. *Sweet Goddess, I need him.*

"You're beautiful, Moira." Aiden's voice warmed her heart.

"So are you." She raised her chin and licked her lips. "I've always thought so."

"Have you?" He stopped in front of her and rested his hands on her hips.

"Yes. Ever since that night I saw you from my window under the tree."

He blinked. "You saw me?"

She smirked and nodded. "The night you left. I saw you in the rain under the tree with your hand around your cock. Jerking off."

A blush stained his cheeks, but his eyes flared with arousal. "And did it turn you on?"

The memory of Aiden under the ponderosa pine outside her window, with his long, dark hair sticking to his face and neck in wet tendrils surfaced. She remembered his wiry body flashing pale in the lightning, each muscle standing out in stark relief. He'd thrown his head back, and one hand massaged his balls while his other stroked his dick in tight agony.

Her pussy grew slick as it had been that night and she licked her lips. "Oh yeah, it turned me on. It made me want more." Her eyes narrowed. "But you were gone. You left me wanting for damn near two decades."

Sorrow tightened the skin around his eyes. "I'm sorry. I was stupid to leave. But that's the last time I'm running from you ever again, Lady Cloudburst."

She gasped. "That's what you called me. I heard you that night."

"Did you?" He tilted his head to kiss her neck, but she pulled back.

"Yes. You said, 'No one but you, Moira Callahan.' And 'Be safe and be loved, Lady Cloudburst' after you'd disappeared. I heard you."

She remembered him standing there, his feet braced apart and his hand still wrapped around his rigid penis. His blazing eyes had met hers through the rainy window, and she felt his need and desire as if they were two halves of a fire burning within her.

No one but you, Moira Callahan.

She'd flattened a hand against the window, wanting him to come to her more than anything and sure she could soothe his heartache. She'd known it in her gut. But when the lightning flashed one last time, Aiden had disappeared and her heart had gone with him.

Be safe and be loved, Lady Cloudburst.

Aiden met her gaze. "I didn't speak those words aloud. I sent them to you through my thoughts."

"But I heard them, at my window. I was there, Aiden. I wanted you to stay. I could've helped."

Sorrow tinged his smile. "I don't think so." He held up a hand as she opened her mouth to protest. "I needed the time away, to think, to learn, to wise up. I was stupid to leave, but it might have been the best thing for me. If I hadn't gone, I wouldn't be ready to love you now." He tilted his head. "And I don't think you were really ready to face off with your brothers then, either."

Moira wanted to argue, but she couldn't find a chink in his conclusion. *Could I have defended him against my whole family?* She admitted she didn't know and sighed, letting some of her remaining tension leave her shoulders.

"Maybe not. They were—are—an overprotective bunch, which irritates the hell out of me. They don't seem to understand I can take care of myself."

"Yeah, they might not." He nodded, his eyes blazing with his arousal. "But for me, while I know you can, I want to make the promise that you don't have to. That will be my job."

"Will it?" She tilted her head. "And how will you take care of me, Aiden?"

"Tonight, I'm going to make love with you." He pushed the tendrils of her hair behind her ears, holding her gaze. "I want to reconnect with you, Moira. I want to show you how I feel and how I felt all those years ago, but was too scared to admit. You've given me the strength to be more than I was, and without you, I'd still be locked away."

She frowned. "But it's only been a few days. How can you say I've done anything?"

"You've taught me a lot in the last few days, and I'm a quick study." He leaned forward and brushed his lips across hers. "Now I want to learn what turns you on and makes you feel good. What are your sexual triggers, Moira?"

"My hard limits or the ones that make me melt?"

He kissed her again. "The ones that make you melt."

This kiss, for starters. She opened her mouth to answer and he slid his tongue in to caress hers, splintering all her thoughts. He tasted of the spicy tea they'd sipped before coming upstairs, and she fell into the mixed flavors of the tea and man.

"So, what makes you melt?" He pulled back from the kiss and she had to reboot her brain.

"Uh, kisses. Lots of kisses." At least she found words.

"What kinds of kisses? This kind?" He tilted his head and kissed her lips in a sweet buss. "Or this kind?" He dipped down below her ear to kiss her neck. "Maybe this kind?" He bent and nuzzled one hard nipple through her shirt. "Or this kind?" He dropped to his knees and grasped her hips, pulling her pussy close to his face. He laid a kiss on her cloth-covered mound and the heat of it sent cream to her nether lips.

"Oh glory, Aiden. Can I have them all?" She'd never sounded breathy, but he'd set her body on fire with a few simple caresses.

"Of course, Lady Cloudburst."

He smiled as he unbuttoned her pants and slid them off her legs. His gaze followed his hands until he helped her step out of her discarded jeans. He took his time, skimming his hands up her legs to grasp her panties at her hips.

"Your skin is so smooth. It's better than my fantasies."

She raised an eyebrow. "You had fantasies of my skin?"

"I had fantasies about you." He met her gaze as he pulled the panties down. "Your skin was only a small portion of them. But now that I have you here, everything about this moment is better than my imagination."

His words heated her as much as his touches. And she wanted more. Her imagination had painted pictures of what it would be like to be his lover, but she didn't want them to cloud the present.

"I'm going to taste and touch and kiss every part of you tonight." He rose and pulled the hem of her shirt up with him. "Let me show you all the ways I've been dreaming of you, Moira."

Aiden gently pushed her onto bed before he stood and whipped his shirt over his head. Moira took her time admiring the ridged muscles of his chest and belly she'd seen in the waterfall. Was it only a few days ago? *Doesn't matter. I'm gonna savor this.* She studied the intricate ink designs on his right pectoral and arm, little flashes of color as he unsnapped the button on his jeans.

Oh, sweet Goddess of the Valley.

The large knotted Celtic raven flashed on his back as

he bent to pull his jeans off, but when he stood she found more ink on his thighs and right calf. Each image seemed to tell a story, though she didn't know how to read it. But she found the art fascinating and arousing as he stood with his dick hard and curving toward his belly.

"You're so sexy."

He laughed as he knelt at the foot of the bed between her legs. "I'm glad you think so. I think the same of you." He dropped a soft kiss on her belly before he grinned. "Are you ready to be kissed?"

"Yes." She pointed to her lips with a smirk. "Come plant a good one here. Use tongue."

"Oh, I'm going to use tongue for sure. Just not there."

And he dipped his head to lick her nether lips.

The first caress of his tongue to her slit made her see stars. She was so primed for his touches, her juices met his mouth as her pussy flexed. Aiden moaned and pressed his lips against her labia, licking up all the cream she offered.

"You taste so sweet, Lady Cloudburst." He burrowed his tongue between her folds and rubbed her clit with the tip.

She whimpered as sparks of light filled her vision. "Good glory."

"Oh yes, it will definitely be good." He hummed as he dove back in to lick and suck on the sensitive flesh between her legs.

Pleasure bloomed in the wake of his sensual assault. She couldn't keep track of all the sensations rioting through her as his tongue caressed her nether lips. Moira moaned and rocked her hips, trying to increase the pressure. He laughed and backed off a little, tickling her clit with deft touches of his tongue.

He built her up toward the peak of pleasure before retreating and rubbing the flat of his tongue against her outer labia. She growled and rocked her hips harder, making him chuckle. But he didn't stop teasing as the arousal increased again.

Just as another wave of sexual energy from the Beltane rituals washed through the room, Aiden shoved a finger into her sheath and Moira's orgasm blasted through her. Pleasure swamped her awareness, allowing her to float in a state of waking perfection for a few moments as her body pulsed with waves of bliss. Aiden rose from his place between her legs and settled beside her, gathering her body into his arms.

"I've got you, my Lady Cloudburst. Take it and fly." He reached down and flicked her clit, sending her into another orgasm.

At last she came back to earth, wrapped in Aiden's embrace. The scents of sex and cedar hit her nose, and she sighed with pleasure. That was the best orgasm she'd had in years and they hadn't even used any kink. She hadn't been sure she could have sex any other way but kinky, but after her disastrous time in Denver, she wasn't sure she could get off at all.

Aiden proved that hilariously wrong.

"That was a helluva kiss."

He laughed, running his hand over her belly and breasts. "So, you enjoyed it?"

"Oh yeah."

"Excellent news." He nuzzled her neck below her ear. "Are you ready for round two?" He pushed his dick against her hip, the tip leaving a trail of pre-cum on her skin.

"If round two includes your hot cock in my empty pussy, then I'm all for it." She met his cerulean blue gaze as she rolled toward him, grasping his hard shaft to rub the head with her thumb.

Aiden closed his eyes and groaned. "I definitely want my cock inside you." He closed his hand around her wrist to stop her. "You have to stop or I'm likely to come like a teenager."

"What, no control?" She teased him as she squeezed

her hand.

"No control around you. I've waited too long to enjoy your body." He rolled away, taking his penis out of her reach. But he returned with a condom held in his hands. "I figured with the surplus of sexual energy going around tonight, it might be wise to take precautions no matter where you are in your cycle."

"You know about that?" She raised an eyebrow as he ripped open the foil package.

"Oh yeah. My mom wasn't shy about being a woman and she made sure I understood how babies were made early on." He rolled the condom down his shaft before meeting her gaze. "I think it's because she had to raise me on her own and she didn't want me fathering any love-children I wasn't ready to take care of. She warned me I carried the Wand of Pregnancy with me, and I had to use it carefully."

"The Wand of Pregnancy?"

"Yup." He rocked his cock against her hip. "You can't get pregnant without it. At least, not without help. And Beltane is famous for making everyone's wand extra potent."

"Which is why you're a Beltane baby."

He tilted his head. "Exactly."

Moira cupped his cheek. "I'm so sorry you didn't know your dad, Aiden."

He shrugged and rocked his hips against hers. "Don't be. It's been a long time, and I've learned how to be a man without a constant father figure. But the lessons my mom taught me stuck, and I'm not quite ready to make a Beltane baby of my own yet."

"Me, either." She pressed her breasts against him. "But since we have the Wand of Pregnancy covered..." She giggled as she rolled over on top of him. "I think we can use the Wand of Pleasure instead."

He raised one charcoal brow. "Wand of Pleasure?"

"Oh yeah." She grasped his shaft and stroked it with a twisting motion. "This right here. I want to use it for pleasuring both you and me."

Aiden arched his back, shoving his dick into her hand with each thrust of his hips. She grinned as she used her other hand to follow his happy trail up to his chest while he bucked beneath her. She loved the ridges of his muscles and the perfect little nipples set in the middle of his pectorals. She squeezed his cock and flicked a nipple, and Aiden responded with a little whimper.

So, my hot Dominant man likes a little slap and tickle himself.

Not that she knew he was Dominant—she only had his word on that—but she'd experienced enough of the lifestyle to get a sense of people, and Aiden wore the alpha cloak.

"You're going to kill me, beauty. Tease your pussy with my cock before you slide it into you."

Even on top of him, he gave the orders, and Moira didn't mind a bit. Rubbing the tip against her nether lips made his electric blue eyes flare. She couldn't help but shiver as her arousal ratcheted up again. She wanted to please him as much as please herself.

Moira rose up on her knees and slid his erect penis between her legs, lowering just enough to feel the head against her folds. She rolled her hips, holding his shaft upright as she dragged her labia over the condom-covered head.

"Oh, fuck yeah, Moira. Wet me with your cream." Aiden growled as he held her hips while she teased him. His eyes glowed with feral pleasure and she wanted to see how far she could push him.

"How wet do you want to be, Sir?" She didn't know why she'd added the honorific, but it felt right.

"I want to slide into you in one long push. Make me that wet, beauty."

His sexy words combined with his electric eyes sent desire surging through her as she rocked her hips. The crown of his dick grew wet with her arousal and increased the sensation each time he slid past her clit. *Oh Goddess, I want to fuck him so hard.* She whimpered and jerked, desperate to drop down on his hard shaft.

"Do you want to fuck me, beauty?" His voice coiled around her like a velvet snake, squeezing her heart. "Do you want to feel my shaft deep inside you?"

"Yes. Please, Sir."

"Do you want to ride me, Moira?"

"Oh glory, yes."

"Then put me in your sweet pussy. But go slow. I want to see myself slide into you."

She whimpered again as she rose and positioned his cock at her entrance. Then she met his gaze as she slowly lowered herself onto his length. The sweet, erotic stretch of his dick in her pussy made her gasp and shiver as she settled onto his lap.

He hissed his pleasure. "Oh, yeah. That's right where I've wanted you for years."

"It's right where I've wanted to be for years, Sir."

A sultry smile curled his lips. "Then we'll have to make this a regular gig." He caressed her thighs. "Now ride me. And keep your eyes on me."

"Yes, Sir."

She didn't need to be told twice. Moira held his mesmerizing blue gaze as she rose and fell on his hard shaft. Each stroke sent pleasure shooting through her, the arousal rising faster than she could control. She wanted to speed up, but his hands gripped her hips and held her to a steady rhythm.

When he thrust up to meet her, her eyes rolled back in her head and she moaned, but he smacked her thighs.

"Look at me, beauty."

She jerked her head down to meet his gaze.

"Keep your eyes on me. I want to see you when you come."

It was terribly intimate and unnerving to watch him while she fucked him, but it was erotic as hell, too. His eyes blazed with desire as they moved together and a feral smile curled his lips as their arousal rose. She wanted to move faster but he wouldn't let her, and the pleasure built inexorably toward her release.

"Oh, glory, I'm going to come, Sir."

"Not yet. Hold on a little longer, beauty." His voice had settled into a gravelly growl she'd never heard from him before, and it sent arousal skittering through her.

"Please, Sir, I need to come."

"No, my beauty. I want you to cover my cock with your cream." He thrust up harder. "I want you to know I'm the one from whom you get your pleasure."

"Oh Goddess." She wanted to throw her head back and ride him harder and faster, but he made her keep the rhythm and it destroyed all her control. "Oh please, Sir, let me come."

"Not yet." Despite his grin, his voice held strain as if he too was losing his fight. "Not yet, my beauty. I want to watch your body flush with your pleasure."

She groaned, but kept her gaze on him as she rocked her hips in the slow rhythm he set. She allowed the slide of his dick to build her awareness of him and set her hands on the muscles of his chest. The ink on his left pectoral made her hand stand out against his skin. The cursive words of the inked missive spelled out "All my heart" between her fingers and a new surge of desire ripped through her. *Yes, I want him. I want all his heart.*

"Oh, glory, Moira. You're the most beautiful woman I've ever seen. Come for me. Come for me now."

She couldn't have held back if she tried. He thrust up hard, slamming into her clit, and she shot in to the stars of pleasure. His electric blue eyes held her as she flew, anchoring her to him despite the bliss overwhelming her senses. She wanted it to last forever, but she couldn't stop the flood of joy as he groaned and thrust one last time. He squinted but kept his gaze locked on her as cum filled the condom between them.

For a moment, she wished she could've taken her words back. What would it be like to chance having his child? But she mentally shook her head. *That's got to be the High Beltane Rituals talking.* She didn't have the time or temperament for a child, especially Aiden's child. She hadn't known him long enough.

Not strictly true.

Maybe, but the man he was and the woman she'd become were effective strangers despite their pasts. Looking down at him as she settled back into her body brought the realization that she wanted to know him now, as the man he'd become.

"I want you, Aiden."

He blinked, his eyes still hazy with his euphoria. "What?"

"I want you in my life. I want to know you better." She stopped before it totally killed the buzz from the lovemaking they'd shared.

He tilted his head. "Isn't that what you say *before* sex?"

"I'm serious, Aiden." She scowled and rolled off him, missing the presence of his penis immediately. "If that's too much for you, get out of my bed and my bedroom."

"Wait, Moira. I didn't mean to make light of this." He rolled to his side and wrapped an arm around her waist. "I'm sorry. Do you mean it? You want me to stay in your life?"

Did he sound hopeful? She narrowed her eyes to take in the details of his expression, hoping for more than flippant amusement. But she only read curiosity and interest in his eyes.

"Yes, I mean it. I didn't get the chance to be with you eighteen years ago." She closed her eyes and took a deep breath. "We're different than we were back then. I want to know the man you are now and see if I like him as much as I did the boy back then."

Aiden studied her for a long time, his expression thoughtful as he let his hand rub her hip.

"I came back to Cloudburst for you, Moira." He nodded when she tilted her head. "Initially, it was to convince you to leave, as I told you. But when I saw what you've created here, I understood this is your home and I couldn't take you away from it. If you're serious and want me to stay, I'm willing to find a place back here in Cloudburst."

She frowned. "Find a place?"

"Find my place. Here. With you." He rubbed the side of her face with his thumb. "I will do my level best to show you I'm here to stay."

A lump formed in her throat. "No more running?"

"No more running. When I said I'm in this for the long haul, I meant it."

Her heart did a little jig, but she covered it with a smirk. "Even if my brothers get involved again?"

He snorted as he rose to take care of the condom. "We're adults now. They don't get to have a say." He strode into the bathroom and she admired the Celtic raven on his back as she thought over his words.

He was right. She was an adult and she could make her own decisions about to whom she'd give her heart. *Not even Lenny Corsica has a right to make this decision.* Of course, it might not be so easy to deter Lenny or her brothers, but it was time to stand her ground for what *she* wanted.

Aiden returned and she allowed herself to enjoy the naked masculine beauty of him as he sauntered toward the bed. He stopped to turn out the light before he settled into the bed beside her. As he wrapped her in his arms again, he let out a contented sigh.

"I've dreamt of this for years."

"What? Having sex with me, or cuddling with me?" She turned her head toward him even if she couldn't see him in the dark.

"Both." He kissed her and wrapped one leg around hers. "I guess it really is Beltane, the time of new life and new beginnings. Thank you for this gift."

"You're welcome."

She smiled into the darkness as she drifted toward sleep, thinking he'd given her the exact same gift. New life, new start. She'd take it with both hands and run.

CHAPTER TWELVE

Morning came far sooner than Aiden would've liked because Tansy and Holly Foxglove were up and demanding breakfast. He would've preferred to snuggle in bed with the woman who held his heart, but the kids were insistent.

"Aren't you glad you wore a condom last night?" Moira scrubbed her face with her hands as he chuckled.

"Yeah, it's probably a good thing." He yawned to hide the strange pang of disappointment.

Whoa back there, dude. Neither of us are ready to share a child. But the idea lodged in the back of his mind and his heart warmed.

"Moira, I'm hungry. Can we have pancakes?" Tansy leaned against the door frame of Moira's room.

Holly looked around her sister's shoulder. "What are you doing in the same bed? Are you like Mommy and Darius now?"

"Well, that explains a few things." Moira's mutter only reached his hears. She raised her voice. "I'm not in the mood for pancakes this morning. But let's see what we can come up with after Aiden and I get dressed, okay?"

"Okay." Neither girl moved.

"How about you ladies go downstairs and fill the kettle

with water." Aiden gave them a smile. "That will be a great help to start tea."

"Okay. I know how to do that." Tansy puffed up her chest.

"Very good. Don't turn on the stove, though. We'll do that when we come down." He gave them a thumbs-up.

"Come on, Holly." The girls dashed away and thundered down the steps.

"I think they were going to wait for us to get up right there." Moira shot him a nervous look.

"Yup. I think so, too." He grinned. "A bit too early for that kind of education, I'd think."

"What, you don't think little girls should see naked men?" She snorted as she rolled to her feet. "You're just a differently shaped body, after all."

"Yeah, well, I'm thinking their mother wouldn't be too thrilled if you told her that." He snorted and sat up, but didn't get out of the bed in case the girls returned to the doorway. "I'm pretty sure she'd never let you take care of them again."

Moira laughed. "Yeah, probably not." She drew on a long-sleeved T-shirt and some yoga pants. "I'll go downstairs and make sure they don't burn down the house. See you in a bit for coffee?"

"Oh yeah. Coffee would be great."

She shot him a warm smile. "Thanks for last night. It was…better than I expected." With that, she slipped out the door.

What the hell does that mean?

He blinked a few times, trying to decide if she'd expected him to suck at sex or if she meant something else. He thought last night was pretty damn good, considering they hadn't used much kink.

Chattering from downstairs made him search the room for his clothes. He eyed the doorway while he rose and found a pair of boxers in his duffel bag. He slipped them on before he closed the door to give him some privacy from little prying eyes. *I better wash my face.*

Moira's scent still clung to his goatee, and he was loath to wash it away. But the last thing he needed was a little girl telling her mother he smelled funny. Hell, just about any other adult would know that scent.

He cleaned himself up in the bathroom and dressed in a sweater and sweats. Hopefully, May Day would allow them a little relaxation time before they had to go into the coffee shop to let folks get their fixes. *I'll definitely need my fix of Moira.* He grinned at himself as he headed downstairs. He didn't think he'd ever get enough of her.

"Oh good. You're alive." Moira shot him a sardonic look as she handed him a cup of coffee.

"I will be. After this. Thanks." He raised the cup and took a sip. "Oh, that's damn good coffee."

"Moira, he said a bad word." Holly shot him a reproachful look.

"No, he said a Mommy Word."

Holly frowned. "What's a Mommy Word?"

"They're words only mommies can use because they know how."

"I know lots of Mommy Words." Tansy raised her chin with a smug smile.

"I'm sure you do, Tansy." Moira nodded sagely. "But knowing them and using them are two different things. You can know them, but only mommies can use them."

"But, you're not a mommy. Do you use them?" Tansy asked.

"Only when I absolutely have to." Moira poured juice into two plastic cups. "Here's your juice. Who's ready to help me make scrambled eggs?"

A chorus of "mes" filled the kitchen as the girls converged on the stove, but Moira managed to direct Holly toward cracking the eggs into a bowl while Tansy watched. Once they got the eggs ready and stirred up, she let Tansy help cook them in the skillet.

Aiden stood back and watched as he sipped his coffee, an odd feeling of love and family hitting him in the chest. This could be his and Moira's family, learning how to make breakfast. It surprised him because he'd never considered having children. Oh sure, he'd thought about connecting with Moira, but not about little people. But watching her with Sabrina's kids made him wish he could have that chance with her.

"Do you want toast or a bagel, Aiden?"

He blinked and looked down into the serious face of Holly. "What?"

"Toast or a bagel? Moira wants to know." She put one hand on her hip.

He raised an eyebrow and shot Moira a glance. She dipped her head to cover her mouth, hiding her smile.

"Toast would be fine. Thank you for asking, Holly."

Holly tossed her hair over her shoulder with a smug smile. "Of course. Just doing my job for a better breakfast."

He couldn't hold back his laughter and Holly's smile widened to a grin. Moira joined in as they prepared the meal. The girls chattered in an ongoing dialogue about Beltane and the brownies their mother had made for Tansy's kindergarten class. Moira asked how Sabrina was getting along with Darius. Both girls said he was fun and made their mommy happy. Moira looked relieved.

After breakfast, Moira let the girls watch some old animated movies she had while they cleaned up the kitchen. He wanted to talk to her about their night together, and about what he'd felt during the morning, but her cell phone rang and she left to answer it. He continued loading the dishwasher and scrubbing the last of the dishes when she came back into the kitchen, wearing a frown.

"Everything okay?" He dried his hands on a towel as she set down the phone.

"I don't know. I guess so. That was Sabrina. She'll be

here in fifteen minutes to get the girls."

"That's good, isn't it?" He turned to face her.

"Yeah, it is." She rubbed her chin with one hand. "She didn't sound very happy on the phone."

"Are you sure she's not just tired from last night?" He smirked and winked. "If she performed the High Beltane Rituals, she might be pretty beat."

Moira snorted, but worry still clouded her eyes. "Yeah, she's gotta be exhausted. Let me go make sure the little hooligans are cleaned up and ready to go."

She disappeared into the living room to get the girls started in the right direction. Aiden watched her gently encourage the younger women to start their cleanup of breakfast dishes and gathering their things. He allowed his mind to paint an image of this being his family with children from Moira, and a curious sensation of pleasure grew in the pit of his stomach.

I want that with my Lady Cloudburst.

But he didn't think she was ready to hear it yet. Was he ready to settle in Cloudburst? *If I can be with her, no question.* He started for the stairs to offer to help her when his own cell phone let out a peal of music by Def Leppard.

"Hey, Sean. What's up?"

"Hey, Aiden. How you doin', son?" His partner's Texas accent sashayed through the phone and made him smile.

"I'm good. How about you?"

"Good, good. You get shit settled at home?"

Aiden shrugged though Sean couldn't see it. "Almost. I'm still working out a few details."

"A few details, huh? Like your lady didn't really wanna see you?"

Aiden snorted. "Not quite, though she took some convincing. How are things at the fort?"

"Yeah, good. We have a few new clients for the security side, and they really liked our presentation. But a couple were kinda interested in the accounting, too."

He and Sean Riordan had started up DACS, a digital accounting and cyber security firm that provided accurate money and tax help as well as security for their money accounts and proprietary information. At first, they'd secured a couple of local Silicon Valley clients and made decent money. But when word got around, they'd gotten more clients than they could handle alone and had to hire more people to help with the load. Now DACS was a Fortune 500 company and had clients everywhere, from New York to Switzerland.

"Okay. Can we get the crew on that? Or do you need me to finesse these clients?"

"Well…" The Texas drawl made Aiden grimace. When Sean used that tone, it meant something needed to be addressed.

"Just spit it out, Cowboy. I don't need your hemming and hawing."

"All right, I'll be upfront. They don't mind the crew workin' on the accounts once they're established. But they want you settin' 'em up and gettin' 'em runnin'. They expressly asked for you to do the initial work."

Shit. He couldn't disappear on Moira now that he'd just gotten back into her good graces. But he didn't want to leave Sean in the lurch either.

"Yeah, I see what you're saying. But I just got my lady to talk to me again." *We did more than talk last night.* "And I promised to help her keep her books, too. Is there any way you can convince them that my team is as good as me?"

Sean snorted. "Ain't no one as good as you, and you well know it."

Aiden chuckled as his compliment. "That's true, but together, the team is pretty damn good."

"You sure you can't come back?"

Aiden shook his head. "Not at the moment. I need to be here." He sighed and rubbed his forehead as he heard the women coming back downstairs. "Look, Sean, if I'm a danger to the company's continued health by being out here in Colorado, I can take a step back and just live off the stock options." He stepped closer to the windows overlooking the street outside.

"Oh, hell no! That ain't the way this is gonna play out." Sean's voice was adamant. "No, we'll work somethin' out. I can have them give me a flashdrive with their login info or even some of their preliminary numbers, and overnight it to you to work on there. I'll convince them there's no reason for you to be physically present when you tend to do your work on the net anyway. You're the lifeblood of this company as much as I am. Ain't no way I'm gonna make you the silent partner in DACS. We've been through too much together."

It was true. He'd been the lonely geek, branded as too shy and too withdrawn. Sean had been the nerd, a Texan much preferring computer puzzles to guns and football. They'd been drawn to each other, making a friendship over megabytes and art. Aiden leaned toward tattoos while Sean liked CG. They'd backed each other up when threatened and bullied, and took the same martial arts classes to beef up their strength and defense.

Sean now looked like a linebacker with shoulders wide enough to make doorways problematic. He had thick reddish-blond hair and a lush beard. Most thought him a dumb jock when they first met him. Then he opened his mouth to talk cyber security and revealed the quick mind beneath the apparent brawn. Clients often underestimated Sean and it made him a master negotiator.

Aiden had grown from the scrawny, gangly kid in to a man with an athletic build. He had strength where Sean had bulk, and it had evened out the team. Sean understood him and he understood Sean. It was a good balance for both of them.

"All right. Tell you what. Why don't you send me their

specs and what they want me to do, and I'll take a look at it. I'll give you an estimate in no more than three days." He could probably do it faster than that, but he didn't want to spend all his time bent over a computer.

I'd much rather spend time with Moira bent over the arm of the couch.

Sean gave an audible sigh of relief. "Thanks, man. I know it's crashin' your family time, but this will really save our asses later on."

"You're welcome." He almost hung up when something occurred to him. "Hey, Sean. Do me a favor when you're not stumping for more clients."

"Oh yeah? What's that?"

"There's this guy who's been bothering my lady here in Colorado. Slippery fucker, too. Seems to be playing the stalker card." Aiden scowled as he stared out the window, scanning the streets in case Corsica decided to make an appearance.

"I hate guys like that. This asshole got a name?"

"My lady calls him Lenny Corsica. Not sure if it's made up or not, but I'd search for Leonard Corsica as well. My lady says she met him in Denver." He rubbed his chin. "I don't know how far back he was there, but she said she ended her association with him two years ago."

"Her 'association'?" Sean sighed. "Is this an ex-boyfriend?"

Aiden scowled at the censure in Sean's voice. "Yeah, I think so. But before you tell me to leave it alone, he suddenly showed up here this week and made some noise about getting back together. My lady told him to fuck off in no uncertain terms."

"Come on, Aiden. I know you got history with this woman, but you want me to investigate an ex?"

"He ignored her safeword, Sean."

Sean hissed a breath. Aiden's partner was a Dominant in the lifestyle, pretty hard-core, too, but what made him so good at it was his attention to detail and the subs he played with. True Doms never ignored a safeword.

"Did this dogfucker hurt her?"

Aiden shot a look over his shoulder toward Moira as she helped the girls get their things arranged for when their mother arrived. "Yeah. Bad enough she left the lifestyle completely."

"Sonuvaprick." Fury seeped through the phone. "All right. Give me his name, the date you think he was in Denver, and the club he visited. I'll track this shithead down and we'll make sure he pays for his ugliness."

Aiden relayed as much as he could remember Moira telling him. Unfortunately, she'd never mentioned the name of the club she'd frequented.

"She did say the Playroom Monitor had to step in. That might make it more memorable for them."

"Okay, I'll do some digging. I have a couple of friends who moved to Denver. They'll know how many places there are to play and which were open in our time frame." He could hear Sean already tapping on the keyboard. "And they'll know who to talk to about this guy. I'll get back to you as soon as I have some good info."

"Thanks, Sean. I appreciate it. The guy has my lady scared and angry. She doesn't know why the hell he showed up now after two years. Frankly, neither do I."

"Think it's a case of 'if I can't have you, no one can'?"

"Could be, but I think it's more than that. I just don't know what put a bug up his ass now."

"Well, don't stress over it. We'll find the fucker and wrap his ass up tight. Don't you worry."

"Thanks, Sean. Send that stuff for the clients to the Cloudburst Coffee & Spa care of Moira Callahan, and I'll get right on it."

"Cloudburst Coffee & Spa?" Sean laughed. "Seriously? What do they do there? Serve hot drinks while you're gettin' a massage?"

Aiden grinned. "Actually, yeah. Well, not during the massage, but before or after."

"Shit-oh-dear. I might just have to come visit to see that for myself."

"Get me that info, and you're welcome anytime."

"Deal. See you soon, son."

"Catch you later, Cowboy."

Aiden shoved his phone into his pocket. It was good for Sean to look into Lenny Corsica. Something about the guy seemed wrong, and having someone to backup Lt. Fitzroy made him feel better. *I'm not going to let anything happen to Moira.* She was now his to protect, his to love.

****

Moira kept an eye on Aiden as she herded Sabrina's kids into getting the stuff collected. He'd gotten a call while she was upstairs collecting the girls, but he'd moved away from the stairs when she come back down. The set of his shoulders suggested he dealt with something he didn't like, and the energy in her house changed from fun to intense, especially around him.

"Do you think Mommy and Darius had a good time last night?" Tansy looked up at Moira, her eyes full of concern.

"I would think so. Why do you ask?"

"Because every time she did it with Tommy, she would come home sad."

Moira tilted her head. "How do you know that?"

"I could feel it in here." She thumped herself in the chest with her little fist. "I don't like it when Mommy's sad."

Moira nodded as she helped Tansy zip up her backpack. *I think we have a budding empath here.* "I wouldn't like it if my mom was sad, either."

"Beltane makes her sad when she has to be with boys."

I seriously don't think Darius is a boy.

"I hope that's not the case this time. She seems to really like Darius."

"Me, too." Holly dropped her backpack beside Tansy's. "He helped us make Beltane wreaths and apple cider."

"That sounds delicious. Your mom is very lucky to have such a helper." She shot a look over her shoulder at Aiden as he stood, still talking on the phone while he looked out the window.

"I think you have a good helper, too." Tansy followed her gaze toward Aiden.

Moira raised an eyebrow. "Oh yeah?"

"Yeah. He decorated your house yesterday, remember?"

"Oh, that's right. I'll have to make sure I thank him."

"Give him a kiss. I think boys like that. At least Darius does when Mommy does it."

Just then, Sabrina knocked on the door. *Oh, thank goodness.* She didn't think she could handle more personal details about Sabrina and her new man. She set their backpacks aside and opened the door.

"Hey, Sabrina. Good to see—" Her voice died at the sight of her friend looking as if the cat had dragged and vomited her up in a nasty hairball. "Good glory. Are you all right?"

Sabrina dredged up a smile, but it only illustrated the puffiness combined with the dark circles around her eyes. "Yeah, I'm all right. How are the kids?"

"They're good." Moira frowned as she stepped aside. "Are you sure you're okay? Do you want some coffee?"

Sabrina shook her head and turned her attention to her daughters.

"Mommy! How was Beltane?"

Tansy distracted her mother for a short time as Moira stood back to watch the other woman. Something had happened. She could read it in every line of Sabrina's body, but her friend never let her attention from her daughters slip.

"Mommy, when we get home, can we go roller skating with Darius again?" Holly shrugged into her coat.

Sabrina stiffened, but managed a small smile. "I'll think about it. I'm pretty tired from last night. Do you have all your things?"

"Yes, Moira helped us." Tansy pulled on her coat. "You look sad, Mommy. Are you okay?"

Sabrina's smile warmed. "I'm fine, Tansy. Just tired. It was a late night last night. We should get home so we can have some of those deviled eggs."

"Oh yeah!" Tansy headed for the door. "Thank you for having us over, Moira. It was fun."

"You're welcome, Tansy." Moira handed her the backpack. "Have a good day with your mom."

"I will." The little girl marched out into the hallway.

"Thank you, Moira." Holly hugged her knees. "See you." She followed her sister.

Sabrina stopped at the doorway and nodded. "Thanks again for taking them. They weren't too bad, were they?"

"Oh no. Aiden and I had a nice time with them."

"Good." Sabrina re-slung her purse over her shoulder. "I'm glad it worked out."

"Hey, are you sure there's nothing going on? If you need to talk, I'm always here." She squeezed Sabrina's elbow.

The other woman managed to look even more tired, but her smile was real. "Thanks. If I need to, I'll give you a call. Thanks again for watching the kids."

She stepped out the door and marshaled her troops before Moira could ask anything else. Moira watched them go before she closed the door and rested her hand against it, frowning. Something had definitely happened at the Beltane rituals last night, but Sabrina made it clear she didn't want to talk about it.

"Everything okay?" Aiden appeared beside her and she straightened.

"Yeah, well, I think it is." She frowned and shook her head. "Sabrina seems sad, like something happened last night. But she doesn't want to talk about it. I'm worried about her."

Aiden nodded as she followed her back into the kitchen. "I suspect it will be fine eventually."

Moira snorted. "You're not going to tell me to relax because everything's okay?"

He shook his head as he put the kettle on to boil. "Nope. Like I said, it'll be okay eventually, but usually at the moment, it needs some working out." He shrugged. "We can't do anything if she doesn't want to talk about it. And maybe it's not really up to us, anyway."

She sighed. "Yeah, I guess so. She just looked so sad." She shook her head, waving away the worries. "Who called? I saw you on the phone, but didn't want to disturb you."

Unease slipped through her gut as his expression shuttered. "It's my friend and business partner, Sean Riordan. He wanted to know when I was coming back."

Her gut sank. Now that they'd gotten together, starting to mend their relationship, he was considering leaving?

"Oh." She tightened her lips over her demand to stay. "What did you tell him?"

He rubbed the back of his neck and leaned against the kitchen counter. "I told him I couldn't leave, that I had too much at stake here."

She frowned. "What does that mean?"

He took a deep breath and met her gaze head-on. "It means that I'm in this for the long haul, like I promised. I'm not going anywhere. I want you, Moira. I've wanted you for damn near twenty years and I'm not giving up my last chance."

She believed him until he grimaced.

"But, I can't leave Sean to run everything himself. So, I'm going to have to split my time between your books, and what my company needs me to do."

She gaped at him. "Your company? As in the one you work for, or the one you own?"

"The one I co-own with Sean."

"Right, you said he was a business partner." She smacked her forehead with her hand. "What does your company do? Or make? Or whatever?"

"We provide digital accounting and cyber security services. I'm the numbers expert and Sean takes care of the security side." Aiden returned to the kitchen as the kettle whistled. "We started it back in college with only a couple of clients. Now we serve hundreds of companies worldwide. Sean gave me the time to come out here to find you and reconnect with my mom. But now that I'm here, I don't want to go back to only working. I want to stay here, but I have to do a little work for Sean, too."

She rubbed her chin as he poured hot water for tea. "Does that mean you'll have to travel back…to wherever your company is based?"

He shook his head as he brought her the mug. "No, I can do the work remotely from here with my laptop as long as I can connect to the internet. But I'll have to get it done in the next couple of days instead of working on your books. Is that okay?"

She blinked. He was asking her permission? She hadn't thought she had that much say in how his life moved.

"Sure, of course. I mean, we're friends, not spouses. You don't need my permission."

He set down his tea and clasped her shoulders in his hands as he met her gaze. "I do need your permission because I want to be more than just friends, Moira. Spouses can wait for a bit, but definitely more than friends."

Spouses can wait. His words jolted something loose inside her and a coil of anxiety or excitement unfurled in her gut—she couldn't quite tell which. Did she want to be his spouse? She mentally shook her head. *Not going there. Can't.* He still needed to prove to her he wouldn't run when the shit hit the fan. *And I need to know I can stand up for him, too.* She didn't like to admit she'd been a coward with her family, but she hadn't fought for him anymore than he'd stayed for her.

Guess we both have some growing up to do.

"I–I want that, too. After last night, I think we're well on our way, don't you?"

"Yep. That's why I wanted to be sure it was okay if I worked on this stuff from Sean. I had him send it to the coffee shop care of you." He released her and picked up his mug.

"You had him send it even if you didn't know my answer?"

"Yeah, I promised him I'd get it done. If it wasn't okay, I would've done it while you were sleeping so I didn't cut into my work time with you." He sipped his tea, his expression solemn. "I'm pretty fast with numbers so it won't take me long."

She didn't know if she felt insulted that he'd do it anyway or impressed that he could get it done so fast that it wouldn't impact his other work. She took a swallow from her own tea to hide her confusion.

"Don't lose sleep. If you're that fast, get it done and then work on my books. To be honest, I doubt my books are much of a challenge if you're working with hundreds of international companies' funds."

He grinned. "I don't work with most of them anymore. I get them started, but then I have a team to pick up and keep close tabs. But this is a new client and they want my expertise to start. Once I've done the initial work, the team can take over." He tilted his head with a smirk. "Besides, if

I'm losing sleep at night, I want it to be because I'm pleasuring you."

His words made blood rush to her cheeks and her pussy tighten. That was the only way she'd like to lose sleep, as well.

"You really want to see if this can work?" She didn't know why she had to ask. He'd told her several times, but the repetition gave her comfort.

"Yes, I do, Lady Cloudburst." He nodded, his cerulean eyes blazing. "I won't be driven off again. This is my time with you. It's up to us. No one else, and I'm taking my second chance to get it right."

She wanted to make him say it again, to confirm his words, but that seemed stupid. Instead she gave him a tremulous smile and nodded.

"Okay."

"Okay?" He raised an eyebrow. "That's it?"

She laughed. "No, but I'm not having much luck finding words."

"All evidence to the contrary."

She laughed again. "Right. I don't know if I'm worth the effort, Aiden." She held up her hand before he could protest. "I know you think I am, but I haven't been very strong in the face of my family when it comes to you. I should've stood up for you, but I was too…" She frowned, searching for the right words. "Scared, inexperienced, sheltered, I guess. I didn't fight for what I wanted. Then you left and it was too late. How can that be worth staying for?"

Aiden lost his smile, his focus centering on her. "You've been my true north since I left. And we've both grown up. It's worth it to me, especially if you say you'll give it a chance."

She took a deep breath. "What about the other thing?"

He frowned. "Other thing?"

"Yeah, the…the lifestyle thing. I don't know if I can

do that again after what happened in Denver." She shook her head. "I know what I am, a submissive. But after that experience, I don't know if I'll ever be comfortable playing. Is that a deal-breaker for you?"

He didn't laugh or smile, but his expression softened. "It's not a deal-breaker because you're the one I want. But would you consider learning your new hard limits? Maybe a different form of the same lifestyle? Something to show you I'm someone you can trust to take care of you and protect you?"

Moira swallowed hard against the fear rising in the pit of her stomach. "I don't know if I can, Aiden." She gritted her teeth against his look of disappointment. "But if you're willing to take the chance on me, maybe I can meet you halfway. Maybe we can learn to trust each other together, and see if this can work without anyone else trying to cut our legs out from under us." She met his gaze and tried to smile. "It might take a long time. I have a few triggers. The biggest one is being restrained to a St. Andrew's Cross. As far as I'm concerned, it's a real torture device and you won't get me near it."

Aiden nodded, his face solemn. "I will never use a St. Andrew's Cross in our play."

"I also have a trust issue."

"Because Corsica ignored your safeword."

She swallowed hard. "Yes." She hissed as the pain from her panic cramped her belly. "Glory, I can't even think about it without wanting to throw up." She shook her head. "It takes a lot for me to trust now. I don't know if I can let go, Aiden." She grimaced. "I don't know if I can be the submissive you need. I'm pretty badly broken."

"You're not broken, Moira. Not by a long shot." He drew her into the living room and had her sit down on the couch. He settled beside her, close enough to touch, but far enough away so he could face her. "You've been abused for the beautiful gift of your submission, and it's hard to offer it to anyone else."

He shook his head, anger in his eyes, but his voice remained gentle. "Corsica is an asshole, not a Dom, and what he did makes me furious. But I will work with you to gain your trust. If you need to use your safeword to make sure I listen, I can accept that. We're both in uncharted territory here. Me, because I've never had to prove I'm trustworthy, and you, because you've only been shown you can't trust your partner. I can tell you I won't hurt you until I'm blue in the face, but you're only going to hear me if I show you." He let out a long breath. "But I can't show you unless you agree to take the chance."

"I want to." She bit her bottom lip. "But not tonight. Can we continue getting to know each other in more vanilla ways? It will help me…"

"To trust I won't hurt you."

"Yes." She blushed. She knew it sounded stupid, but actions spoke louder than words.

He squeezed her hand. "I get it, and I'll wait for you to be ready as long as you don't push me away."

She leaned forward to wrap her arms around him. She rested her head against his chest and closed her eyes, listening to his heartbeat. He'd given her the gift of time, and it was more than anyone had ever given her. It also meant he gave her *his* trust, and that was huge.

"Thank you."

"Oh, my sweet beauty, thank you for trusting me enough to ask." He kissed the top of her head. "We'll do this our way, with our own rules about what's right and wrong. And this time, no one can stop us from making our own path."

She settled into his words and his embrace. Maybe they'd both get their second chance at love and it would stick.

CHAPTER THIRTEEN

True to his word, Aiden kept his courting of Moira to vanilla ways. Moira spent the next couple of days cleaning her apartment to welcome in the energies of new life and renewal. Aiden worked on the project Sean had sent him while she arranged her home. During breaks, they shared meals and talked about their lives apart. He told her about his times in college and with Sean. She talked about her own college experiences and how the energy of Denver drove her to seek the oblivion of subspace in the BDSM world.

And then that shithead Corsica fucked it up for her.

It still infuriated Aiden that her natural and beautiful submissive nature was damaged so badly. Not just because he couldn't have his time with her, but because she didn't deserve such damage. He wanted to beat the living daylights out of the asshole, but it wouldn't change what he'd done to Moira.

A couple days after, Moira's brother Kieran dropped by the coffee shop, his gaze seeking out Aiden as soon as he stepped through the door. Aiden snorted to himself, surprised it had taken this long for one of the Callahan brothers to check up on him. He'd expected the rest of the clan to descend on Moira's place after he stopped in the bar when he first arrived, but Kieran must not have told anyone he'd arrived in Cloudburst.

"So, this is where you ended up." Kieran settled himself on one of the counter stools beside the desert display. "I guess you weren't kidding about reconnecting with Moira."

Aiden grunted. "No, I wasn't kidding." He raised his gaze to Kieran's mouth. "What brings you by today, Kieran? Just checking up on me?"

"Nah, I'm here to see my sister." Kieran winked. "And get a good cup of coffee. What's been brewed today?"

He didn't believe Kieran's motivation. "We have Brouha-Java, Spine-Stiffener, and Caramel Carnival, light roast."

"Oh, yeah, after the night I had, I could use some Spine-Stiffener. Large please."

Aiden moved to filled a paper to-go cup. He left room for cream. "After the night you had?"

"Yeah. One of the horses at the resort got tangled in a barbed-wire fence and tore himself up pretty bad." Kieran took a sip of the coffee and sighed with pleasure. "Oh, yeah, that's good." He shook his head. "The poor critter damn near lost his hind leg. Ivan, the head wrangler, and I had to decide if we'd have to put him down."

Aiden's heart sank. "Did you?"

Kieran dropped his head and his shoulders sagged. "Yeah."

"Damn, I'm sorry, man." Aiden reached out to grasp the Kieran's forearm. "That's terrible."

Kieran nodded with a grimace. "It came down to a choice between quantity and quality of life. The stupid fool had hurt himself so badly, he wouldn't have had much quality." He shrugged. "I did what I could to keep him calm until he left."

Kieran's sorrow must have been vibrant because Moira

appeared from the back room with concern on her face.

"Kieran, hey. What are you doing here this early in the day?" She paused beside Aiden.

"He had to put down a horse last night." Aiden poured himself a cup of coffee to ease the pain he read in Kieran's body language.

"Oh glory, Kieran. I'm so sorry." Moira came around the counter and wrapped her brother in a tight embrace. "Did you ease the critter across?"

"Yeah." Kieran's voice sounded strangled as he hugged Moira back. "Yeah, I did."

"Oh honey, I'm sorry. I know those horses mean everything to you." She held him and Aiden realized Kieran had a deeper connection to animals then he'd thought.

"I couldn't save him, Mo. I tried, but it was too late." Kieran's shoulders shook as he buried his face against his sister's shoulder.

"I hear you. I'm sure he was glad you were with him at the end. You know all those critters trust you." She held on, easing her brother's pain with her own brand of strength. "What have you got going on the rest of the day? Do you have to get back to work?"

Kieran shook his head as he pulled back, wiping his eyes with one hand. "No, Ivan gave me the rest of the day off. He said I should rest and take time with loved ones."

"Wise man." Moira nodded with approval. "You know what you need? A massage. Let me check with Talia and see if she has any openings today."

"Oh, you know, Moira, I'm okay. I don't want to get in the way." Discomfort crossed Kieran's face along with a blush.

"No, no. It'll do you some good. She's really amazing at relieving stress and sorrow. Let me just ask her." Moira ignored his protests as she ducked back toward the massage room.

"No, Moira, wait—aw hell." Kieran grimaced before he caught Aiden looking at him. "Shit."

"You don't want to see Talia? She's actually really good. I'm sure she can help you." Aiden kept his gaze away from the man's eyes, but it didn't take a genius to read what was going on.

"It's not that. I'm sure she's great. It's just…"

"It's just you don't want to see her when you're all jacked up and looking like you've been run over by a train?"

"Yeah, something like that."

Aiden nodded then leaned on the counter. "Would you take some advice?"

Kieran paused, his shoulders tightening as he scanned Aiden. "Sure."

"If she has the time, take the appointment. You like her, right?"

"Yeah…"

"Women are protectors just as much as men, only they protect the heart rather than the body. Take the massage. Then you'll get two things out of this."

Kieran narrowed his eyes. "What two things?"

"Her hands on you, working out the knots from the stress, and her empathy and compassion for the pain you're feeling." Aiden clicked his tongue and tilted his head. "Guess that was three things. Can't go wrong with any of them, though."

Kieran opened his mouth to respond when Moira and Talia came back to the front of the coffee shop.

"All right, it's all set. Talia can take you in the next ten minutes for an hour-long massage."

"Oh, hey, you know, I wouldn't want to impose—"

"It's not an imposition, Kieran. I can tell you need some work done." Talia smiled as she reached out to take his hand. "I can help, I promise."

"But I smell like horse and sweat and…I should really

150

take a shower first." Kieran shot Aiden a pleading look as Talia drew him to his feet. "Really, I smell awful."

"I think you smell fine. Besides, I'm not going to massage you with your clothes on, silly. Come on." Talia tugged on him to follow her.

"Just go with her, Kieran. It'll help." Moira gave him another hug. "See you in an hour, yeah?"

"Uh, yeah. Okay."

The younger Callahan followed Talia toward the massage room and Aiden smothered a laugh behind his hand.

"What are you laughing at?" Moira nudged him with her shoulder.

"Kieran. I'm pretty sure he's got a thing for Talia." Aiden cleaned up some spilled coffee grounds

"No way. Can't be. They've been friends forever, since we were all kids."

Aiden snorted. "Maybe the friendship has shifted on his part, 'cause he's got it bad for her."

"Really? I haven't noticed it from him. But I've seen it on her part."

He grinned at her. "And maybe you're not seeing enough in your brother." He sobered as he shot a look out the windows. "Speaking of which, any sign of Corsica recently?"

She lost her smile as she shook her head. "No, why? Have you?"

"No, and that worries me a little. He didn't strike me as a guy who'd give up that easily."

"No." She shot a look at the door where Talia worked. "Did you tell my brother about him?"

Aiden shook his head. "Not yet. Do you want them to know or keep it quiet?"

She grimaced. "I'd rather keep it quiet, but if Lt. Fitzroy knows, Mum and Da will know, too."

"I don't think so. Fitzroy gives me the impression he

won't pass on information unless the injured parties give permission." He finished pouring the new bags of coffee into their respective containers. "So, if you don't want your family to know, he won't share it. He's not your typical cop who tries to get in good with the town leaders."

Moira sighed. "Yeah, well, my family owns this town and everyone wants to cater to them, or at least to my parents and older brothers. The moment I wanted to do something against my family's wishes, I was stonewalled."

"You can make your own path now, Moira."

She snorted. "Yeah, maybe, but now I have Corsica encroaching on my hard-won freedom, and if I get my family involved, I'll never be able to do anything on my own. They'll walk around saying they had to save me again."

Aiden frowned. "Did they save you before?"

She shrugged. "I came 'running home to mama' after things went south in Denver. I think pretty much all my family would say that trying something new was foolhardy, and if I'd stayed home, nothing like this would've happened." She gave him a significant look. "Because I came home, they saved me from the problems outside of Cloudburst."

"That's ludicrous. If you hadn't left, you would've been stifled and never learned your true nature."

She shrugged again. "But I wouldn't have learned business and started my own coffeeshop away from the family bar. And they could've kept better tabs on me. They wanted me under their thumbs."

Aiden scowled. "Do they do the same to your brothers?"

Moira shook her head. "I don't think so. My parents are rather old-fashioned and think that women stay home to make families while the men go off and start new ventures, or have adventures. They didn't like it when I made my own choices. And they really won't like it when I tell them you're back."

He snorted. "Kieran seems okay with it."

"He and Thomas were the only ones who didn't have a problem with you, but they were younger than both of us, and didn't feel the need to protect their sister in that way. Stephen, Patrick, and Kallen still have those issues."

"That's fuckin' sexist."

"Yup." She patted the counter. "Gotta love the Callahans. They believe their own good press, and the old ways are how things should be. I'm going to check my email and see if the order lists are good to go for this week." She gave him a sad smile and headed toward the office.

He watched her go, but decided to stay at the counter and help a few customers as he waited for Kieran. Aiden empathized with Moira's younger brother at the loss of the horse, but he wanted to talk to him about the Callahans, and what information he would relay to them about Moira.

He also wanted to keep an eye on the street to see if Corsica came back. Something about the guy suggested he was worse than even Moira described. Aiden would have to check in with Fitzroy to find out what strides had been made toward finding the guy.

Before he could do more than throw out the old coffee bags, his phone rang.

"Hey, Sean. Everything okay?"

"Yeah, everything's great. Thanks for getting on that work so quick. The clients are singing our praises and we got the contract. You rocked it."

Aiden grinned. "Good, I'm glad to hear it. They had some interesting mathematics in their books, and they might want to consider getting a forensic accountant to look them over. Someone might be embezzling."

"Shit, really?"

Aiden shrugged. "That's the sense I got. Something hinky's going on there. Of course, if they're embezzling themselves, they might not want you to notice. It's your call." He'd finished the work and sent it early that morning, so getting a call now seemed fast.

"Yeesh, okay, thanks. Maybe I'll have someone I trust take a blind look at it to see if they see what you did." Sean sounded disappointed. "I don't really want to get involved in a hostile corporate takeover."

"Yeah, makes me glad I'm in Cloudburst, frankly."

"Yeah, speaking of that, you got a minute to talk about the guy whose name you gave me?"

Something in Sean's voice had Aiden's hackles up. "Yeah, give me a moment to get somewhere it's not as loud."

Aiden headed outside and turned to open the door up to Moira's apartment. He paused to look around, his gut told him he needed to be aware of who watched him. No one loitered within sight, so he ducked in the door and up the stairs. He let himself into Moira's apartment and locked the door behind him before heading to the windows to scan the street. The outdoor noise settled into a dull rumble.

"Okay, I can hear you know. What have you found out?"

"Okay, here's what I got. This guy's a real whackjob. I looked up Lenny Corsica, AKA Leonard Hugh Craven, AKA Leo H. Carver, AKA Lenny H. Conklin."

"Holy shit, that's a lot of names."

"Yeah, and he's got a reason for all them. He's wanted on some outstanding warrants for assault and battery, mostly on women. This shithead's a real piece of work."

"How do you know it's the same guy?" Aiden scowled.

"Two reasons. The first is you sent me that still of his face from your security cameras. We cleaned the image up and got a real clear picture of him to compare to pics from other sources." Sean shuffled some papers around in the background. "Second, I took a look at Body Politic, the local BDSM club in Denver for the dates you said your lady was a member there. They take pics of all their members for security reasons, kinda like what we've got goin' on right now. The name didn't match to anything, but your pic from the security cameras and the pic from the club both matched the pic on Lenny Corsica's Colorado driver's license. He's our guy."

"Sonuvaprick. Where is he wanted and for what, specifically?"

"Looks like he's wanted for assault and attempted assault in Miami, Florida, Camden, New Jersey, Champaign, Illinois, and assault and battery in Pahrump, Nevada, and Phoenix, Arizona. Our boy's stepping shit up."

"We can add stalking to his resume."

"You think your lady will press charges?"

"I can only hope she will. If we can find him. He hasn't been around lately, but I'm not buying he's gone."

"Well, if you get this info to the cops, there's enough of a trail and a facial similarity to at least bring him in for questionin'."

"Yeah. How old are the charges from the other states?"

"Let's see. Those from Miami, Camden, and Champaign are from the early 2000s, but the Pahrump and Phoenix charges are from the last two years."

"From the time when Moira came home."

"Yup, looks that way."

"And now he's here, trying to hook up with her again. Why the hell would he come looking for her after all this time?"

"I dunno. Seems kinda weird that he'd go back to one of his victims." Sean paused, sitting back in the chair from the sounds of creaking leather through the phone. "Unless, she's become his unicorn."

"His what?" Aiden raised his head and frowned.

"His unicorn, the one who got away before he could do

real and lasting damage."

"Sean, he's done lasting damage. She got out of the lifestyle because of it."

"For good?" Sean's voice held sorrow and disbelief.

"I don't know, honestly. We're keeping things vanilla at the moment. I can't push because I'll lose my chance with her, and I already fucked up once."

"Did you hurt her?" Sean's voice grew sharp.

"Not the way you're thinking. I ran away. There were reasons, our youth being one of them, but they seemed a lot more important at the time. Now they look stupid." Aiden sighed and shrugged. "It doesn't matter now. But Corsica, or whatever the hell his name is, is in Cloudburst, and he made it very clear to Moira that he wants to get back together."

"She ain't fallin' for it, is she?"

"Hell no, she told him to get out and stay away from her, but he didn't seem to get the hint."

"Good for her. Did you tell the local PD?"

"Yeah, and the lieutenant has a man out looking for him. Some sort of PI who works with the department here." Aiden shrugged. "I haven't met him, but Fitzroy thinks he's competent."

"Good. Given how slippery this asshole is, you're gonna need all the help you can get." Sean paused, leaning forward again. "Although, if he fucks up enough this time, the FBI's gonna get involved 'cause he's crossed state lines."

"Hey, as far as I'm concerned, they can have the dogfucker. He should be thrown away in a dark hole and forgotten about." Aiden ran his hand through his hair as he watched the street. "Can you send me all the info you managed to dig up? I want to turn it over to Lieutenant Fitzroy so he knows everything we do."

"Yeah, sure, will do. Hey, brother, watch your back. There's no info on whether he beat up any boyfriends of the women he assaulted, but just in case, keep an eye out."

"Yeah, will do. Thanks, Cowboy. Let me know what they find out about those accounts."

They hung up and Aiden let the information settle into his consciousness. Lenny Corsica was a rabid animal that needed to be put down. Aiden didn't often have violent thoughts, but anyone who tried to hurt Moira would answer to him. Corsica had returned to hurt Moira. Aiden had no doubt about that.

The question is, how will we stop him?

****

Moira leaned back against the wall behind the counter and let out her breath, long and slow. She cradled a hot cup of coffee in her hands as she let her gaze and mind drift. Aiden had gone off somewhere and Talia worked on her brother Kieran, so she was left alone with her thoughts for a few minutes.

She thought about what Aiden had said concerning Kieran and Talia. Could her brother have a sweet spot for her best friend and business partner? She knew Talia liked him, but she hadn't seen him reciprocate. *Maybe that's changing.* He'd been reluctant to take Talia's help. *Maybe I did Talia a favor by letting her get her hands on my brother.* Moira couldn't help but laugh at the thought.

But the ugly specter of Lenny Corsica rose in her mind and she shivered. Sure, they hadn't seen him since he'd delivered the flowers and stopped by the coffee shop, but he was still out there. Lurking like a troll come out from the rocks. Anger rose in her chest. Why the hell did she have to run and hide? She hadn't done anything to encourage his assholery. In fact, she'd walked away from her life in Denver to free herself from his ugliness.

She turned her gaze to the street outside the windows, watching people walk by, but she didn't catch sight of her tormentor. *Why is he back now? Why after two years?* It didn't make sense. She hadn't contacted or encouraged him. She didn't send him texts, emails, phone calls. She didn't know him on social media and she didn't engage him in any way. Why here and now?

She wanted to scream, to throw something, but it wouldn't stop Corsica from coming after her. It wouldn't change the torment he heaped on her shoulders.

She shook her head and turned to look for anything to distract her from her impotent fury when Kieran came back out to the coffee shop. He wore a dreamy expression, and most of the sadness had left his face.

"Feel better?" She shot him a smile.

"Oh, yeah. Did you know Talia has magic hands?"

Moira laughed. "Yes, sir. Why do you think I agreed to go into business with her? I knew she could deliver the perfect complement to coffee and tea relaxation."

"She can definitely do that. Hell, I think she managed to loosen a kink in my spine I've had for years." He rubbed his neck and met Moira's gaze. "Where's Aiden?"

"At the moment, I don't know. Why? Do you need to talk to him?" She frowned.

"No, I need to talk to you about him."

Moira swallowed hard. "Okay. Do you want to go into the office?"

He shook his head. "No. Can we just sit in those comfy chairs over there?" He pointed toward two wing-backed loungers. "After my massage, I don't want to sit on hard wood or plastic."

"All right." She followed him and sat down, grateful she'd made this nook a place where two people could talk intimately. "So, what do you want to talk about Aiden?"

"How is he treating you, Moira? Tell me honestly."

She frowned. "Good. Better than good. Great, actually. We're working on our friendship." *And more.* "Why?"

"Because when he arrived in Cloudburst, I asked him

what his intentions were for being here. And I told him that if he wasn't planning on staying, he needed to avoid talking to you."

Moira scowled. "Why the hell would you do that?"

"Because I didn't want you to get your hopes up in case he took off again."

"Oh, my glory, you are so selfish and assholian right now."

Kieran blinked. "What?"

"What were you trying to do, make my decisions for me? You're *younger* than me."

"I was trying to protect you."

"Fuck you, Kieran. You don't get that job. Do you even know why he left all those years ago?"

He wordlessly shook his head.

"Aiden left because Mum, Da, Stephen, Patrick and Kallen all threatened him and made him unwelcome." She pointed at him with a sneer. "Our 'loving' family chased him off because they decided he wasn't good enough for their precious little daughter. A daughter they planned on keeping all wrapped up in cotton wool so she wouldn't be damaged." She snorted. "Newsflash: I was damaged by them running Aiden off. So, you see, he didn't break my heart, the Callahans did."

"They'd never—"

"Stop. They'd never do it to you or our brothers, I'm sure. If you haven't noticed, our parents are sexist and elitist. They know what's right for all of us, and have made decisions about who's good enough to be our partners." She tilted her head. "Didn't they make you break up with Liz Bradford back in high school?"

"Yeah, but she didn't really like me that much, it turned out."

"Is that true? Did you ask her? Or is that what Mum and Da, and your brothers told you?" She shook her head. "They believe their own press, Kieran. They think they're the chosen ones and have to keep their bloodlines pure. Whatever that means. But they do make an effort to accomplish it, including running Aiden off and breaking up your relationship with Liz."

Kieran sat back in the chair, a frown marring his features. "You really think that's true?"

"I know it's true. I can feel the energies, remember? Our family's animosity toward certain members of this town was and is strong." She scowled. "They don't think Aiden's good enough, and when I was sixteen, I wasn't strong enough to tell them off. But I'm strong enough now. And I'm telling you. You leave my relationship with Aiden alone. It's up to me and him. No one else gets a say. If I want to be with him, I will. And if we decide to break up, it will be mutual. Got it?"

"Yeah, I got it." He nodded as he rubbed his chin.

"Let me ask you a personal question. Are you interested in Talia?"

"What?" Panic flashed across his face and his shoulders tensed. "Why would you ask that?"

She shrugged, trying to downplay her question. "Because I'm pretty sure she's sweet on you and if you break her heart, it's going to hurt our business. So, I'll give you the warning you gave Aiden: If you're only planning on fooling around with her, don't. But if you're truly interested in her, I'll back your play."

Kieran tilted his head. "You'd really be okay with me going out with Talia?"

"Yeah, if you mean it. She's a good person, Kieran. And my best friend and business partner." Moira nodded. "I don't know what the family will think about you hooking up with her, but it's not really their business if you really like her. I'm pretty sure she likes you."

Kieran settled into silence, his gaze distant. Moira smiled to herself. *Guess he never considered that.* She really didn't know how the family would take it, but it was time for the Callahan kids to make their own decisions about whom they loved.

"What are you going to tell the folks?"

Kieran blinked. "What?"

"What are you going to tell the family about me and Aiden?" She needed to know so she'd be ready for the onslaught of her family demanding to know her business. And they would.

"Oh, uh, how do you know I'd tell them anything?"

She dropped her chin and shot him a dry look. "Seriously? The other half of your mission in coming here today was to scope things out for the family. I need to know what you're going to tell them so I can be prepared for their visits."

He frowned. "What do you think the first half was?"

She shrugged. "Either it was to check up on Aiden for yourself, or it was to hit on Talia. I'm not sure which."

He shook his head. "You're scary, you know that?"

"It's a gift." She winked. "So, which is it?"

Kieran had the grace to blush. "A bit of both. I like Aiden, but you know how the family feels about him. I wanted to be sure I hadn't screwed everything up by sending him your way. But seeing how you are, and hearing you say it's good, makes me think I did something right."

"I think what you did right was get out of the way and let me figure it out myself, little brother."

He grimaced. "Yeah, I'm starting to get that. You don't want to be protected, do you?"

She shook her head. "Not in that way. I want you to have my back, not warn off other men you wouldn't choose to go out with."

"I wouldn't choose to go out with any men, Moira."

She scowled. "The point is, just because you don't like the guy doesn't mean you get to choose who I get to be with. What Da and our brothers forget is I'm a person who can make my own decisions. Instead, they see me as a valuable, something to be defended and held, not a person like them."

He frowned. "I'm sure that's not true. They see you as a person."

"Think so? They chased off Aiden because they didn't approve of him, and the damn near destroyed any chance for me to start my own business in town. Did they ever do that to you or Thomas, when he wanted to start his own music school?"

"That's different. He didn't start a business in competition with theirs."

"Neither did I, Kieran. I don't serve alcohol or greasy food."

He opened his mouth, but nothing came out as he thought over her words. She understood her parents' belief in the idea of men leading, but she'd seen what could happen when no one balanced that, and her brothers all benefited from the imbalance.

"You're right. Mum and Da never said a word to get in Thomas's or Kallen's way."

"Exactly. So, I'll ask you again. What are you going to tell the family about me?"

Kieran sat back and let his gaze swing away from her. He seemed reluctant to answer, but she wouldn't let him squirm out of this one. She needed to be prepared, because it was time her family understood she'd make her own way.

"I'm gonna tell them you're doing well. You're successful, happy, and have reconnected with Aiden." Kieran returned his gaze to her face. "But I do have one question. Do you love him?"

Now it was her turn to slide her gaze away. Did she?

Memories of what he'd said about their relationship came back to her. He said they'd do it their way, without interference from anyone else. They'd make their own rules because others' rules didn't work for them. He'd listened to her, understood her needs and fears, and let her take her time. Did all that equate to love?

She met her brother's gaze. "It's too early for me to answer that honestly. But he has my respect, my admiration, and my affection. He treats me as a person, Kieran, which is more than I can say for my older brothers and parents. He doesn't see me as a stepping stone or a bargaining chip for better things. And he doesn't make unilateral decisions for me." *At least outside the bedroom.* "That means a lot to me."

Kieran's gaze shifted away from her and she turned her head to follow it, meeting Aiden's. She had no idea how long he'd been standing there or how much he heard, but his expression suggested he'd heard enough. Pride and pleasure filled his eyes, and she suppressed a shiver that she'd managed to please him.

"I think I'm going to tell them you're doing fine." Kieran's eyes sparkled as he turned them to Moira.

"And are you going to mention Aiden?"

"Of course." He nodded as Aiden came to stand beside her chair.

"Kieran—"

"They're going to find out, Moira. Besides, they need to understand there's a good likelihood he's going to be a permanent part of your life." He held up a hand to stop her protest. "I know it's not a done deal yet, but just the things you've told me make me think it won't be long. And I'm very happy for you."

"Are you going to tell them about Talia?"

Kieran lost all expression. "Why would I?"

She held up her hands. "All right, I'll leave it alone. But here's the thing, Kieran. Whatever you feel for Talia, you best tell her. Because either you're leading her on, or you're being a coward and not facing up to your own needs. Take it from me, the second option isn't fun, either."

His gaze drifted back to the door of Talia's massage

room. "Yeah."

"Right, well, I gotta get back to work. I'm sorry your day started off so bad. Hopefully it'll get better from here on out." Moira stood and smiled at her brother. "I'm glad you stopped by and we had this talk."

"Hey, Moira. Don't tell Talia anything, okay?"

For just a moment, her confident younger brother looked like the little boy she'd taught to fly fish in Oro Creek, all uncertain and a little afraid. He stood beside the chair, his shoulders hunched and his hands shoved into his jean pockets.

"I won't. But don't play any games with her, little brother. She's a person I value and deserves honesty."

"Yeah, I know." He nodded. "Thanks." He rubbed the back of his neck and grimaced. "I better get home and take a shower before I catch a nap. I'll see you around, yeah?"

"Yeah." Moira waved him out the door, feeling Aiden at her back. "What?"

He dropped a soft kiss on the top of her head. "I don't see you as a stepping stone or a bargaining chip. You're an amazing person and I love being with you."

"Thanks, Aiden." She turned around and smiled at him. "Where did you head off to?"

"I got a call from Sean and needed some quiet to talk to him."

"Oh, okay. Everything all right?"

He grimaced. "Yes, and no. I gotta to talk to you about Corsica, but it might be a conversation better left till when we're alone."

Her stomach sank and her throat dried out. "Corsica?"

"Yeah." Aiden rubbed the back of his neck much like her brother had done earlier. "I want to talk to you about him. You might consider telling your family he's here in town. He's a lot worse than you knew."

"Oh, glory." She shot a look out the front windows as if Corsica would show up, conjured by her thoughts. "He's bad, isn't he? I knew there was something wrong two years ago, but I figured moving back to Cloudburst was the best option. Now he's followed me here. Sweet Goddess, they have to catch him."

"They will. I'm going to email this to Lt. Fitzroy. I want him to see what I've found out." He rubbed her back. "I don't like the idea that he's targeted you after all this time."

Moira swallowed back bile. "What is he, Aiden? Why is he here?"

He shook his head. "He's a predator, but I don't know why he's here for you."

"Yeah, I don't either." She hissed as she rubbed her arms with her hands. "It's hard to feel safe when I know he's out there, waiting for me to let down my guard."

He tilted his head. "Come with me." He held out his hand and she had the odd feeling he meant more than simply following him. If she gave him her hand, what did it really mean to her? She took his hand, refusing to think about it as he led her into the office. *It's just him wanting to protect me, nothing more.* But she didn't quite believe it.

"All right, here's what I learned about Lenny Corsica."

She read over the email he'd received, and her gut sank lower and lower with each new paragraph. Multiple assaults, all involving some sort of pain or rape. And women from all over the country, even after she'd left him.

"Sweet Goddess of the Valley." Moira turned to Aiden with her hand over her mouth to keep from throwing up. "He's a monster. They have to catch him."

"Yeah, no argument there." Aiden typed at the computer to print the information as well as email it on to the Cloudburst PD. "Once Fitzroy sees this, he'll probably step things up. He might even inform the FBI since it spans across state lines."

"Great."

"Hey, it's going to be okay. They'll catch him and all

we'll have to deal with is your family." He grinned.

She wished she could be so confident, but in truth she worried it would be a lot harder than he said. "Glory, I don't want to face them, either."

"Come on. Let me make you a meal and pamper you."

Moira gaped at him. "I can't just leave. It's still the afternoon. We don't close until eight."

"And you have folks to do that, right?" He pulled her out of the office toward the front. "Besides, I'm just going to make you a meal, pamper you a bit, and then you can come back and close up for the night, if you're so inclined."

She huffed a laugh as he paused just outside of Talia's room. "You're serious."

"Yes. Tell Talia you need a breather, and I'm sure she'll tell you it'll be fine."

Moira narrowed her eyes. "Did you cook something up with her?"

"No, ma'am. But I'm pretty sure she'll think it's a good idea anyway. Why don't you go ask?"

He grinned so infuriatingly sweet, she couldn't help but laugh. "All right, I'll ask, but be prepared. She's busy today. More than likely she'll say I need to be back here to close."

CHAPTER FOURTEEN

"I can't believe she told me to take the rest of the day."

Aiden swallowed a chuckle as he led Moira into the living room of her apartment and sat her down on the couch.

"You totally set me up with her help, didn't you?" She shot him a narrow-eyed look.

"Nope. I didn't do anything." He grinned as he headed for the kitchen. "But I'm pretty sure she's noticed how dealing with your family along with the threat of Corsica is wearing on you. I've noticed."

Moira's shoulders slumped. "It's a lot to take in."

"Yes. Have you thought about telling them? They could be helpful with keeping an eye out for him."

She shook her head. "That means they'll ask questions and tell me it's my fault, and do the whole, 'well, if you hadn't left...'"

"I think you're selling them short. They're your family and they care about you." He set the kettle on to boil and pulled out some pasta and sauce to prepare a comfort meal.

She barked a laugh. "Why are you defending them? They ran you off because you weren't good enough for them. Not me, them." She scowled. "If they truly cared for me, they wouldn't have a problem with you being my boyfriend."

He couldn't argue with her there, but he needed to know one thing. "Does that mean I'm your boyfriend?"

"What?" She gave him the perfect 'deer in headlights' look.

"Do you consider me your boyfriend?" He didn't mean to hold his breath, but he needed her to say yes. *And if she does, I'll be her slave forever.*

That was all he'd ever wanted. To serve her to the best of his ability, not only in life, but in Dominance as well. Of course, when he left Cloudburst, he hadn't known her proclivities and figured his were way out of left field. But now that he understood her submissive nature, he needed her to need him. He was desperate to serve her as her Dom.

"I—"

"Because I want to be." He came around to kneel in front of her and take her hands. "I want to be your lover. The man who brings you to orgasm with loving attention to detail. I want to be the one who stands at your back, lending support, or stands in front of you in defense. I want to be the one who receives the gift of your submission and earns it every day, by showing you I'm worthy of it."

For the second time, Moira gaped at him. "Showing me *you're* worthy?"

He nodded, losing his smile. "There's no need for Dominance if there isn't a submissive to serve. It's my job to please you and to give you what you need. If I'm worthy of your gift, you'll come back to me for more." He gave her a half-smile. "To be honest, I need to be needed. I serve you by giving you what you need."

"And what do you think I need, Aiden?" She didn't smile, but her tone wasn't hostile.

"I think you've had a lot to deal with, making your business run, fighting for your independence, always making decisions. The buck stops with you." He pushed some errant tendrils of hair behind her ears. "I think you need someone to take those decisions away from you in bed, so you can fully relax. Someone you can depend on to make sure you get the most pleasure."

Her pupils dilated and her breathing quickened, but she swallowed and tilted her head. "You think I need someone else to make my sexual decisions?"

"Oh, no. I know you can make those on your own. What I think you need is someone who knows what you want and gives it to you every time without you having to tell or direct him."

"Oh glory." She took a deep breath, the expansion of her chest raising her breasts, and consequently, his dick. "I left the lifestyle, Aiden. I don't think I can go back to it. I know what I need, but I still have nightmares of being tied down and…and…"

"Raped?"

"Yes." She swallowed hard and looked away. "I know I'm broken, so you don't have to say it. But this is where I am now. I can enjoy vanilla sex, but that will slowly kill you and you'll resent me."

"Moira, stop." He grasped her face in his hands and turned her to look at him. "You're not broken, and vanilla sex isn't going to make me miserable. Not if it's with you. But you know BDSM is more than physical restraints and pain. And we make our own rules, remember?"

She grimaced. "We can make our own rules, but certain tenants have to be observed."

"True." He nodded. "But Dominance and submission are states of mind and agreement, not toys, straps, or accessories."

"I–I don't know if I can do that, Aiden."

"Will you take the chance on me? Will you trust me?" He held out his hand to her.

And then held his breath as she stared at it.

Would she take him up on his offer? Would she push

aside all her fears to trust him to take care of her? He'd wanted her before as an eighteen-year-old kid, but he'd never wanted anything more than he wanted her trust.

She opened her mouth, but nothing came out. She swallowed hard before nodding and taking his hand. "I trust you, Aiden."

He let his breath out so hard, they both laughed. "Thank the Goddess."

"Did you believe I'd turn you down?"

He shot her a rueful smile as he pulled her up and led her toward the stairs. "I wasn't sure what you'd do, but I was going out of my mind with the thought that you would."

She nodded again. "I wasn't sure what I'd decide, either, but I definitely trust you."

"Good." The Dominant persona he developed over his time away from Cloudburst filled his voice. "This afternoon, you're mine to please. Do you accept the role of my cherished beauty, who will take all the pleasure I plan to give you?"

She took a deep breath as they paused in front of her bedroom. It was up to her. He couldn't force her to take this step, but she if she balked now, she might never get beyond her fears. *Please, Lady Cloudburst. Please trust me not to hurt you.*

She licked her lips as she shot a look at her bedroom. It appeared innocent enough, but once they stepped across the threshold, they'd enter the world of Dominant/submissive play.

Moira turned her gaze to him. "I accept my role of cherished beauty, but I also accept your role as my Dominant, the man who's only job is to take care of and please me, by giving me what I need." And she stepped into the room without looking back.

****

Moira's mouth dried out as she took her first steps back into the lifestyle she'd left two years earlier. *But this time it's with Aiden.* She could trust him. She felt it deep in her gut, but memories of the time before still made her stomach flutter with fear.

"Calm, my beauty. You're safe."

Aiden's voice held control, warmth, and confidence. The cadence tore the fear from her and settled her into a place of ease and understanding. *How does he do that?* It didn't matter. All that mattered was his ability to take her to a place of pleasure and calm.

"Sit on the bed. We need to make some ground rules. Are you ready?" He stood in front of her and met her gaze.

"I'm ready, Sir."

He smiled in approval and she damn near wriggled in pleasure. "Very good. Let's start with your safeword. I need to know that so there's no question about what you do and do not like."

She swallowed hard as panic built up with his question. "I don't…I can't use the last one..,It didn't work." She rose to her feet, determined to get away as the fear came roaring back. "I can't do this. I'm not going to do this!"

She took two steps toward the door before he caught her and pulled her back against his chest.

"Deep breaths, Moira. We aren't in Denver. You're safe and I have you."

She closed her eyes and tried to slow her breathing, but the panic festered in her belly. "I can't. I can't."

"Yes, you can. You'll listen to my heartbeat and breathing, and mimic it. Come on, breathe with me."

She tried to listen to him, but the fear lay on her chest like a wet wool blanket and she struggled to find her breath. She tried to yank away, but only succeeded in turning to face him.

"Moira!" His sharp rebuke brought her eyes open to meet his cerulean gaze. "Breathe with me. Focus."

She watched his eyes and regulated her breathing to his, following his deep breaths. He nodded in time and his intense focus on her dismantled the panic. She kept her gaze on him, following his breaths and the ringing in her ears stopped. Her heart rate returned to normal and she was able stand on her own.

"Come sit down again." He tugged her back to the bed and forced her to sit before he settled beside her. "I want you to pick a safeword that is different from the one you had before. A word only you and I know. It's just for us. It has nothing to do with Denver or the other times you've been in the lifestyle."

She swallowed as the fear began to rise again, but she fought it back. "What if it doesn't work? I promised I'd never do this again. I promised I'd never let myself get hurt again."

"Who did you promise that to?"

"Myself." The whispered word held all of her dread and remorse. She couldn't break a promise to herself.

"That's a good person to promise. But I'm not the man from Denver. We agree on your safeword and it will stop everything, no questions asked. You have complete control here, Moira." Aiden met her gaze and squeezed her hands. "You have all the control. I serve you, and when you are done, we're done, no matter what."

"But you're Dominant…I thought I served you." That's what she'd learned. That's what Lenny taught her.

"Oh, my beauty, did Corsica tell you that?"

She nodded, the corners of her mouth pulling down.

Aiden swore under his breath. "He lied to you. Dominants are the slaves to their submissives. They can't help but do everything their sub wants or needs. And if the sub is done or can't go on, the game ends, even if the Dominant hasn't reached their climax. You have all the power, Moira. I live to serve you."

She shook her head. "That doesn't make any sense. Submissives are...well, submissive."

"But the Dom is the one who serves to make sure, in this case, *he* is giving his sub all the pleasure she wants." He didn't smile. "Do you understand you're the one in control?"

She blinked. Did she? Did she know she could stop the game whenever she wanted? Could she trust he would stop when asked?

"Yes, Sir, I think I understand."

He nodded. "All right. Tell me your safeword first. Then we'll talk about hard limits, and find a way to enjoy our play time without hitting them."

She took a deep breath. "Rhinestone."

His lips quirked. "Rhinestone?"

"Yes, Sir."

"Why that word, my beauty?"

"Because they're fake diamonds, and if our play hits my hard limits, it'll be clear to me that your word is just as fake as rhinestones."

Aiden lost his smile and she expected to see anger in his eyes, but he nodded. "A good reminder for us both. Rhinestone, it is."

She let out a breath she hadn't known she'd held. "Okay."

"Let's talk about hard limits. You said you can't be restrained, is that true?"

She nodded. "I start to panic. I still have nightmares of being bound on a St. Andrew's Cross and I can't move." She shook her head hard as she closed her eyes. "I can't put myself in that kind of position again, Sir. I won't."

"Keep breathing, my beauty. I won't use a cross, or even restraints unless we both think it will benefit you. And right now, it won't. But that means you're going to have to keep your hands and feet where I tell you to."

She swallowed hard and her heart rate picked up, but not from fear. She'd have to hold her limbs where he wanted them without help? Excitement skittered through her and she shivered.

"Does that frighten you?"

"No, Sir."

A warm smile curled his lips. "Good. How do you feel about impact play?"

"What kind of impact play, Sir?" She shivered again with a little less pleasure.

"Floggers, riding crops, paddles, canes?"

"I don't mind floggers and paddles, but I don't like crops, canes, or whips, Sir."

"What about dildos, vibes, and butt plugs?"

"I'm fine with all of them, Sir."

He raised his eyebrows. "Are you? Very good." Another warm smile curled his lips, his gaze filling with anticipation. "I'll be sure to find some of my favorite toys, then."

She sighed, her pussy tightening with excitement.

"But today we're going to establish how we both want this to go. No toys, no restraints, just me pleasing you and taking pleasure from you. Is that what you want, Moira?" He met her gaze steadily, no smile, but his expression held no hostility, either.

"Yes, Sir. Today, that's what I want."

"Excellent. Let me take care of you, my beauty. Up on your feet now."

She rose and he pulled her a bit away from the bed before standing in front of her. "Let me take care of you the best way I know how. Will you grant me this gift?"

She met his brilliant blue gaze and saw all his hope and fear mixed in a jumbled mess. She understood the emotions. She wanted the pleasure and connection, but feared the damage and emotional pain. The question came down to trust. Did she trust him to keep his word?

The moment stretched on as he waited. She let the question bounce around in her gut, waiting for the echoes of its ramifications to come back to her. Could she trust Aiden in this?

Yes.

The answer was both simple and huge. She could give him this chance to take her trust and make an investment, allowing it and their relationship to grow.

"Yes, Sir. I grant you the opportunity to take care of me today, to show me you're worthy of my gift."

She had no idea where the words came from. She'd never spoken so boldly during a play session, but her gut said it was the right statement to set the tone. Her submission was a gift, and one that could be easily revoked. She was done receiving nothing but pain and fear.

He raised his chin, approval flashing in his eyes as he nodded. "And if I show you I'm worthy, will you allow me to care for you again?"

She tilted her head, offering him a half-smile. "I think we should take it one session at a time, Sir."

"Wise words, my beauty. All right, one session at a time." He leaned forward to kiss her on the forehead. "Then let's begin. Are you ready?"

"Yes, Sir."

"I love how sweetly you say that, my beauty."

Aiden smiled and reached for her shirt front, grasping the top button and pushing it through its hole. He never dropped her gaze as he slid each plastic disk through their corresponding holes until he could open her shirt. She inhaled when the cooler air of her room touched her bare skin, but his gasp of pleasure made it worth it.

"No bra, my beauty?"

"No, Sir. I stopped wearing bras a few years ago."

Sorrow flashed in his eyes. "Because of Denver?"

She shook her head. "No, Sir. I read a study that showed women who stopped wearing bras had breasts that were firmer. I decided to do my own experiment and took mine off." She thrust her chest out toward him. "What do you think, Sir?"

Now his gaze dropped to her chest and he slid his hands over her breasts. Heat and arousal blazed through her as he gently squeezed and molded her flesh to his palms. He'd grown to be an expert in caresses and she reveled in them.

He raised his gaze to hers with a smile. "While I have nothing to compare it to, I'd say your experiment has worked. Your breasts are beautiful, full, firm, and make my mouth water. Hold them up for me to worship, my beauty."

Aiden grasped one of her hands to fit it under her breast and hold it until the nipple pointed straight at him.

"Oh yeah, just like that, my beauty. Same with the other one."

The stark arousal in his voice made cream rush to her folds as she pushed both breasts up where he could see her nipples, hard and ready, waiting for his ministrations. He trailed one finger over the tops of them, building pleasurable fire along her skin. She moaned with his simple and tender touches, locking her knees to keep from melting to the floor.

"Your skin is softer than I imagined." He slid his fingers over the taut nipples and gently tweaked them. "After I'd learned how to give a submissive her ultimate pleasure, I dreamt of doing this to you, Moira. You've always been my North Star, the one I hoped to return to." He sighed his delight. "I'm glad I finally did."

Moira was glad, too, as he bent and sealed his mouth around one nipple while his hand caressed the other. Hot, wet pleasure filled her awareness and she gasped, swaying on her feet. Holy Goddess of the Valley, having a man sucking on her nipples had never filled her with such delight before. He swirled his tongue around her areola before gently closing his teeth on her nipple while he squeezed her other with his fingers.

Electric pleasure shot through her and she threw back her head with a low squeal. Breast play had never been her thing, but Aiden's skilled hands and mouth pulled pleasure from her she hadn't known she could feel. He growled and moved to the second breast, allowing his hand to take over on the first. Cool air swirled over her wet areola, but his warm fingers massaged the chilled flesh while his hot mouth settled on her second nipple.

They moaned at the same time, and his obvious enjoyment sent more cream to her nether lips. She dropped her gaze to watch him lave her second nipple and suck on it, while his hand squeezed her first with more enthusiasm. Pleasure and arousal filled her chest, and she whimpered as he closed his teeth around it, adding a tiny spark of pain. Instead of killing her pleasure, it increased it, and she arched her back, thrusting her breast into his mouth.

Aiden pulled back and smirked. "So, you like your breasts played with, my beauty?"

"Yes, Sir." Her breathy voice surprised her. "With you, Sir. No one else has made them feel this sexy or good."

"I'm very pleased to be the first." The subtext of *and only* floated in the air, but he wisely kept the words to himself. "They are sweeter than my favorite wine. I will suck on them as often as possible." He put his words into practice by returning to the first breast and pulling the nipple into his mouth to tease it with his tongue.

Moira moaned and writhed in his grip, not sure if she wanted to get closer to his hot mouth or away from his massaging tongue. Either way would bring her pleasure and she allowed herself to fall into the sensations. Until he released her and stood.

She whimpered and he grinned. "You're so beautiful, Moira. Do you see what you're doing to me?" He reached between his legs and grasped his cock pushing against the front of his jeans. "I'm aching for you, my beauty."

She licked her lips and moaned. "I want to taste that, Sir."

A smile curled his lips and he tipped his head. "I might give you the opportunity. But first, we must see to your pleasure."

"Tasting you would give me pleasure, Sir."

"Would it?" He raised his eyebrows, but his knowing smile never slipped. "That's good news. But right now, I need to see you in all your glory."

He knelt in front of her to unsnap her jeans and slide them off her hips. He helped her step out of them as she rested her hands on his shoulders. The silkiness of his hair in his ponytail slid over the backs of her hands when he turned his head, and the sensations sent cream to her labia.

But when he peeled her panties off to her thighs and placed a soft kiss on her mound, she damn near melted to the floor.

"I can smell your arousal, my beauty. And it makes me want to taste you." He rose and let her step out of her panties before drawing her onto the bed. "Scoot all the way to the headboard and spread your legs. I want to see your beautiful pussy before I taste it."

His erotic words made her shiver. He jerked back the covers and watched hungrily as she crawled into place. She settled onto her back and spread her legs so he could inspect her sex.

"Grasp the headboard and keep your hands there. Don't let go until I tell you, Moira. Do you understand?"

"Yes, Sir."

She raised her arms above her head and wrapped her hands around the thick wooden posts of her headboard. The action thrust her chest out and his nostrils flared as her breasts arched up. His reaction sent cream to her pussy and tightened her nipples. When his gaze dropped to her crotch and he licked his lips, his appreciation made her moan.

"Oh, my beauty, you're more than I'd hoped for and so

responsive, just to the sounds I make." Aiden licked his lips again and pulled his shirt over his head.

She had to remember how to breathe.

She'd seen his chest several times in the past few days, but it never ceased to turn her on. The ink on his left pectoral brought a rainbow of color to the hard muscle as it encircled the perfect little nipple. She licked her lips in the desire to suck on it. *If he lets me.* Anticipation had her squirming. The Celtic raven flashed again as he pulled off his jeans, but he left his boxer briefs on, containing his hard, curved dick. She swallowed against disappointment.

"Don't worry, my beauty. I'll show you my cock here soon enough. But for now, I want all your attention on what I'm going to do to you." He crawled onto the bed between her legs and settled onto his belly. "Don't let go, now."

"No, Sir."

He grinned. "Good lady."

He lowered his head and his breath on her pubic hair sent pleasure shooting through her.

"Oh, glory."

"I love when you say that, my beauty."

More than likely she'd say it a lot more once he put his lips and tongue on her labia. *Please make me say it a lot more.* The moment the heat of his mouth hit her folds, she her hips jerked and she whimpered. He chuckled against her sensitive flesh and stroked with his tongue from the base of her slit to her clit. She groaned and her hands tightened on the headboard's posts.

"You're so delectable, Moira. Like sweet apricot syrup on my tongue." He licked her again, taking this time to massage her clit with the tip of his tongue. "Oh, so hard and sweet. I need more. Don't let go, now."

Aiden dove in to licking and tasting her pussy like a rare delicacy. He used his fingers to peel apart her labia majora so he could reach her inner labia, stroking each with his skillful tongue. Hot, sweet pleasure coiled in her gut

179

and warned her she wouldn't last long under his onslaught. She keened a breathy wail and rocked her pelvis against his mouth, but he moved his hands to her hips and held her still.

He moaned as he licked and sucked on her sensitive flesh, massaging her folds and clit with determined motions. She whimpered and writhed, wanting to get closer to his teasing lips and tongue, and yet overwhelmed with the sensations. Frustration built with the focus he had on her clit, yet she worried she wouldn't be able to hold out if he chose to drop his lips to her aching slit. Her dilemma kept her on the edge of pleasure as he took his time sampling her pussy.

He pulled back from her and she whimpered in protest.

"There will be no coming until I let you, my beauty. You must hold out." He ran his fingers through her pubic hair on her mound with a smirk. "Not until I say. Do you understand?"

She whimpered and gave a quick, jerky nod as her body came down. "Yes, Sir."

"Good lady."

He returned his mouth to her pussy and started again. Moira tightened her hands on the headboard and tried to think of something other than what his tongue was doing. But he sucked on her clit and her rational thoughts splintered into bright shards of pleasure. Despite that, she groaned and bit her lip, hanging on.

When he shoved a finger into her clenching slit, she damn near levitated. "Oh, sweet glory."

"You're so wet for me, my beauty. Such sweet apricot cream coating my hand. Oh yeah."

Aiden dove back in, sucking on her clit while he pumped his finger in and out in a measured rhythm. When she whimpered and squirmed, he added a second finger, stretching and filling her in a delicious way. She rocked her hips, trying to get more out of his caresses, but he slowed down, setting her arousal on fire.

"Oh, glory, Sir. Please."

He raised his head and grinned at her. "Please what, my beauty?"

"Please, may I come?"

"Oh no, we're not nearly close enough yet."

She wailed as he chuckled and went back to torturing her with pleasure. She almost forgot what to do with her hands when he thrust his fingers in and sucked on her clit. She started to let go of the headboard, but a stern voice reminded her she'd promised her Dom to hold on until he said to let go. Fear of what he'd do if she broke the promise skittered through her and added to the erotic excitement building within.

Then he curled his fingers and she wailed, digging her fingers into the headboard.

"Oh, please, Sir. May I come?"

"Uh-uh." He didn't take his lips off her clit or his fingers from her pussy, but continued to stroke her G-spot until she saw stars.

She whimpered and writhed in his grip as he tortured her with relentless pleasure. Just when she didn't think she could take anymore, he pulled back and gave her a sultry smile.

"You may come, my beauty." Then he sucked her clit into his mouth and grazed it with his teeth.

Moira screamed his name as her orgasm exploded through her. He hummed and moaned, lapping up all the cream of her release as she flew. Pleasure soaked her mind and set it adrift in satin waves of bliss. He kept sucking and finger-fucking her, encouraging the ecstasy to continue, and the waves carried her far from herself.

When she returned, her body trembled, and he gathered her against his chest, holding her while she settled into boneless calm.

"I have you, my beauty, my Lady Cloudburst. You're

safe and loved. I have you." He whispered the soft words into her hair, his calm voice at odds with the raging hard-on pressed against her hip.

For the first time in the world of BDSM, she didn't want to laugh with derision. Aiden made her believe she was safe and loved. She'd never felt that before. With previous partners, she'd felt pleasured, or used, or even meh. Aiden changed everything she knew about the lifestyle and how it could be.

"Thank you, Sir."

"Oh, Moira, I should be thanking you. Watching you take your pleasure, drenching my face with your cream, that was truly a wonder to see." He licked his lips, his eyes heavy-lidded with arousal. "I'm honored with your gift of submission."

He rocked his hips against her and she remembered he hadn't gotten his pleasure. She stiffened, guilt swirling through her for relaxing in his embrace when his dick still sat hard between his legs.

"I'm sorry, Sir. I should've realized you needed me. I'm ready." She struggled to turn toward him, but he held her still.

"Just enjoy for the moment. You deserve this bliss, Moira." He kissed her shoulder. "Take your time. I enjoy watching you relax." He let his hands slide over her chest, rubbing her nipples with his palms while his fingertips skimmed the edges of her breasts.

She wanted to protest, but his eyes held warmth and something else. Something she wasn't sure she was ready to define.

"May I touch you, Sir?"

His lips quirked into a warm smile. "You may."

She brought her arms down from the headboard and hissed with pain. It had been a while since she'd left her arms above her head for any length of time, and the muscles protested their unaccustomed use.

"Easy, my beauty. Let me help." He grasped her nearest arm and rubbed the shoulder and biceps to loosen their stiffness. He laid her arm at her side before treating the other arm to the same ministrations. "I guess we'll need to be more careful about leaving your hands up on the headboard too long." He shot her a cheeky smile. "Maybe I'll have you keep your hands on my thighs while I fuck you slow."

She gasped and her mind slid back into the space of arousal and anticipation. But before she would submit to him again, she needed to touch him. To tell him with her caresses that she appreciated what he'd done.

Her shoulders and arms still hurt from holding them above her head, but she pushed through the pain to lay one hand on his cheek as she stared into his electric blue eyes.

"Thank you, Sir."

His brows lowered as he smiled in confusion. "For what are you thanking me, my beauty?"

She shook her head. She didn't have the words to make what she felt clear. It was more than pleasure, more than safety, more than being cherished, yet it was all of them together.

"You need to speak it, Moira." His voice hardened, though the warmth remained in his eyes. "For what are you thanking me?"

"For everything." She whispered the only word that made sense. "Everything."

"For pleasure?"

"Yes." She nodded.

"For direction?"

"Yes."

"For…" He trailed off, waiting for her to supply the next noun.

"For understanding my needs and my hang-ups, and still having sex with me." She tried to keep from squirming, but her limitations embarrassed her.

"Oh, my beauty, I haven't had sex with you."

Her face heated as she realized it was true. "Oh, I meant—"

"I've made love with you."

"What?"

Aiden slid his hand over her hip to rest on her belly above her mound, his fingers idly playing with the hair there.

"I've made love with you. Sex is for strangers scratching an itch. What I've done with you is made love, finding our common ground, and fulfilling our needs." He leaned forward to kiss her lips, brushing his against hers gently. "And I'm not finished making love with you. You are here for my pleasure, and my pleasure is making sure you get yours, completely. I want you floating in satisfaction so deep, you can't move after."

She gaped at him as he rolled over and stood up, shucking his briefs, revealing his hard penis. She loved the curve as it rose from the dark curls around it, and she licked her lips with the hope that he'd let her suck on it.

"I see you staring at my cock, you little minx. But I don't want it in your mouth today. I want to bury myself in your hot pussy and make you come again." He reached into his jeans pocket to pull out a condom, rolling it over his hard length. "Are you ready to receive my cock, Moira?"

She whimpered and nodded. "Yes, Sir."

"Very good." He smiled as he crawled over her body to rest with his hips between her legs. "You will keep your hands on the bed and not move them until I tell you. Is that clear?"

"Yes, Sir." She didn't want to agree, but the approval and pleasure in his eyes made the wait worth it.

"Good lady."

He grasped his latex-covered shaft and lined it up with her wet slit, teasing her clit with the tip. She whimpered and spread her legs wider to allow him closer, but he merely pulled back to continue his tease.

"Do you want my cock, Moira?"

She bit her bottom lip, drowning in his eyes. "Yes, Sir."

"How badly do you want it?" He tilted his head, still brushing the tip of his dick against her labia. "What do you need me to do with my cock?"

"I need you inside me, Sir. Please."

"Here?" He rubbed her clit with his finger, making her throw her head back and hiss as her sensitive nub throbbed with pleasure. "Or here?" He shoved a finger into her clenching sheath and she wailed with erotic need.

"In my pussy, Sir. Please."

"Tell me what you need, my beauty." His eyes blazed with feral desire. "Tell me what you want."

"I need you to fill me with your cock, Sir."

"This cock? Like this?"

He lined the head up with her slit and thrust home hard, filling her to the hilt. Moira screamed with joy. Sweet Goddess, he filled her completely and sent ripples of pleasure through her just from stretching her around his shaft.

But he didn't move.

"Aw, shit, you're still so damn tight after my finger fucking." Aiden closed his eyes and shivered, but it wasn't enough movement to shift his dick.

She tightened her hands into fists in the sheets, but she needed him to move soon or she'd go out of her mind. He leaned closer until they were almost nose-to-nose, and kissed her on the lips. A quick teasing buss that didn't mellow her need at all.

"You want me to move, my beauty?"

"Yes, Sir." She managed to force the words between her clenched teeth as her pussy clenched around his shaft.

He nodded, but dropped his gaze to her breasts, trembling with her breaths as she fought to hold still while his cock throbbed in her sheath. Bracing himself with one hand, he used the other to brush her chest with his fingers, a light teasing touch meant to heighten her sensitivity.

But she was almost at her limit. She didn't want more teasing. She wanted him to fuck her, and fuck her deep. She let her grip on the bedsheets relax as she concentrated on her inner muscles. *Tease me, will you, Sir? Fine.* She used her Kegel exercises to squeeze his dick.

His eyes widened and returned to hers. "What are you up to?"

"Nothing, Sir. I haven't moved my hands or my hips." But she squeezed him again.

"Oh, you naughty minx. You're trying to make me move, aren't you?"

"No, Sir. I'm lying here quietly, just as you asked." She smiled and squeezed a third time, gratified when he groaned and hissed.

She wanted to sit up and kiss his chest, licking his nipples, but she didn't dare move. She kept up her internal ministrations until he groaned and pulled his cock out of her pussy. She almost cried with his departure, but he shoved it back into her waiting sheath, his eyes mere slits as the pleasure took control.

"Is this what you wanted, my beauty? You want me to fuck you?" He pulled out and slammed back in, sending shock waves of ecstasy through her.

"Yes, oh glory, yes, Sir."

"Say it, Moira. Tell me what you want. Don't hold back. Tell me, my beauty."

"I want you to fuck me, Sir. I want you to fill me with your cum, Sir."

"Oh yeah. Put your hands on my thighs, Moira, and take my cock."

Aiden grabbed her hands and positioned them on his legs above his knees before he began to thrust in earnest. He drove into her, his thick shaft rubbing against her clit with each retreat, driving her release higher. She dug her fingers into his hard flesh as he pounded her pussy, his jaw clenched and his eyes ablaze.

Her own pleasure threatened to erupt, but she held on, keeping the orgasm at bay by the skin of her teeth. *Oh sweet glory. Must hold out, must not come.*

"Moira." His voice had grown gravely and rough, his eyes full of lust and desire. "You will come for me. You will scream my name, do you hear me?"

She didn't have the breath to do more than nod as he reached between them and strummed her clit with his thumb as he thrust home. Stars exploded behind her eyelids as she shot into the pleasure swamping her whole being.

"Aiden!" She screamed his name, just as he'd requested and the part of her dreading serving a new Dom withered and died away. She let herself go and sailed into freedom.

"Oh yeah, Moira, come for me. Squeeze my cock. Oh fuck yeah!"

He roared out his own release and thrust a few more times before he collapsed on top of her. He lay there for several seconds, his breathing loud in her ears as she settled back into her body. His exhaustion matched hers, but in that moment, she knew she'd found the person she'd been looking for in Denver. This was her true Dom, the man who could direct her body in bed just the way she needed it.

I love you, Aiden.

She wasn't ready to say it aloud, but she understood he'd stolen her heart, her secret heart, the one that needed a Dominant man to protect it.

"Are you all right?" Aiden raised his body so he could look down on her. "Moira, are you well?"

"Yes, Sir. Thank you, Sir." She smiled, more grateful for his loving than anything.

"Give me a moment to clean you up."

He pulled out of her body and pulled the condom off, tying a knot in it as he headed for the bathroom. She languished in the sensations of her body floating in euphoria and the knowledge that she'd found the one person she needed most. She'd known he was special since she was a teenager, but now it settled into her gut, as solid as a piece of granite. *He's mine and I'm never letting him go.*

Aiden returned with a warm washcloth and tenderly cleaned her labia and mound before he threw the towel in a hamper and settled back into the bed with her. He drew the covers over them as the rainy afternoon light made the room soft, gathering her into his arms.

"You're perfect, Moira. My perfect match. Thank you for your submission."

"You're welcome, Sir."

She closed her eyes, secure in agreement with his assessment. She was his perfect match, and he was hers.

CHAPTER FIFTEEN

Moira washed down the counters of the Cloudburst Coffee & Spa, a smile curling her lips. Satisfaction, pleasure, and joy settled around her as she worked, her mind on the last several days. She and Aiden had found their rhythm, both in bed and in day-to-day life. And damn, it was good.

They slept together each night so they could touch each other. Moira found she needed his presence for the comfort it brought her, and the reassurance. They didn't always play, but the times they did, she found peace and connection that branded her soul. Aiden admitted he'd hoped they would reach this point, but it had worked out even better than he'd expected.

Her smile broadened as she scrubbed some built up gunk under one of the coffee makers. They'd taken the time to talk about what they wanted and needed from each other. Aiden needed to be Dominant in the bedroom, but he insisted his dominance required a submissive to serve. He needed to bring her pleasure to receive his own. Without her, he felt lost and empty. *Totally counterintuitive.*

They'd agreed to only play at home when alone, but in the day-to-day interactions, they'd remain vanilla. *Mostly to keep our families from freaking out more than they already do.* Mainstream society frowned on D/s relationships of any form, equating it to slavery and tyranny. She'd known some Master-slave relationships when she'd played in Denver, but the couples always seemed happy to her. *Guess Aiden's right. We all make our own rules.* She'd also met some "One True Wayers", people who insisted they knew how BDSM should be performed and only their way was correct. But she'd found them to be more worried about rules than the connection between the players. *Safe, sane, and consensual. That's all I need.*

She grimaced, thinking about Lenny. Definitely the antithesis of safe, sane, or consensual.

"Hey, Moira. What's up with that look?" Talia stopped at the counter with a basket on her hip of clean linens for her massage table.

Moira shook her head. "Just thinking about the past and how stupid I was. What's going on with you?"

Now it was Talia's turn to grimace. "Just doing laundry. It's like a never-ending chore, worse than at home."

"Ain't that the truth."

"Hey, I wanted to give you a heads-up. Kieran called to tell me that Kallen is on his way."

Moira raised her eyebrows. "Why?"

Talia shrugged. "Kieran told the family that Aiden's back in town and working with you, so Kallen said he'd set that straight in a hurry." She shook her head. "They've really got a hang-up about him, don't they?"

"Yeah, but that's not what I was asking about. Why would Kieran call you and not me?"

Talia blinked before a scarlet blush worked its way over her cheeks. "I dunno. Maybe he couldn't get through on your phone?"

Or he'd rather talk to the woman he's attracted to

rather than get an earful from his sister.

"I'm sure that's it." Moira snorted. "I'll definitely have to check my phone for missed calls. Thanks for giving me the warning."

"You're welcome." Talia's cheeks remained rosy, but her expression grew serious. "Have you told any of them about that guy from Denver? I was surprised when Kieran didn't mention him."

Moira sighed and some of her good mood evaporated. "I'm hoping I'll never have to mention him to them."

Talia gaped. "Why not?"

"Because they'll make it all about how I should've stayed in Cloudburst where I was 'safe' from guys like Lenny. I don't need their self-righteousness right now."

"That's bullshit."

"I know."

"No, I mean it's bullshit you aren't telling your family, people who care about you and want to protect you." Talia scowled as she set her basket down. "They could help keep an eye out for this guy. The more people who are looking for him, the harder it will be for him to hurt you."

"Maybe, but they won't do this for free. It will be about how much I owe for this inconvenience to *them*. How my past actions are making *their* lives harder now because they have to make efforts on my behalf."

"Kieran doesn't feel that way, and I'd bet Thomas doesn't either." Talia raised her chin.

"Maybe not, but they still carry around the self-righteousness of being men and Callahans to boot." Moira held up her hand to Talia's mounting defense. "I'm sure Kieran doesn't treat you like he's the Goddess's gift to the world, but he's pretty secure in his position in Cloudburst. My point is, being the only girl in a group of entitled boys has left an impression, and I prefer to leave my family out of this if I can."

"I think you should still tell Kieran so he can help if he

wants to." Talia frowned. "Explain to him why you hesitate to tell the rest and let him make the decision to inform the family. Make it clear you don't want the strings attached, and if he tells them, they're helping *him* help you, not helping you directly."

"That's semantics, Talia. Eventually the bill comes due and I'll be the one required to pay."

Talia sighed and picked up her basket. "Just consider it. How would you feel if your younger brothers had a stalker issue and never asked for your help? Despite what you think of your family, and as lousy as they may show it, they really do care about and love you. At least tell Kieran, okay?"

"Tell Kieran what?" Aiden appeared with a couple of boxes filled with the day's orders of coffee beans.

Moira sighed as Talia crossed her arms over her chest.

"Talia wants me to tell Kieran about Lenny."

"Ah." He nodded and opened one of the boxes to get out the beans.

"'Ah?' That's all you have to say?" Moira blinked.

"Yeah." He gave her a guileless smile as he pulled out the bag of coffee beans. "I didn't hear the whole conversation, so I don't have anything useful to add."

Moira gaped while Talia grunted with an amused smile.

"He's smart, this one. I can see why you like him." Talia picked up her basket again. "I'm going to make sure the room's ready for my next client. But think about it, Moira. I think it would help, and keep an eye out for Kallen. Kieran said he's all fired up about Aiden."

Moira rubbed her forehead. "Great. I'll think about talking to Kieran."

"Good." Talia nodded and headed for her massage room without a backward glance.

Moira shot a look at Aiden as he finished with the second bag and gathered up the empties to take out to the trash.

"You really didn't have anything to say about telling Kieran about Corsica?"

Aiden shrugged, his expression solemn. "I have plenty to say, but here and now isn't the time. Let me get the rest of the grinders filled and we'll talk more about it."

"All right."

She watched him go, her smile returning. Aiden understood her better than even Talia. He'd make his case and hear her out, until they both understood the other's position. She liked that about him. Her family wouldn't do that. They'd railroad things through, telling her how it had to be and why they were right. Her wants and perspectives wouldn't come into their considerations at all. *They never have.*

She turned back to cleaning the counters as the door to her coffee shop opened and her older brother sauntered in. He paused long enough to swing his judgmental gaze around the comfortable décor until it rested on her. His lips tightened in annoyance as he continued to the counter.

She had to admit her brother was handsome when he managed to lose the scowl. Dark hair cut short along the sides the same length as his trimmed beard gave him a rustic look. Combined with full lips and piercing blue eyes, he was striking. Add in the broad shoulders and muscular legs encased in denim, and the women fell at his feet. *Too bad he's a controlling asshole most of the time.*

Moira rested her hands on the counter and raised her chin as she waited for her brother. She didn't smile or scowl, but she braced herself to stand up to him. The old armor fell into place around her like a familiar cage.

"Hi, Kallen. What can I do for you?"

Kallen paused, surprised she'd made the opening salvo. Usually he took control of their communication, dictating how it would go before she'd even had a chance to speak.

"Hi Moira. I, uh, wanted to stop by and see how things were going."

Oh yeah, I'm sure you wanted to do that. She nodded. "Good, thanks. And you?"

"Uh, good. Yeah, good." He scanned the room around her as if searching for things to criticize, and finding none, found himself on uneven ground. "Mum and Da are having their annual Memorial Day party on the Sunday before and wanted to be sure you were invited. Talia, too."

She tilted her head with her best polite smile. "Thanks. I'll be sure to tell her, though I suspect she'll receive an invitation from Kieran."

"Oh yeah?" For a brief moment, Kallen's expression lightened and warmth filled his blue eyes. "It's about time he made his move. She's a nice girl, and the folks like her."

"She is a nice woman. I'm glad to hear the family approves."

"What the hell does that mean?"

"You'll figure it out." She paused as Aiden returned carrying the next two boxes of coffee beans.

Kallen's gaze sharpened on the other man and his scowl returned, lowering his brows. Aiden ignored him like he would any other customer at the counter and kept working. Moira waited for Kallen to say something, but his gaze seemed permanently locked on her lover's form.

"What the hell is he doing here?" Kallen glowered as he pointed at Aiden.

Moira looked over her shoulder while Aiden continued to stock coffee flavors. "Working. Was that all you wanted, Kallen?"

"He shouldn't be here. He left a long time ago."

At least his memory's still good.

"Do you really want to get into this here and now?" Moira waved to the servers and customers in the coffee shop. "Because I'm pretty sure this is more of a private discussion."

"It's not a discussion, Moira. He needs to go. He already left once." Kallen crossed his beefy arms over his chest, making himself look bigger.

Like he needs help at 6'2" and 210 pounds.

"Yes, he did, and why do you think he left? What would make him want to pull up stakes and take off?" She dropped her chin and opened her eyes in mock-surprise. "Would that be because you, Da, Stephen, and Patrick decided he wasn't good enough for me? Or maybe it was something more sexist? Maybe it's that I'm nothing more than a pair of tits and a vagina for you to protect from encroaching dicks. Sound about right?"

Kallen's jaw dropped. "Ew, Moira. That's disgusting. You have a foul mouth."

"No, I'm pointing out to you how you think of me with regards to Aiden. I loved him and he left because you chased him off."

"You didn't love him. You were sixteen and didn't know anything about love."

She scowled. "That might have been true, but you didn't give me a chance to find out. Besides, you were eighteen, and didn't know any more about it either. But Aiden's dick wasn't good enough for my tits and vagina, and you all were going to make sure he knew it." She stared her older brother down as the coffee shop bustled around them, somehow ignoring the family drama. "So, here's the deal. This is my place of business, not beholden to the rest of the Callahan clan, and while you're in my place of business, you'll treat me and my employees in a professional and courteous manner. Otherwise, I'll have to ask you to leave, and I'll call the cops to make sure it happens, brother of mine or not. Are we clear?"

"Moira—"

"Are we clear, Kallen?" She crossed her arms over her chest.

He opened his mouth to cuss her out, she was sure, but

Aiden stepped up behind her and waited with her. His warm strength buoyed her up and made her gut do flips of joy. Kallen scowled and crossed his arms, mirroring her stance, but she merely raised an eyebrow.

"Dammit, Moira. He still can't even meet my gaze and you know what Da says about that." It sounded lame and Kallen seemed to realize it because he closed his mouth and shook his head. "Look, I just came to invite you and Talia to the Memorial Day party Mum and Da are throwing at the homestead. It's on Sunday."

"Thanks."

"Are you going to come?" He waited, expectation written in every line of his body.

"Can I bring a date?"

His scowl deepened. "Who are you dating?"

"Still defending the precious vagina from wandering dicks, are you, Kallen?"

"That's not what I'm doing. Some men aren't good enough for you." He shot a look over her shoulder. Aiden stiffened, but rested his hand on her hip. Kallen's gaze riveted to the gesture, his eyes glowing with anger. *Glory, doesn't he have any other emotion?*

"Should I be dating you or one of our cousins, then? Are they good enough?" She raised her eyebrows as his outraged gaze returned to hers. "I'm thirty-four years old. I'm pretty sure I can make my own decision about who's 'good enough' for me." She shook her head. "Thanks for the invitation, but I think we're done here. Give my best to the other men whose dicks are 'good enough' for me."

She patted the counter and turned away from her brother without a backward glance, her heart pounding in her chest. She'd never spoken so brashly to any of her siblings, but damn, it felt good. They'd ruled her life since she was born, even making it difficult for her to get her own business started. But throwing his inherent sexism into his face lifted a weight off her shoulders she hadn't known she'd been carrying.

****

Aiden couldn't have been more proud of Moira if he'd tried. Standing up to her brothers hadn't been part of her repertoire when he'd known her two decades earlier, but she'd grown up. And he liked the woman she'd become.

"Did you teach her those nasty words, Westmorland?" Kallen snarled. "She never would've said shit like that to me before you."

Aiden barked a laugh. "Are you serious? You do know she's not sixteen anymore, right?" He shook his head, keeping his gaze a little to the left of Kallen's shoulder. "Stop treating her like a little girl, or worse as she said, a precious set of tits and vagina. She's not a possession, Callahan."

"She's *my* little sister."

"She's not *your* anything. She's a person and a member of your family. Have enough respect for her to see that." He snorted. "Hell, have enough respect for yourself and your parents. I'm pretty sure they taught her how to take care of herself."

"This from a man who can't look me in the eye when he's talking to me." Derision dripped from Kallen's voice, an insidious poison meant to coerce.

Taking a deep breath, Aiden steeled himself against the rush of personal stats he knew would come, and met Kallen's gaze.

Blood type B positive, BMI twenty-six point eight, two-hundred ten pounds, life expectancy eighty-nine point two years, ninety-eight percent chance he will marry outside his profession, outside his comfort zone.

Before he could stop them, Kallen's internal thoughts intruded. *This motherfucker thinks he knows everything about Moira, but I know him. I know men. He's just thinking with his dick...like I do about Sophie Forrest in nothing but her turnout gear.*

Aiden swallowed back the bile reaching into his throat. "I can meet your eyes, Callahan, but you gotta stop thinking about Ms. Forrest like that or I'm gonna hurl."

Kallen's face blanched white and he took a step back. "What did you say?"

Aiden returned his gaze to the left of his shoulder. "Forrest, the firefighter you have the hots for. Stop thinking about her sexually for the moment." He scrubbed his face with his hands, before returning his gaze to Kallen's chest. "There's a reason I don't meet people's gazes, Callahan. I get way too much information just from looking at you. You know that saying about the eyes being the windows to the soul? Yeah, that. I learn things I don't want to know. So, I'm gonna give you this opportunity to relay to your overbearing family that Moira is doing fine and unless you want to bare all your ugly little secrets, you *don't* want me to meet your eyes. Got it?"

Kallen swallowed hard. "I got it."

"Good." Aiden nodded. "See you around, Callahan." He didn't wait to see if the other man left before he headed into the back office to find Moira.

That felt damn good. It wasn't often anyone got one over on the Callahan family. But at least they'd know they weren't the only ones with special talents in this town. *And damn, I hope Ms. Sophie Forrest puts that jackass in his place if he ever hits on her.* Something from Kallen's thoughts suggested she was tougher than most women and Kallen liked that about her. *Maybe there's some hope for him.*

Aiden found Moira sitting in her desk chair with her feet propped up on the desk, a cup of chai in her hands. A secret and satisfied smile curled her lips, and Aiden wanted to kiss it off them. He liked to see his beauty happy and strong.

"You look happy." He stopped in front of the desk and resisted the urge to run his hands over her legs.

"I am." She grinned. "I just told one of my big brothers to fuck off because he was being a sexist pig, and it was awesome."

Aiden nodded. "Awesome is the word. Will you go to the Memorial Day party?"

She shrugged. "I don't know. Not without a date, especially if the date is you."

"You really want to bring me to the party with you?"

She frowned. "Of course, I do."

"Even if your parents and other brothers don't approve of me?" He raised his eyebrows. He believed her, but he wanted to hear her say it.

"Even then. I don't care if they don't approve. It was never their choice whom I loved or wanted to be with. If you're planning to stay and work this out with me, I want to make it work with you." She raised her chin. "I'll say it out loud in front of all of them. I just need to know you're in this despite them and aren't going to run the first sign of difficulty."

"I'm not going anywhere, Moira. Being with you is the whole reason I came back to Cloudburst." He leaned forward with his hands on the desk. "You know, you could run from this place, too. If you wanted."

She shook her head. "No. This is my home and my place of business. I won't run. Not from my family, and not from Corsica. They don't have to like my choice, but they do have to respect it. At least Kieran's on my side."

"Yeah, I think your younger brother understands you better than the others."

Moira shrugged. "He might. It's hard to tell."

"Not that hard." Aiden tilted his head. "Talia suggested you should tell him about Corsica. Is that right?"

She grimaced. "Yeah. She thinks he'll be able to help."

He nodded, shrugging. "I think she's right."

Moira sighed. "If I tell him, he'll share it with the family, and the sanctimonious I-told-you-sos will start. I really don't need the same old arguments about why I shouldn't have left, yada yada yada." She raised her gaze. "Did you turn in all that stuff Sean gave you about Corsica over to the police?"

"Yeah, and I heard back from Fitzroy." Aiden rubbed the back of his neck. "They've been looking for him, but whatever he's doing, he's currently lying low. Fitzroy said MacLaren has been researching this guy to see what his patterns are. But I'm pretty sure he hasn't given up."

"No, predators never do. They seem to think they're untouchable." She sighed and rubbed her face. "How did he find me?"

"When you left Denver, did you erase every piece of your existence there?"

Moira frowned. "Not exactly. I mean, we didn't have any friends in common, just acquaintances, and I didn't tell them where I was going. But I didn't go dark like Witness Protection or anything." She dropped her head to her desk. "Ugh. What did I do to attract this asshole?"

"You once knew him, that's what."

"Everyone says you shouldn't lead anyone on, but I haven't, Aiden." She shot him a pleading look. "Seriously, I made it clear it was over and I *moved across the state*, two years ago. It's not like I left a trail of bread crumbs for him to follow."

"No, but you didn't make it impossible, either."

"I didn't know I would have to."

Aiden patted her hand. "Leave it to Fitzroy and his man MacLaren. I have a feeling they always get their guy." He hoped. Fitzroy was crafty in ways that made his hair stand on end, but the man also had to play within the laws of the U.S. *Maybe MacLaren doesn't have the same rules.*

"I hope you're right because I shouldn't be the one always looking over my shoulder."

"No, you shouldn't. But you could have some help."
He raised his eyebrows, hoping she'd take his suggestion.

"You mean my family."

He nodded. "More eyes on the lookout for him. We know what he looks like and what name he's using. At least tell Kieran. Maybe the guy's staying up at the Cloudburst Resort. That's where Kieran works, right?"

"Yes, but he works in the stables. If Corsica doesn't go riding, he won't see him."

Aiden rubbed his chin. "But your family lives in town. If at least Kieran and Thomas know what to look for, that might mean he gets caught sooner. The problem with the other women Corsica hurt was they had no one looking out for them. Corsica made a mistake chasing you here. Too many people know you." He tilted his head. "But you have to tell them."

Moira sighed and put her feet on the floor. "All right, I'll tell Kieran and Thomas, and leave it to them to mention it to the family. But I don't need the I-told-you-sos, and I really don't want them to know the details about our relationship."

"No one has to know about our relationship, Moira, just that we have one." He moved around the desk and crouched in front of her. "That's none of their business, anyway. But I want you to be safe and having more people who can keep an eye out for this scumbag will really help."

She closed her eyes as her shoulders sagged. "Okay."

"Okay, what, my beauty?" He used some of his Dom's voice to encourage her strength.

"Okay, I will call my brothers and tell them about Corsica."

"Good lady. Do you want me there when you do?" He'd back her play no matter what it was.

She shook her head. "No, I don't need you to be there. I can do this on my own."

"You don't have to, you know."

She nodded and opened her eyes. "I know. For the first time in a long time, I feel like someone has my best interests at heart."

"Oh, my beauty, that's true. And I always will."

She raised her gaze to his. "Always?"

"For as long as you let me. You're my world and my heart. Whenever you need me, I'll do my best to be there. No matter what." He reached out to cup her cheeks in his hands. "I'm here for the long haul, Moira."

"Say it again, Aiden, please." She tilted her head against his palms.

"I'm here for the long haul and I have your back, no matter what."

And he would. Come hell or high water, he'd be there for her. He wasn't going anywhere.

CHAPTER SIXTEEN

Despite the pressure of Lenny's silent threat, it took a couple of days for Moira to find the courage to call her brothers. She'd had to fight for her independence so hard. Asking for help now felt like she was going back on the promise she'd made to herself. But Talia and Aiden were right. The more people who knew about Lenny, the harder it would be for him to cause trouble.

She'd agreed to meet Kieran and Thomas at the House of Clouds Music School, a modest little store that sold music and rented instruments. Thomas also offered discounted classes for anything from violin to cello, trumpet to trombone, and a host of wind instruments. He'd started the business just before Moira graduated from college and he'd done well teaching the local kids their band and orchestra instruments.

Moira pushed through the doors and took a deep breath. Thomas had an affinity for natural scents, but his favorite was cedar despite it being a rare tree in the Rocky Mountains. Today there wasn't anyone else in the store except her brother Kieran and he turned from the racks of acoustic guitars to greet her with a smile.

"Hey Moira. Good to see you." He wiped his hands on

his faded jeans, brushing off the excess dirt left there by one of his equine charges.

"Yeah, you too. Is Thomas here?" She shot a look toward the practice rooms in the back.

"Yeah, he went get an old cello he's repairing. He said he needed to do it while we talked."

As if conjured by their conversation, their youngest brother Thomas strode in with a cello held in his hands by the neck. The strings were missing and some of the pegs, but otherwise the instrument looked sound.

Thomas himself looked a little rough around the edges. He was the tallest of the Callahans at six feet six inches, and had the red hair and emerald green eyes of their paternal grandmother. He had broad shoulders Kallen, but his body was long and lean, rather than robust.

"Moira, it's very good to see you. Been way too long." Thomas's musical voice could sooth a rabid wolverine, and she was a far less fearsome being. "Do you still play the piano?"

Chagrin wormed through her gut. "I can still play, though I haven't in a long time."

He *tsked* as he sat down on a stool in front of a stand meant to hold the cello while he repaired it. "You shouldn't let those skills go. Music is the language of the heart."

"I thought that was love." Kieran took another stool.

"They're one and the same," Thomas remarked as he pulled out a cello D string. "So, what brings you to the shop in person, Moira?"

She sighed as she snagged a nearby chair and sank into it. "I wish it was just because I haven't seen you both in person much since the coffee shop opened. But it's more than that."

Thomas looked up from where he'd been winding the end of the D string to the pin. "More than just wanting to see your brothers?" He smirked. "This sounds interesting."

"Scary is more like it." She scrubbed her face with her

hands, wishing she didn't have to talk about it. "You know how I came home from Denver two years ago?"

Kieran snorted. "Uh, yeah. You're here and own the Cloudburst Coffee & Spa. We kinda noticed."

"Don't be a smartass, Kieran." Thomas shook his head at his older brother. "There's a reason she's starting slow."

Kieran raised his eyebrows and lost his smile. "There is? How do you know?"

Thomas inclined his head to Moira. "You might understand horses, but you ignore the energy of the humans around you."

"That's because there are too many of them, and horses are a lot nicer."

"Guys, I need you to listen." Moira clapped her hands to get their attention. "I came home from Denver because I had a really bad experience there. I'm not going to go into it, the details aren't important. What is important is the guy I broke up with has shown up here now and wants to get back together."

"Why is that a problem? That happens all the time." Kieran frowned.

Moira sighed. "Yeah, I'm sure it does, but there was a reason I broke up with him and moved home. And it wasn't to have him chase me down to get reacquainted. He's got a rap sheet that makes me glad I got away."

"'Rap sheet'? You've been watching too many cop procedurals on TV." Kieran snorted, but his body language spoke of unease.

"Would you focus, please?" She rubbed her arms. *This is why I didn't bother to tell them.* They either wouldn't take it seriously or they'd give her the third degree about leaving. "He's hurt a lot of women from several different states. But now he's here, trying to get back together with me. I don't want to. I've told him so, but he hasn't listened."

Thomas's gaze sharpened. "He's contacted you

already?"

She nodded. "Yeah, he came to the coffee shop twice. Once to drop off flowers and once to talk to me when no one else was around." She rubbed her arms again. "The flowers had poisoned energy."

People outside her family would've laughed, but Thomas' chin came up and Kieran swallowed as his lips tightened.

"Have you seen him since?" Thomas set the cello aside.

She shook her head. "No, but I know he's still here somewhere."

"Have you told the police?" Kieran had finally gotten the seriousness of her situation.

"Yes, that's why I know about his rap sheet. Lt. Fitzroy knows and is keeping an eye on things, but no one has seen or heard from him recently." She shrugged. "Aiden said I needed to tell you about him so there would be more eyes out looking for him."

"Aiden was right. You should've told us as soon as he showed up, Moira." Kieran scowled.

"Maybe, but if I had told you, what would Mum, Da, and our older brothers said?"

Thomas sighed. "They would've said it wouldn't have happened if you hadn't left Cloudburst in the first place."

She pointed at him. "Exactly. They would've used it as a way to make it about them, how they have to save me at their inconvenience, and require me to owe them something." She rubbed her forehead. "I'm leaving it up to you to tell them if you want to, but only to get more people aware of this guy."

"They just want to protect you." Kieran wore unease like a shirt.

"Maybe that's what they tell themselves, but I think it's more they want to be in control. You know how highly they hold their standing and reputation in this town."

Kieran grimaced while Thomas nodded. "Do you have a picture of the guy stalking you?"

She fished the pictures out of her pocket and handed them to her brothers. "His name is Lenny Corsica, and he's average looking, well spoken. No one would think him a predator. The two times he came to the coffee shop, he dressed in a suit and tie."

Thomas nodded, studying the image. "Do you mind if I show this to a friend of mine? He's an expert in finding people who are hiding."

"Sure, the more who know what to look for, the better. Fitzroy said he has his best man on the job, but so far they haven't come up with anything."

"Are you sure you don't want me to tell the rest of the family?" Kieran rubbed the back of his neck. "They might be your best bet in terms of knowing who's new in town."

She shrugged, though her stomach clenched. "I'm leaving that up to you. But I want it very clear it's only to make sure the police can find him. I don't want them thinking I owe them anything. I didn't ask them for help because I don't want to pay their price for it. Keep that in mind."

"They're not like that, Moira. Stop seeing them as adversaries."

She raised her chin and faced Kieran down. "When you've walked my path and faced the same struggles I have as the only daughter in this family, then you can tell me how they are. You're one of their golden boys, Kieran. They expect you to go out on your own and have adventures. They'll back you up without question, and know when you ask they'll be expected to help."

She held up her hand when he opened his mouth to protest. "But for me, they want to marry me off to a man of their choosing, wrap me up in cotton batting, and keep me safe. If I go against those expectations, like I did, they consider any consequences of that to be my fault, and will only reluctantly help me deal with it. But they'll expect me to pay them back later. They don't need you to pay them back."

"Because I'm family and that's what families do." Kieran shot Thomas a look. "Back me up here, Thomas."

But their younger brother shook his head. "You're both right. Mum and Da groomed Moira to be the 'stay-at-home' child so they could make sure she'd be taken care of and protected. And they made sure their sons, us included, had opportunities to get out and do things. They'd have our backs no matter what. But then Stephen became the stay-at-home child along with Patrick, and Moira wanted to strike out on her own. Hell, she's the only one who ever left Cloudburst. All the rest of us are still here."

"She came back." Kieran mumbled the words and Thomas grimaced.

"I came back to start over, but now the past has followed me." Moira scowled. "Look, if you don't want to help, that's fine. Give me the pictures back and I'll ask Talia if she knows anyone who would be willing." She held out her hand for the picture.

"You've involved Talia in this?" Outrage laced Kieran's words.

"She knew long before you, jackass."

"But now she's in danger."

Moira blinked. "He's stalking me, not her. And why is it you're more worried about my best friend than you are about me, your sister?" She snatched the image out of his hands. "I knew it was a mistake to tell you. Look, do whatever you want. Hopefully Fitzroy and his friend MacLaren will catch Corsica without needing anyone's help." She picked up her purse. "Thanks for meeting with me."

"Moira, wait." Thomas caught her before she made it to the door.

She blinked back her tears of frustration and betrayal.

Guess the old adage of you can never go back is true. No one ever promised they'd have her back. *Aiden did. Talia, too.* But her own family was too worried about their reputations to make such promises.

"What do you want, Thomas? I need to get back to the coffee shop."

"Hey, it's going to be okay. MacLaren is the friend I was telling you about. Having a picture to show him will really help."

Moira nodded. "I'm glad to hear that."

"You don't believe me, do you?" Thomas frowned, but it was full of sadness. "I guess we haven't done much to back you up over the years, so there isn't a precedent for you to believe in." He sighed, squeezing her shoulders. "Want to hear an ugly truth?"

She frowned up at her brother. "To be honest, I don't know if I can deal with more ugly truths."

Thomas grimaced. "Yeah, well, this one might help us both." He drew her back to her chair. "I was pretty pissed off at you for leaving. You were my sister and my friend, and you up and left." She gaped at him and he shrugged. "I was a young, dumb, self-centered kid. I was the baby, remember? The whole world revolved around me."

She snorted with amusement, but his admission hurt. "You know I didn't leave you, right?"

"Yeah, I know that now, but at the time I was too stupid to understand you were doing what you needed to do to be the best you possible." He gave her a self-deprecating smile. "I was still in high school and you'd always been there for me. To have you leave was a shock."

It had been a shock to her, too. The bigger towns were so much different than Cloudburst, and her family couldn't make things better. She'd been on her own, but freedom came with that, too. For a while, it had been a good balance. *Until I met Lenny.*

"Did you feel the same, Kieran?"

209

He scowled and shrugged, but nodded. "Kinda. I guess I believed the unspoken expectation that you'd always stay in Cloudburst, and your choice to leave shook me up. But I kinda understood it, too. I wanted to get out from under Mum and Da's thumbs and do something other than run the family bar. That's why I went to live with Uncle Marcus on the Golden C Ranch."

Moira sighed and rubbed her thighs with her hands. "I didn't leave you. I wanted my own adventures before I chose to get married, if that came to pass. And it still might. But right now, there's a guy after me who won't take no for an answer, and I'm asking you to keep an eye out for him. Because if you don't back me up now, you might not have me around to reprimand later."

"I have your back, Moira. I'll talk to MacLaren, myself." Thomas pulled her into a hug. "I don't want to curtail you, but I don't want to lose you, either. I love you."

Some of the tension left her shoulders. "I love you, too, Tom-Tom." The old nickname came back with a warmth she'd definitely missed. "I appreciate the help and backup."

"No strings attached, okay? You're family and my favorite sister. I'd back you up anytime."

"I'm your only sister." She snorted, but gratitude filled her heart. "Thanks."

He nodded and released her as she surreptitiously rubbed the tears that threatened to overflow.

"You're welcome. Sorry it took me so long to make it clear." He shrugged with a grimace. "Sometimes I'm a little slow on the uptake. But I'm here for you."

"Me, too." Kieran raised his head to meet her gaze. They shared the same hazel eyes of their mother, but he had the dark hair of their father. "I'm sorry I'm such a selfish jackass. And I am worried about you. I don't want you or Talia to get hurt." He took a deep breath. "I'm gonna tell the folks about this guy Corsica, but I'll mention I heard it from Talia that he's creeping her out. Maybe that will keep them from harping on you."

"Thanks, Kieran." She nodded. "I'll let Talia know. She's the one who insisted I call Fitzroy first."

He beamed. "She's a smart one."

"Yeah, must be why she's my best friend." She winked as she rose. "Thanks for hearing me out, guys. I'm hoping it will all be over soon and Fitzroy catches him before anything else needs to be done. But better to let you know."

"And we'll let you know if we hear or see anything." Kieran stood as well. "Give me Aiden's cell number. That way I can text him, too."

She shared the number with both her brothers before heading outside into the sunny day. Some of her anxiety had faded. She hadn't realized how worried she was about telling them until it was a done deal. Now, she admitted it was the right choice.

She still worried her parents would get involved and try to lean on Fitzroy with their big-shot status, but it seemed like a small price to pay now that her brothers had her back. Maybe they would all find Lenny before he did anything ugly and frightening. Despite her hope, her gut clenched in dread. She never wanted to see the creep again.

Her unease at being out in the open hurried her steps until she reached the Cloudburst Coffee & Spa, and she ducked inside with a sigh of relief.

Until she saw the large bouquet of flowers sitting on the back counter beside the coffee grinder.

Oh, sweet glory. Not another one. Her stomach dropped and her hand shook as she reached for the card held by a three-pronged plastic stand. The flowers reeked of sinister energy and she yanked her hand back before she'd even touched the card. *They're from him.*

She shot a look around to see who might have witnessed the delivery and caught one of the servers.

"Did you see who brought in these flowers?"

"Yes, Ms. Callahan. The delivery guy came in about

twenty minutes ago." The young man she remembered had a S name, like Seth or Sam.

"Did he work for the flower company or was he dressed ordinary?" She had to know if Corsica had come himself.

"He was wearing a Durango Flower Power uniform." Seth/Sam loaded the dirty dishes into the dishwasher.

She nodded. "Thanks. Is Talia here?"

"I think she's in with a client right now."

"Okay, thanks. Have you seen Aiden?"

Seth/Sam shook his head. "I haven't seen him since you left. He might be in the office."

She nodded and headed straight there, pulling out her cell phone as she went. The noise from the coffee shop faded the closer she got to the back, but her call to Lt. Fitzroy connected immediately.

"Cloudburst Police Department. This is Janice. May I help you?"

"Hi, this is Moira Callahan from the Cloudburst Coffee & Spa. May I speak to the lieutenant please?"

"Can I tell him what this is about, Ms. Callahan?" Janice sounded professional, but Moira remembered she was a friend of her mother's and would be all too happy to gossip about Moira's life.

"I'm calling to talk to him about the disturbance at the coffee shop a few days ago." That sounded plausible and hopefully would throw Janice off the scent.

"Of course, let me put you through."

The phone clicked into hold-mode and some classical music filled the line. She'd heard it was supposed to relax the caller, but the flowers sitting on the counter in her coffee shop kept her on edge. She pushed through the door to her office and caught Aiden's eye. He raised his head with a smile that died as soon as he saw her face.

"This is Lt. Fitzroy." The man's voice never ceased to calm her down.

"Hi, Lieutenant. This is Moira Callahan. Corsica sent more flowers." She met Aiden's gaze and a frown settled on his features.

"Did he bring them in person, Ms. Callahan?"

"Not according to one of my servers. I wasn't here at the time they were delivered." She shook her head at Aiden's questioning gaze. "He said it was a delivery guy from Durango Flower Power who brought it in."

"Is there a card with it?"

"Yes, sir."

"Don't touch it until I or one of my officers can get there. We might be able to verify it's from Corsica." She heard some scrambling in the background on the line.

"How will that help?" She couldn't imagine how fingerprints or whatever they'd look for would help them find Corsica.

"It will verify that he's the one who keeps contacting you even though you've asked him to leave you alone. I'm calling one of my men right now. Please wait for him to get there before doing anything with the flowers."

"Okay."

"He'll be there in no more than fifteen minutes. If the flowers are in the way, wear gloves to move them."

"Will do, Lieutenant. Thank you."

She hung up and faced Aiden, his eyes narrowed.

"What's going on?"

"Corsica sent more flowers through a delivery service. They're out in the coffee shop." She waved back the way she'd come. "I didn't touch them. They have the same toxic energy the first set did."

"He sent them here?" Anger filled Aiden's eyes as he headed for the door. "And you didn't see how they arrived?"

"No, I was talking to Kieran and Thomas."

He stopped and turned back to her. "How did that go?"

She shrugged as she threw her coat on the hat tree.

"Good enough, I guess. My brothers will keep an eye out for Corsica. Kieran wanted to tell the family, too."

Aiden nodded. "I think it might be a good idea. What did you tell him?"

"I told him it was up to him." She grimaced. "But he said he'd tell them Corsica creeped Talia out and we should keep an eye out for him." She shrugged again. "It's close enough and will keep my family from bugging me about leaving Cloudburst."

He wrapped her in his arms and held her. "Is Fitzroy sending someone to look at those flowers?"

She nodded against his chest, wishing she could close her eyes and make it all go away. "Yes. He said someone would be here within fifteen minutes."

"Let's go out front and wait for them. I know I could use a cup of coffee."

She shook her head. "Not yet. Please don't go yet. Just hold me a little longer."

Aiden's body froze as if he hadn't expected her request, but his arms never loosened. She closed her eyes and stayed in the circle of his arms, allowing his heat and strength to seep into her. She inhaled his scent. This was where she wanted to be, not the horrifying world of a stalker's threats.

"Hey, are you all right?"

"Yeah, I'm fine. I just needed a breather from the fear. Thanks for giving me a few moments."

"Moira." He pushed her back just enough so he could meet her eyes. "Anytime you need that break, I'm here for you. All right? Anytime."

"Thank you." She could use all the help she could get.

Ten minutes later someone knocked on the office door and Aiden opened it to find a tall man with broad shoulders and piercing brown eyes. A leather jacket stretched across those shoulders and faded jeans covered his legs. He paused at the threshold and inhaled deeply before meeting

Moira's gaze.

She froze.

The intensity of this man both scared her and engendered respect. He was definitely more than he seemed. The energy around him spoke of immense strength and power, a predator who could take down powerful beings, but a discerning hunter who picked his prey carefully.

"Ms. Callahan? My name is Alex MacLaren. Lt. Fitzroy sent me." Mr. MacLaren's rich voice slid over her, promising protection.

She understood what he was doing, but appreciated it nonetheless.

"Yes, Mr. MacLaren. Thank you for coming. The flowers are out in the coffee shop." She didn't reach for him, conscious of his strengths and uneasy with experiencing them close up.

He sniffed the air as if he had allergies, but his gaze never wavered from hers. "Can you show them to me? I'm here to collect evidence."

She nodded and shot a look at Aiden. He'd narrowed his eyes as he watched MacLaren, but he too kept his distance.

"Please come with me. I'll show you where they are."

MacLaren fell in beside her as they headed for the front. "You're afraid of me."

"Shouldn't I be? That's what you project when facing unknown people, right?" She swallowed as he nodded slowly. "Besides, I can tell you're more than you show." She let him behind the counter in the coffee shop. "I once met a guy in Denver who'd retired from the Army. He said he was in the SpecOps side, and I believed it because he had the same sort of predatory watchfulness you do. I decided I didn't want to know more about him then, and I don't want to now."

MacLaren laughed. "Fair enough." He pulled out latex

gloves as they neared the bouquet. "Are these the flowers Corsica sent?"

"Yes." She shuddered. She could feel their malevolence even standing several feet away.

"Have you touched them or the card?"

"No. I almost grabbed it, but decided to leave them be. I don't even know if he wrote anything on the card."

Aiden came up behind her and rested his hands on her hips, both providing protection and comfort.

MacLaren studied the flowers before he touched anything. He seemed to be reading more from them than she had. When he did touch them, he used the vase to turn them around until the card could be easily plucked from the blooms. Corsica had again chosen a mixture of pink roses, white carnations, and baby's breath, but he'd added one blood-red rose in the center. Moira shuddered again.

"I'll take the card back to the station as evidence. Do you want to know what's written on it?" MacLaren plucked the card from its three-pronged holder and held it up.

Moira shook her head. "No, please just take it and find out all you can. I can't let his ugliness ruin my life."

MacLaren nodded before he lifted the card in its envelope to his nose and sniffed it. It seemed strange that a man as observant as MacLaren would use his nose so much, but Moira hadn't trained as an investigator. She figured all the senses were beneficial if one knew how to use them. He opened the envelope and pulled out the card. She could see black writing on the stark white surface, but she forced her eyes away before the words made sense.

MacLaren grunted and scowled before he put the card back into its paper covering and dropped it into a little plastic resealable bag. He pulled out a pen and marked the bag before he raised his gaze to hers. For a moment, she thought she saw his eyes glow as if flames burned behind them, but when she looked again, they were the normal brown she'd seen at first. *Must have imagined it.*

"I'll take this to the techs at the station and we'll see if we can get anything useful from it." From the way his eyes raised to look over her shoulder at Aiden, she suspected he already had something. "In the meantime, keep an eye out for him and if he comes back, call us immediately. I'll let Lt. Fitzroy give you a call if the Cloudburst PD finds anything."

"Thank you, Mr. MacLaren. I appreciate the help."

"You're welcome, Ms. Callahan. I promise, we'll get this guy."

Something in the way he said the words made her think he didn't mean 'catch and release.'

****

Moira shivered but stepped away from Aiden and he tried to ignore the helplessness he felt. He didn't usually feel so useless or out of his depth, but dealing with someone who attacked from the shadows stole his usual confidence.

"Thanks again for coming, Mr. MacLaren. I'm going to just throw these out if that's okay with you." She pointed a shaking finger at the flowers and Aiden wanted to wrap her up in his arms.

"That's fine. Here, use paper towels to carry it. I'll take the vase, too, just in case he touched it."

Moira nodded with a grimace, but wrapped paper towels around the glass vase and carried the whole mess toward the back door.

As soon as she was out of site, MacLaren turned his gaze back to Aiden. "You need to know what's on the card."

Aiden raised his eyebrows. "I do?"

"Yeah. I sense you're her mate and she'll need your backup when the time comes."

MacLaren's use of *mate* threw him a little, but the

older man pulled out the card again and showed him the writing. In precise, all-caps writing, the black words marched across the card.

We'll be together again. See you soon. XOXO LC

Aiden's gut curdled as his anger rose. "What the hell does that mean?"

"I don't know. Maybe she does, but if I'd received this, I would think of it as a threat." MacLaren stuffed the card back into the bag and tucked it in his jacket pocket. "She doesn't want his attention, so why is he sending her flowers and suggesting they'll be together? Definitely a threat."

Aiden swallowed hard. He had to agree, but he didn't know what to do about it.

"What can I do? I'm going out of my mind, but he's like a ghost. He shows up, leaves stuff for her, and disappears for weeks."

MacLaren fished out another card, this one with his name and a phone number. "You'll keep your eyes open and your ear to the ground, and call me if you see anything suspicious. The cops will do all they can, but they have to go through proper channels, and that might make it easier for this bastard." His intense gaze bored into Aiden's. "I have his scent in my nose now. If he's anywhere in Cloudburst, I'll find him first."

Something about this man made Aiden believe him. "I'll let you know if I see or hear anything."

"Good." He looked up as Moira returned with only the vase still wrapped in a towel. "Thanks, Ms. Callahan. I'll get that to the lab as well. Maybe it'll lead to other clues and we can track this guy down."

He took his leave and they remained behind the counter, watching as he disappeared into the people walking by outside. Moira didn't say anything until she'd poured herself a hot cup of chai and offered him one. He shook his head.

"Do you think his visit will help?"

Aiden shot a look out the windows, looking for any sign of Corsica. "Yeah, something in my gut says he'll be more helpful than even Lt. Fitzroy."

"You think so?"

"Yeah." Aiden took a deep breath and faced Moira. "I got a look at the card Corsica wrote."

All the color leached from her face. "Was it bad?"

"Not on the surface, but the meaning rang through loud and clear."

"What did it say?" She whispered the words, her eyes going wide.

"We'll be together again. See you soon."

Her hands tightened around her mug. "Oh glory. I don't want to see him soon. I want him to leave me alone. I made it really clear. What the hell do you think it means?"

"I don't know. But MacLaren knows about it and will step up his vigilance."

She shook her head, her expression bleak. "I hope it means he catches Corsica and scares the living shit out of him."

"Oh, MacLaren could do that. He's a scary guy." The guy wasn't human, Aiden was sure. He didn't know what he was, but for now he was on their side, and that had to be enough.

CHAPTER SEVENTEEN

After MacLaren's visit, Moira remained on edge about Corsica's promise. When would he show up? What did he have planned? Where was he? But days passed with nothing out of the ordinary happening and some of her tension waned. She kept looking over her shoulder whenever she went anywhere, but the energy of town was sanguine and no more gifts showed up for her at the coffee shop.

Lt. Fitzroy had called back within a week to tell her the finger prints on the card indeed belonged to Corsica, but he'd paid for the flowers using cash and the delivery guy had never seen him. Fitzroy said they'd keep an eye out for him, but unless he made an appearance, there was little they could do. MacLaren had contacted Aiden to tell him there hadn't been any traces in town, but he was expanding his search area. All they could was wait.

But after two weeks of nothing, Moira started to think Lenny had moved on. With Fitzroy and the Cloudburst PD on the lookout, and MacLaren out sniffing around, quite literally, it would be hard to get close to her. She allowed herself to relax.

She and Aiden had grown closer sexually as well as emotionally. She found herself happy to see him in her bed in the mornings, and she loved it when he Dominated her. She'd found her partner, the one who understood her soul, and she didn't want to give up on it.

She'd also strengthened her relationships with her two youngest brothers. Thomas often stopped by the coffee shop both to and from his music store to chat and buy coffee. He met Aiden and told her afterward that he thought they looked good together. The small token of approval warmed her heart and she'd thrown her arms around her tall brother. Thomas had blushed, but his shoulders had straightened and he'd damn near strutted out the door.

Kieran had made his visits more regular, but Moira suspected it had more to do with Talia than it did with her. Still, her brother made an effort to spend a little time with her and talk about mundane things like the family and the horses at the Golden C Ranch. Their uncle Marcus had raised a good crop of "dependable mutts", mixed-breed horses good for riding, ranching, and pasture pets. Some were rescues, some wild herd culls, but all were smart, gentle, and good with people. Marcus made sure of it.

As the Memorial Day weekend approached and the days grew warmer, the worry about Corsica took a backseat to her concern about how her parents and three older brothers would react to her bringing Aiden with her to the party. Kieran and Thomas had accepted him without much reservation, but they were younger than her, and she was the wiser big sister in their eyes. Her older brothers were less convinced with her ability to pick worthy men.

As if they know anything about being worthy men.

Stephen was divorced, Kallen still single, and Patrick, last she'd heard, was licking his wounds after a bad breakup. Not exactly the poster boys for successful relationships.

I'm not exactly an expert, either.

No, her failure with Corsica made her suspect as well, but she and Aiden worked well together in many ways, and he made her heart pound from the smallest things. Like when he rolled out of bed and looked over his shoulder at her, a sexy smile etched on his lips. Or when he would bring her a cup of chai in the middle of the day just when she needed a pick-me-up. And the nights together wore her out with their explosive pleasure.

The Saturday of Memorial Day weekend opened up rainy and gloomy despite the warmer weather they'd had during the week. For some reason, Moira's mood reflected the weather and she found herself restless. The wet day had kept most people at home and she'd done all the ordering, shift scheduling, and stocking she could think of to keep her busy.

"I'm going to go for a walk." She swung her hooded jacket around her shoulders.

"Now? In this weather?" Talia shot a dubious look out the doors. "It looks cold and wet." She shivered.

"It won't be bad. Just a spring rain. It's already sixty degrees out there." She waved Talia off. "I'm feeling cooped up in here and need some fresh air."

Talia frowned and rubbed her arms. "Fine, but don't go too far, okay? The day is giving me the heebie jeebies."

"I won't. I'm just going to walk near Oro Creek. I'll be within town and close to the road." She gave a cheery smile as she headed for the back door. "I'll be careful, I promise."

To be honest, she needed the space to think, and the Cloudburst Coffee & Spa, while relaxing to her patrons, took too much of her attention to let her clear her head. She climbed into her Jeep, dug out her cell phone and threw it in her purse, before inserting the key. The Jeep rumbled to life and the purr of the engine soothed some of her restlessness. *This is a good idea.*

She backed out of her spot and headed toward the creek running along the south side of town. The trees were still bare, but the air had the quality of hope despite being cool and wet. Mist sprinkled her windshield with water droplets, but she rolled one window down to catch the spring freshness.

Traffic was light and it didn't take her long to reach her favorite spot with a trail that led to the creek. Though the trees grew thick along the gentle slope to the water, the season made everything visible through the trunks. It was open here and no one would be able to sneak up on her. She parked the Jeep and got out, breathing in the wet air full of spring promise.

Moira headed for the creek's edge, hoping the currant would soothe some of her familial concerns. Tomorrow she'd have to face everyone at the annual Memorial Day party. She suspected her older brothers and her father wouldn't like her choice to be with Aiden. And her mother hadn't said word one.

I'm sure she'll have some words tomorrow. It would definitely be an event packed to the gills with tension.

She sighed and tightened her hooded jacket around her chest. It might be spring, but the Colorado Rockies seemed to have forgotten. Despite the lateness of season, they still had patches of snow on the ground from the last storm that came through a week ago. She paused on the rocky beach of Oro Creek and admired the reflection of the trees on the water. The air sat still, allowing the mist to coat everything. She closed her eyes and inhaled slowly. Here she could relax and let the creek take some of her worry and restlessness away.

Moira loved her family, even as overbearing and controlling as they were. She'd moved out of her parents' house as soon as she could, ready to find her own path. She'd left long before her next oldest brother, and had to fight to find a way to live on her own terms. Her father had written her off, but her older brothers still thought she needed to be guided into whatever they pictured as the perfect life for her. *Except they don't know me very well anymore.*

None of her family knew she had a submissive nature and enjoyed BDSM. *Well, with Aiden.* Lenny and his brand of sadism had damaged that side of her.

She could see her brothers' expressions if they found out what she'd been doing in Denver when she needed relief from the pressures of city life. Disgust, disdain, dismissal. They wouldn't understand the lifestyle, and probably blame her for any harm that came to her.

Only Aiden really gets it.

She bent and picked up a rock to skip it across the still waters of the creek's eddy. It bounced five times before it skidded beneath the water's surface. Aiden. The man she'd loved since she was a kid, and now knew better as a woman. He was the partner she wanted, a man who could love her for her quirks, her abilities, and even her hang-ups. He'd been so patient with those she'd gathered from her life before him. It made the decision to give him her heart very easy.

Who am I kidding? He already has my heart.

She laughed in the silence of the gray afternoon. Now all she had to do was find the courage to stand up to her family. *With Aiden beside me.* They'd run him off two decades ago, but now she was stronger. She'd defend him and their love. Even if it meant she'd be disowned.

It doesn't matter. I have the Cloudburst Coffee & Spa with Talia. She didn't need the family's approval to survive. *And I have Aiden.*

Moira threw another rock into the stream before she heard footsteps on the rocky beach behind her. She turned to see who intruded upon her solitude, but she only caught sight of someone wearing dark clothes before something collided with her head.

Stars and pain exploded across her vision, and she went down with a cry. Disorientation rattled her awareness and she tried to crawl away from her attacker, but he kicked her in the side. Her breath whooshed out, stealing her ability to scream, and her vision swam.

Oh glory. Goddess help me.

The man bent down until his face was close to hers. "Hey gosling. I told you we'd be together again. No one leaves the lifestyle, Moira. And now you'll be mine forever."

She tried to reach for her cell phone, but she remembered she'd taken it out of her jeans' pocket and thrown it in her purse. The one on the front seat of her Jeep. She tried to roll to her hands and knees, but he clocked her in the head again and grabbed her arms.

"Oh, there'll be plenty of time for that, gosling. You can crawl across my floor. But for now, I need you to come with me." He bent down in front of her, pushing her hair away from her face. The scent of his sweet and cloying cologne filled her nose and brought back horrible memories from the nights he hurt her. "Are you ready, gosling?"

Glory, she hated that nickname and she opened her mouth to tell him to fuck off. But the pain and disorientation grayed out her vision as her world tilted. *Am I flying?* The creek spun off to her left and faded into a thick black cloud, and her awareness went with it.

CHAPTER EIGHTEEN

"Have you heard from Moira?"

Talia's anxious face filled the office door as Aiden looked up from the books. "What?"

"Have you heard from Moira?" She rubbed her hands on her thighs. "She said she was going for a walk down at the creek to clear her head, but that was over an hour ago and she hasn't responded to my texts."

Aiden frowned, trying to think of when he'd last heard from Moira. "Let me check my phone." He fished it out of his pocket, but saw no messages of any kind. "No, nothing. Where did she say she was going?"

"Oro Creek. She said she'd stay in town, close to the road." Talia ran a hand through her hair. "She always answers my texts." She swallowed hard.

Aiden's gut tightened as unease slithered through him. Something was definitely wrong. He lifted his phone and dialed the number he'd put in almost three weeks earlier.

"MacLaren."

"Mr. MacLaren, this is Aiden Westmorland. Moira is missing and isn't answering her phone."

A short silence sounded. "How long has she been gone?"

"Over an hour. No texts or voicemails answered." Aiden grabbed his coat and headed for the coffee shop, Talia trailing behind.

"Does anyone know where she went?"

Aiden held his phone with his shoulder as he shoved his arms into the sleeves of his coat. "She told Talia she wanted to take a walk down at Oro Creek."

"Her favorite place is at the Willow Park trailhead. It's on the south side of town and it's not even a hundred yards from the creek." Talia drew a quick map on a napkin.

"Willow Park trailhead on Oro Creek. Know it?" Aiden relayed the information as he studied her crude map.

"Yeah. I'll be there in ten minutes. Have you talked to her brothers?"

"My next calls." Aiden grabbed his keys and gloves. "I'm headed that way."

"Okay, see you there." MacLaren hung up.

Aiden shot a look at Talia, her face a mask of worry. "I'll find her, I promise."

She nodded and he headed out the back to start his truck. He let it warm up a few moments while he punched numbers into his phone.

"This is Kieran, what can I do you for?"

"Kieran, it's Aiden. Moira's missing."

A short paused sounded. "How do you know she's just not answering her phone?"

"She's been gone over an hour after taking a walk and hasn't answered texts or calls." Aiden put the truck in reverse and backed out of the parking lot.

"Maybe she forgot her phone somewhere?" Kieran sounded hopeful.

"I don't think so, Callahan. I'm on my way to look for her now."

"Do you know where she went?" It sounded as if Kieran stepped into a room and closed the door.

"Talia says she went for a walk down by Oro Creek."

Aiden glanced at the map and turned the truck to the south. "Oh yeah, that's her favorite place since she got back to Cloudburst. Look for the sign to Willow Park."

"Will do. I'll let you know if I find her. Can you call Thomas and tell him?"

"Yeah, I will. Thanks for doing this. I can't get away from work at the moment. But I'll come as soon as I'm done here."

"At the end of the work day?" That was several hours away.

"No, as soon as I'm done." Annoyance laced his voice. "Find Moira." He hung up.

Aiden cursed and threw his phone into his pocket as he roared through a yellow light. Unease and worry cramped his gut and he couldn't help speeding toward the creek. He hoped Fitzroy would forgive him if he broke some speed laws. He glanced at the crude map and turned the wheel, his tires squealing as he skidded into the parking lot to Willow Park. Moira's Jeep sat near the break in the fence and he pulled in beside it.

He threw himself out and looked into the Jeep's interior. Nothing looked disturbed. The doors were locked and her purse sat on the front seat. Her cell phone stuck out of the top pocket and lit up as he watched. *Probably someone calling her.*

"Fuck!" He backed away from the Jeep and looked around. No one else had braved the cool, gray day to visit the park. He stood alone, trying to figure out what to do.

Before he made a move one way or another, a cherry red Jeep Wrangler pulled up beside his truck. Alex MacLaren rolled from the seat and headed his way.

"Anything?"

Aiden shook his head. "Her purse and phone are in the Jeep. No outward signs of struggle and the vehicle's locked. She must have the keys with her."

"All right. Let's look around. You said she went down

to the creek."

Aiden nodded. "That's the assumption."

MacLaren swung toward the stream. Aiden followed the other man, unnerved at how quick and quiet he moved. MacLaren was big, broad, and muscular. How he managed to say so silent was a mystery.

Focus on finding Moira.

They made it to the rocky beach, but the stretch of cobbled shoreline remained empty in either direction. He hadn't expected to see her, but disappointment made a hole in his gut. They swung their gazes over the calm expanse of the empty beach.

"There." MacLaren pointed to some gouges left in the gravel.

"Oh sweet Goddess." They hurried to them and Aiden's gut sank. "Those are drag marks from someone's feet."

MacLaren nodded. "Yeah. And the ground is roughed up over here. I'd say they were attacked before they were dragged."

They found the scuff marks and a flat spot where something adult sized had hit the ground. The furrows led away from the spot toward the trees along the beach. Aiden's fury rose.

"Looks like they head back up toward the parking lot. Is there any way to track where they went?"

MacLaren nodded. "At least until the parking lot. After that, I don't know." He pointed to the drag marks. "Let's follow them."

Aiden grimaced, but followed behind MacLaren, careful not to disturb the tracks with his own footprints. While MacLaren led the way, his attention at his feet, Aiden wondered what more they could do. Moira had disappeared off the face of the earth, and while he knew who'd taken her, he couldn't think of way to track where they went.

Come on, Aiden. Think!

"When you found out Corsica had a record, did you get a warrant to search his cell phone records?"

MacLaren threw a look over his shoulder before he returned his gaze to the ground. "Yeah, actually. Fitzroy got one to help track where he was."

"Give me the number." An idea popped into Aiden's head. Not strictly legal, but he'd do anything to bring this bastard down.

"Why?"

"I got a buddy who can do things with a computer that'd make your head spin. Maybe we can track where he is now." Aiden held up his phone, ready to call Sean.

"You don't know Corsica has her." But MacLaren didn't sound convinced.

"Then we'll just swing by to see if he needs coffee, and if she's not there, we'll leave him alone." Aiden didn't believe it would be that simple, but on the record it sounded fair.

MacLaren grimaced before his gaze stuck to the ground. "Shit."

"What?" Aiden froze in the act of finding Sean's number.

"Blood." He pointed to a dark patch on the ground. Aiden wouldn't have seen it in the grass and old leaves from last season.

Aiden swallowed hard. "Is it human blood?"

"Yes." MacLaren met his gaze. "Female, too. Call your buddy."

"Shit." He dialed the phone, fear making his hands shake.

"Hey, Aiden, how's it goin'?"

"Not great. Can you trace Corsica's cell phone number for me?"

The creak of Sean's chair sounded as he sat forward while the phone was jostled. "Yeah, give me just a sec."

The clicking of keys followed. "Okay, hit me with it."

MacLaren rattled off the number and Sean's fingers flew. "Okay, it looks like he still has his phone on. He's on Highway 160 between Cloudburst and Chimney Rock. Accordin' to the satellite maps, there ain't nothin' out there, but I'll give you the coordinates and you can have at it."

"Thanks, Cowboy. I owe you."

"No way. This shit's gotta end. He's an asshole and should be put down like a rabid dog. Let me know when you've got him."

"Worried you'll be stuck behind a screen and out of the action?" Aiden teased to lighten the panic in his gut.

"Hell no, I just wanna know when my work saves someone's ass. You take care of that lady, y'hear?"

"Will do, Cowboy." Aiden shoved his phone in his pocket and turned to MacLaren. "He's to the west, off Highway 160 between here and Chimney Rock."

MacLaren put his own phone away. "Okay. I'll drive. Lt. Fitzroy will have a forensics crew out here and I've marked the blood spot. We'll leave them to it."

Aiden followed him with his gut churning. Sweet Goddess of the Valley, they had to get to Moira before Corsica did anything to her. *Nice try, jackass. He's already done something to her.* He'd attacked and kidnapped her. They had to get to her before he did more than that.

****

Moira floated in a space of darkness and pain. Her head swam like she rocked on rolling seas and the world didn't quite hold still. Even with her eyes closed, she felt unstable. Some part of her recognized she stood upright, but discomfort reigned over her.

Everything hurt. Her ribs stabbed her with each breath, her shoulders throbbed, and her legs ached. Pain existed as one big warning sign wrapping her up in spikes that advanced and retreated with each breath.

Where was she? She opened her eyes, but had to slit them against the bright spotlight shining into her face from above. The floor at her feet was concrete and smooth with some sort of sealant she'd seen in artsy-fartsy grocery stores. Nothing else appeared close to her and she tried to lean forward to sit down.

Her wrists snagged on something and her shoulders screamed in protest. What the hell? She turned her head to find her right hand belted securely to an upright beam of wood. *No.* She looked at her left hand and found the same. *Oh glory, no. Not again.* Dropping her gaze to her bare feet, she realized why everything hurt and she couldn't change position. She was strapped, naked, to a St. Andrew's Cross.

She moaned and fought her bounds, the anger and fear morphing into panic. *I can't do this again. I said no.* She fought, but only succeeded in causing herself more pain. A scream of rage erupted from her throat at her impotence.

"There, there, gosling." Lenny's sickeningly sweet voice slid over her like slime mold and she shivered. "God, you're intoxicating all trussed up like this. I recall how good it was to be with you, but my memories pale in comparison to having you here again."

He stood just outside the circle of light. She could barely see his silhouette.

"Release me, Lenny. I said no. I don't want to do this again." She tried to ignore the bile working up her throat from her belly. He'd tied her to the cross naked, vulnerable to his hands and anything else he planned to use on her.

"Oh, gosling, I know that's not true. You're a pain slut and you love it."

"No, I'm not. I never was. I told you. I made it clear, I even left town. The answer is no." She twisted her hands in the straps, but they'd been tightened down too much to

eave slide against her skin. "My safeword is Andromeda."
She took a deep breath. "ANDROMEDA!"

"Sweet little bitch." He smiled at her with derisive
affection. "We haven't agreed on your safeword. Old ones
don't count. Besides, it's too late to use one. You're
already here and strapped in. I'd hate to waste such a
precious commodity when it's before me." He extended his
arm with a riding crop, using the leather flap at the end to
gently slap her breasts.

Moira stared at him with no expression. She wouldn't
accept his attempt to degrade her. And she felt nothing but
disgust.

"Come on, gosling. We've been apart too long and I've
missed you." He inhaled deeply, but frowned as if he
hadn't found the scent he'd been expecting. "Hmm. I think
we need to make some adjustments here."

She raised her eyebrows. Adjustments? Did that mean
he'd set her free?

Lenny stepped up to her dressed in leather pants with a
harness containing metal rivets crisscrossing his naked,
hairless chest. A small paunch pushed its way through the
harness and hung over the waistline of the pants. Disgust
wormed its way up her throat and she swallowed against
vomiting.

Instead of freeing her, he reached up and tightened the
straps around her hands, grinning as she squeaked with
pain. He bent and did the same to her ankles, pausing to
sniff her pussy on the way back up. She wished she could
twist and slam her hip into his cheekbone, but he'd secured
her too tight. Frustrated fury boiled beneath her skin and
she forced herself to hold still. If she had one leg free, she'd
have kneed him in the chin.

He stepped back, his expression reverent as if he
enjoyed not only the pain she experienced, but the smell of
her cleft. She resisted the urge to scowl. She wasn't even
wet.

"You smell good, gosling. But I know you can smell better, wetter, ready for my knob." He smiled up at her. "I know you crave pain—"

"I don't. I never have."

He scowled with her interruption. "You forgot to call me Master. And you should never interrupt your Master. You'll need to be punished." His eye lit up and he licked his lips in anticipation.

Without warning, he stepped back and cracked the riding crop against her left breast. Burning fire shot through her chest and she screamed as she jerked against the tight bonds. He reversed his stroke and slapped the crop against the right breast, adding a new brand to the previous one.

"Oh yeah, look at how beautifully your skin blooms with my caresses." He grabbed one nipple and squeezed until she moaned. The pain from his grip added a new layer to her constant throb.

Lenny inhaled again, a beatific smile curling his lips. "Oh, yeah, I can feel it now."

Feel what now? What the hell was he getting out of this?

He stepped back and pulled out his phone from his back pocket. He aimed the little device at her and she heard the electronic shutter sound confirming he'd taken some pictures. He moved from one side to the other, clicking away before shoving the phone back into his pocket.

"You were always my best, Moira." He shivered with pleasure. "You always gave me the most strength and vitality. I shouldn't have let you go." He gave her a mock-frown. "But I didn't know what I'd lost until I found my next slut. She didn't give off the same sustenance as you and she couldn't satisfy me."

"Wh–what are you talking about?"

She was surprised her voice worked at all. The excruciating pain kept throbbing like a migraine, except it sat in every muscle and bone.

"Energy, my gushing slut. Yours is delectable, satisfying, and sustains me for days at a time." He shrugged. "Of course, at the time you ran away, I didn't know that, and it took me several more bitches and sluts to make the connection. They just didn't have enough delicious pain power to keep me going. But you, gosling." He swung the crop again her hip and she cried out. "Oh, yes, your power is intoxicating." He shivered as he inhaled, as if sucking in her pain with each throb of her body.

Holy Goddess of the Valley, he's an energy vampire.

She'd heard of such beings, but most of the time they were people who sponged off the positive beings in their lives, draining them of their energy and vitality like human blackholes. She'd also met people who thrived off the negative power of fear and anger, usually from the news and internet. But she'd never met anyone who actually lived off or grew stronger from it like that green character in the comic books did from anger.

Lenny gets stronger from pain.

Her pain.

Holy shit.

"Now, we're going to play a little game. It's called, "Right Answer or Punishment." You must give me the correct answer to my questions, or you'll be punished." He pinched the other nipple until she squirmed in her bonds and he grinned. "You get three tries to answer correctly. If you don't, you get punished. The more times you answer incorrectly, the more severe the punishment will be. Do you understand, gosling?"

Glory, she hated that fucking nickname. She refused to answer him.

He grabbed her chin in a vice-like grip and forced her to look at him. "Do you understand?"

"Yes."

He cracked a palm across her cheek, adding new pain and making her see stars. "Answer me respectfully, slut.

You say 'yes, Master'."

She'd rather spit in his face, but she had to resist somewhere. Giving him the title would decrease the chances of him hitting her. And if he didn't hit her, he wouldn't get that extra dose of pain to buoy himself up.

"Yes, Master." She scowled as she said it, her lips dripping in a sneer, not entirely of her doing. If her mouth hadn't been so swollen from his blows, she would've had more expression to show.

"Good girl."

I'm not a girl, you sick fuck.

Anger was her only weapon. Did he need fear to go with his pain, or was the pain enough? He'd hurt her as much as he could to get his rocks off, but she wouldn't give him the pleasure of seeing her scared. Dread pooled in her gut as she realized she might not survive this encounter. Or worse, she would, and he'd keep torturing her forever.

Let's not give in to panic quite yet.

It was a good line and she'd like to believe it, but watching Lenny disappear into the darkness beyond the light then reappear with a long bamboo cane made the words seem empty. With enough force, the cane would leave welts and break bones. Its flexibility made it a very effective tool for inducing agony. She swallowed hard and he grinned.

"All right, gosling. Are you ready for your questions?"

She shook her head. "No, Master. ANDROMEDA!"

He waggled a finger. "Ah ah ah. I told you. No old safewords. I think it's time to remind you." And he swung the cane hard into her broken ribs.

CHAPTER NINETEEN

Aiden's tension escalated the farther west they drove. MacLaren kept his gaze on the road and his thoughts to himself. Aiden watched the rainy forest pass by as they wound their way down the hills toward the little town of Chimney Rock. When he was a kid, Chimney Rock had been nothing more than a Forest Service station with a Ranger in it to keep the tourists from doing damage to the natural monolith. But as the popularity had grown, so had the population.

But between Cloudburst and Chimney Rock, Forest Service roads wove into the San Juan National Forest with campsites and old abandoned buildings dotting the few cleared areas. From what Sean had sent, Aiden suspected Corsica had found one such building to use for his needs, some place well off the road where no one would hear Moira scream.

He brought up the coordinates Sean had sent him to check how close they were getting.

"How long have you known Moira?"

MacLaren's question came out of nowhere. He hadn't expected the man to speak, much less engage in chit chat. Something about him suggested he hunted alone and silently, but was making an exception for Aiden. He shot the man a surprised look.

MacLaren caught it and snorted, smiling ruefully. "My wife tells me I need to be more communicative. We have to work together to find this mudfucker and I can smell the tension rising off of you."

Odd turn of phrase, but Aiden appreciated the distraction.

"We've known each other since high school, but our lives took separate roads there for a while. I've only recently come back to Cloudburst."

MacLaren nodded. "You planning to stay now that you're back?"

Aiden took his time before he answered. The time he'd spent there helping her with the coffee shop and getting to know her brothers made him realize he didn't want to leave. Cloudburst was her home, and she was his. He didn't want to be anywhere she couldn't be with him.

"Yeah, I'm planning to stay."

"Good." MacLaren nodded with satisfaction. "Very good."

"Why?"

"Because this woman is your mate, your true connection. I could smell it on you and her when I came to collect the card and vase." He gave Aiden a mysterious smile before turning his gaze back to the road. "I think you already knew that, but weren't going to say it because you don't know me well enough, right?"

Aiden blinked, surprised at his perspicacity. "There's a road coming up to the right in about a hundred yards. Looks like it will get us closest to the last coordinates of Corsica's phone."

MacLaren chuckled, but slowed on the wet pavement just as the little green Forest Service sign showed up in the rainy gloom on the far side of dirt road. He turned right and surged up the rutted track until they got enough grip in the slick mud. The trees grew closer together here and while the road remained relatively straight, visibility was hampered by both rain and vegetation. The Jeep's headlights showed watery ruts and soaked dead grass under the trees, but no other roads or buildings. Aiden told himself to be patient.

She has to be out here. I have to bring her home safe.

He couldn't think of any other outcome.

"Yeah, I already knew Moira was special and important. I didn't quite know how much until now."

MacLaren nodded, his smile gone. "We'll find her and take down the mudfucker. How close are we to the coordinates your buddy sent?"

Aiden glanced at his phone. "We're getting closer. It's hard to tell. It looks like it will be up ahead on the left-hand side. There's nothing marked on Google Maps, but the coordinates say there's something there. Or at least the phone is."

MacLaren grunted, his gaze fixed on the road ahead of their headlights. The track between the dark trunks of trees seemed to go on unbroken, but after a few more minutes of driving, the trees opened up to a grass meadow gray with rain. Aiden scanned the open area to the left and they both spotted the aluminum-sided equipment shed. It was long, enough to park several large vehicles or farm equipment inside, and had no windows. A small charcoal gray SUV sat parked between the vehicle and human doors halfway along its length.

"There." Aiden pointed. "That's where the phone is."

"It could be in the vehicle." MacLaren stopped the Jeep just off the main dirt road and killed the headlights.

"Even if it is, we know it's his vehicle." Aiden shoved his phone into his pocket and reached for the door handle.

MacLaren laid a hand on his shoulder. "We have to go slow and quiet. If we run in, guns blazing so-to-speak, he'll have time to get away and we'll lose him. I don't want this mudfucker to come back to my town."

Aiden gritted his teeth and nodded. "Okay."

"I'm going to scope out the perimeter, make sure there aren't any other doors. Just sit tight for a few and I'll be back."

Aiden shook his head. "I'm going to get closer, but I won't make any moves until you check the place out."

MacLaren tilted his head and scanned Aiden's body. Though it wasn't sexual in nature, the perusal raised the hair on Aiden's neck. MacLaren's eyes glowed for a moment, a red-gold he'd seen in campfire flames, before he nodded.

"Just keep quiet. We won't have much time after we break through the door."

Aiden opened his mouth, but MacLaren was already out of the Jeep and trotting toward the shed. He shrugged and got out, closing the car door as quietly as possible. MacLaren disappeared behind the shed and Aiden took a deep breath, letting it out slow as he listened to the forest around them.

The rain made a shushing sound, much like static on old radios, and the wind periodically brushed through the trees. Otherwise, the forest remained silent. He checked his coat pocket for his Leatherman tool and headed closer to the shed, listening for any human sounds. He kept his gaze locked on the door to the shed as he moved closer, hoping the silence wouldn't mean Moira was dead.

If she was dead, Corsica would be gone. While it wasn't a cheery thought, it did give him a little hope.

MacLaren appeared around the far end of the shed and ghosted to him, shaking his head.

"No other entrances, and the only windows are on the short sides, higher up toward the roof."

"Did you hear anything?"

MacLaren grimaced and nodded. "Yeah, you're not gonna like it."

Aiden swallowed hard as his gut sank. "What?"

MacLaren sighed and looked toward the door to the shed. "He's in there torturing her."

"Sonuvaprick! We have to get in there and take him down." Aiden advanced for the door before MacLaren caught his arm.

"If it's locked, we'll make too much noise that way. He'll know we're coming."

Aiden held up the Leatherman tool. "We'll try the door, and if locked, I'll pick it."

MacLaren grunted in amusement and followed Aiden to the door. He grasped the doorknob and after shooting a glance at the other man, slowly twisted. The latch turned silently and he eased the door open with a small sigh of relief. One obstacle down, unknown number to go. They stepped inside and closed the door softly behind them, MacLaren twisting the knob lock.

The space inside sat in darkness more profound than the rainy forest outside. The scents of oil, mud, and cold metal hit his nose, and dim shapes of a tractor and some oil drums filled the space to the left. Light poured from the right and he turned his gaze toward it.

Holy fuck!

Moira hung from her wrists and ankles on a St. Andrew's Cross, completely naked. Bruises and welts marked the skin on her ribs and legs. Her head dropped forward, her hair a tangled mane draping over her chest. He wasn't close enough to see what other damage had been done, but whatever he found, he'd exact on Corsica's body.

Rage rolled over him and he headed toward lighted end of the shed. He'd take down the mudfucker who'd hurt his friend, and make sure he'd never get up again.

"No, Aiden, wait!" MacLaren whispered, but Aiden was already moving.

"Oh yeah, gosling. Each mark, each blow, they make your skin glow in such wonderful colors, and your pain is a fine wine." Corsica's sing-songy voice made Aiden roar as he hurtled toward the man.

The creepy fucker in black leather pants turned at the last second and backhanded Aiden in the head with a negligent wave. The impact knocked the wind out of Aiden and threw him hard against the front wall of the shed. *What the fuck was that?* It felt like he'd been hit by a bus. He slammed to the floor with a painful grunt and Corsica laughed.

"Do you see, gosling? Your would-be lover isn't strong enough to have you. Your energy makes me invincible." He took a step forward and swung a bamboo cane into Moira's left side.

She grunted in pain and he hissed as if bathing in hot water. "Oh yeeessssss. God, you're magnificent. I could live on your pain forever."

Holy shit, he's an energy vampire.

"Aiden." Moira had turned her head to look search for him through the one eye that wasn't swollen. Her lips were cracked and bleeding, but she could still wheeze out words. "Pain. Pain."

At first he thought she meant she was in excruciating pain. *Yeah, I can see that.* He was right there with her. The impact with the wall had tweaked his ribs and made him see stars. His head rang like a bell, but the pain had started to recede. He struggled to his feet, wondering where MacLaren had gotten to, but his focus remained on Corsica.

The man seemed to glow with vitality and strength. Even as he watched, Corsica's muscles on his back grew more defined as if he'd been visiting the gym lately.

"Pain, Aiden." Moira's words ended in a wail as Corsica

slammed the cane into her right leg, leaving a bloody welt from torn skin.

"Leave her alone, you stupid mudfucker." Aiden raised his head and squared his shoulders. "She's not yours."

Corsica laughed. "Oh, she's always been mine. I didn't know what I'd lost until she ran away, but now that I know, I'm never letting her go." He reached out to caress her breast, ending in a tight grip on the nipple and twisted, hard. Moira groaned as he shivered with pleasure. "Oh yeah, never letting you go, gosling."

Tears streamed down Moira's bruised face but she turned her one-eyed gaze toward him. "Aiden, it's about pain...You know about...pain."

"Oh, yes, my sweet vessel of power. It's all about the pain, isn't it?" Corsica stroked her between the legs, but Moira's gaze never flinched from Aiden's.

You know about pain.

Pain made Corsica stronger, like some sort of strength serum. Moira's pain. He frowned. How could he break the connection between them? Corsica fed off Moira's injuries and agony. Could he distract the crazed man enough to take him out? *Where the hell is MacLaren?*

Aiden had used pain to control his sexual urges for the years. While he'd been with Moira in Cloudburst, he hadn't needed it. But pain seemed to be Corsica's drug of choice. Was it just Moira's pain or would anyone's pain do? Given the many women he'd hurt, Aiden suspected any pain was good for him. Moira's just happened to be the most powerful.

Aiden pulled out the Leatherman and unfolded the knife blade inside. *I'd like to give him all the pain he can take.* Preferably with a knife buried in his gut and his intestines dangling. Given the strength Corsica exhibited, there was no way Aiden could overpower him in a hand-to-hand fight. But maybe he could distract him enough for MacLaren to do something. He hadn't seen the other man, but he was sure MacLaren had caught the feat of strength Corsica displayed.

"Hey, Corsica, you're a weakling." Aiden called as he held the knife in his right hand. "You hurt women. That just shows you're a bully and a coward." He twisted his lips into a sneer as he watched the man strut around the cross. "No wonder Moira left you in Denver. She knew you'd never be able to please her."

Corsica brayed an evil laugh. "Please her? You got that backwards, *Aiden.* I'm the Dom and she's the sub. It's all about pleasing me. If you knew anything about the lifestyle, you'd know that."

You got that backwards, you sick mudfucker.

Corsica was nothing more than an abusive bully. But telling him so wouldn't change his actions. Aiden had to figure out a way to distract him.

"Hey, you like pain, right?" He moved closer, but remained out of the light.

Corsica laughed again. "I don't like pain, I like others' pain. Moira's the best pain slut I've ever had. Aren't you, gosling?" He slapped her face, rocking her head to the side. Blood sprayed across the concrete floor from her lips and nose.

A snarl sounded in the back of the shed and Aiden swallowed hard. Even Corsica noticed the predatory sound and turned to look behind him. Nothing appeared in the darkness, though Aiden held his breath to listen for any movement.

After a few more seconds, Corsica turned back to Moira, intent on hitting her again. Aiden picked up a loose clod of dirt left from some vehicle tire, hurled it at the wannabe Dom. It hit him in the shoulder and made him turn toward Aiden with a sneer.

As long as he leaves Moira alone.

"You can't have her, she's mine." Corsica hoisted the cane and came at Aiden, swinging.

Aw hell. He hadn't expected to have to defend against a stick, but hand-to-hand combat wasn't out of the question. He'd taken martial arts to deal with bullies like Corsica. And if he could distract the man long enough, maybe MacLaren would be able to free Moira and take her home.

He feinted to the side and ducked under Corsica's swing, the cane whistling over his head.

"She's not yours. She's her own person. You need to leave her alone." Aiden brought his arm up to stop the return cut and grabbed the cane with his other hand, intending to tear it from Corsica's grip.

But the man was too strong and Aiden was forced to let go, stepping back.

"You're nothing, you little, skinny shit. You're worthless and weak. You thought you could defend her?" Corsica snorted as he came at Aiden again. "You can't even defend yourself."

Aiden didn't bother to respond as he focused on blocking the swings of the cane. While Corsica was strong, and his blows rattled Aiden's body, he had little skill at hand-to-hand combat. Aiden kept blocking and ducking, trying to wear Corsica out rather than take the brunt of his strength.

Frustrated with Aiden's deflection, Corsica swept the cane downward and hooked his forward foot. Aiden tried to shift his weight to his back foot, but he wasn't fast enough, and the blow dumped him on his ass. He scrambled backwards, hoping to find something he could use to defend himself. The Leatherman wouldn't do anything against the cane.

"Now, she'll get to watch you die." Corsica shot a look toward Moira, who hadn't uttered a word, but her one good eye squinted toward them. "See, gosling? This is where I kill your weak-ass lover and no one will ever take you from me again. Get ready."

He raised the cane to swing it at Aiden's head when a hair-raising snarl filled the room. Everyone shot a look toward the tractor and Aiden swallowed hard.

"What is that?" Corsica paused, his muscles tense as he peered into the darkness. "What the fuck is that?"

Before Aiden could answer, a huge wolf, easily the height of a Great Dane with the girth of a Mastiff, launched itself at Corsica. Corsica screamed like a toddler as the wolf latched onto his throat, taking him down to the floor. Corsica screamed again, trying to fight off the animal, but despite his increased strength, he was no match. Snarls filled the space as the wolf savaged the man under it, tearing at him with powerful jaws.

Aiden scrambled to his feet and headed for Moira, not sure he'd be able to defend against such a creature, but he'd do what he could to protect her. He wanted to kneel at her feet and release her ankles, but he didn't want to be caught with his back to the great beast.

"Hold on just a little longer, Moira."

He faced the wolf just as the huge creature tore out Corsica's throat. The man's shriek ended and his body went slack. Blood soaked the floor beneath him as the wolf stepped back, shaking this head as if to rid itself of the taste of Corsica's blood. The glowing gold eyes raised to Aiden's and he braced for impact.

But the wolf didn't attack. Instead it sat back on its haunches, threw its head back, and howled in jubilation for victory. The sound was both victorious and eerie, and Aiden shivered at the power in it.

"Sweet glory."

Moira's whispered made him turn halfway, keeping one eye on the big canine.

"How are you?"

"Not sure. We gonna die now?"

"Not sure. Hold tight."

Despite her obvious pain, she snorted. "Don't have a choice."

Aiden watched the wolf as it dropped his head and stared straight at him with glowing golden eyes. He swallowed hard, but frowned as the tip of the wolf's tail seemed to sparkle, like little flames danced at the ends of the guard hairs. But it didn't surprise him as much as what happened to the corpse in front of the animal.

It, too, began to sparkle, but not with flames. This light appeared like a gathering of energy or pixie dust he'd seen in those animated fairy movies. More and more specks of light pulled off the body and swirled together in the shape of a spiral, floating lazily in the air.

More strange, the corpse crackled, the sound reminding Aiden of the wood in a fire breaking down as the flames consumed it. Under the light of the sparkling swirl, Corsica's body slowly desiccated, the vitality left the muscles and the skin turned black. The lips pulled back from the teeth as the eyes sunk into the skull. Most of the hair fell off the crown of the skull to pile around it in an eerie halo. Eventually, all that remained was a blackened mummy in leather pants and a harness.

"Holy Goddess." Aiden swallowed hard.

The wolf got to its feet and snapped at the swirl of sparkles like a playful puppy, but Aiden didn't have any illusions about what kind of play the creature would engage in. *No running.* He snorted. Like he'd get very far. The damn thing was the size of a pony.

But the swirl of sparkling energy took one last rotation before it shot toward Aiden and Moira. Aiden ducked and the light splashed into Moira's chest. She cried out in surprise, rather than pain, and threw her head back.

Aiden gaped as the wounds on her face, arms, torso, and legs healedThe energy disappeared into her body and restored as much health and vitality as Corsica had taken from her. She grunted as the energy straightened her ribs. The wounds from the tight straps at her wrists and ankles faded and healed before Aiden's eyes.

"Glory be." He'd never been much of a devout person, but this was nothing short of the Goddess's magic at work, he was sure.

At last the process of revitalization ended and Moira hung on the cross, breathing hard. Aiden did the same, the changes made him breathless. He shot a look toward the wolf, but the huge creature had disappeared during the transformation. All that remained of its work was the mummified skeleton on the floor.

"Aiden?" Moira's voice sounded tired. "Will you please untie me?"

"Oh, yes." He dropped to his knees and slowly unbuckled her ankles, not wanting to cause more damage from their overtightened grip.

He massaged each foot, allowing the ankles to resume a natural position so she could put weight on her feet. Unfortunately, the bonds on her wrists remained too tight to allow her to stand. She perched on her toes and met his gaze with both eyes.

"Thank you." She gave him a lopsided smile, the bruising around her right eye still puffy.

"You're welcome. Just hold on a bit more and I'll get those off your wrists." He rose and bit his lip. Her shoulders were going to hurt. "You've been there a while. I'm going to do one wrist at time and rub your shoulder and arm. It's going to hurt."

She nodded. "I know. But I need to get away from here."

"Okay. Right wrist first."

He reached up and carefully unbuckled the cuff. Corsica had tightened it down so much her fingers were tinged with purple. *You ugly, sick, mudfucker.* He wished he could punish the bastard even more for what he'd done but desiccating into a brittle mummy in leather pants was pretty bad.

When he released Moira's right arm, he held it carefully, inspecting the skin as he let the joint move. Her wrist no longer bled and only showed the indentation of the cuff. She whimpered as he massaged the biceps, triceps, and deltoid, trying to loosen them before they seized.

"Oh glory, that hurts."

"I know. I'm sorry, Moira." He laid her arm against her body and moved around her to release the second wrist. "Ready for this one?"

"Yes, please." She sounded tired but determined.

He loved her refusal to give up, to give in, and wallow in pain. He loved her continued defiance and endurance.

Hell, he just plain loved her.

"I love you, Moira."

"What?" She looked up at him as he unbuckled her left wrist.

He slowly drew it down to her side as he massaged her muscles. He met her gaze, trying to ignore the winces she gave as he worked her stretched joints.

"I love you. I want you. I need you in my life." He swallowed hard and worked her deltoid, but he didn't drop her gaze. "I want to stay here in Cloudburst with you, take care of your financial books, and make love with you every chance I get. Will you let me stay?"

Tears sparked in her eyes. "Are you sure you want me? After what Corsica…after what just happened? I might be completely broken, Aiden."

"No one's completely broken." He drew her against his body and wrapped his arms around her. "I know your hard limits, I know your safeword, and I'd never betray your trust." He leaned his chin on top of her head. "We'll do this together, remember? Our rules, our way."

She sighed and rested against his chest. That was the only warning he received before the sobs and tears flooded from her. His heart ached and he wished he could take her pain away. Instead he held her close to his chest, offering her his comfort and strength for the moments she needed them.

After several moments, she quieted, their breathing the only sound inside the shed. But new sounds from outside intruded on their solitude. The rain on the roof came hard and fast, but the pattering gave them a sense of comfort as if Mother Nature washed the filth away. Sirens blared in the distance and the door to the shed opened and closed.

"Aiden?" MacLaren's voice boomed in the silent space.

"Yeah, back here." He called as he looked down at Moira. "MacLaren brought me. We tried to get here sooner, but didn't know where he'd taken you."

She nodded. "I didn't know, either. In fact, I still don't. Where are we?"

"An equipment shed in the San Juan National Forest."

She stepped back just far enough to look up at him with a frown. "Did I see or hear a wolf in here earlier? I could've sworn there was one."

MacLaren's footsteps drew closer as Aiden nodded, lowering his voice. "Yup. I'll tell you more later."

"Are you two okay? The police and paramedics are on their way." MacLaren stepped into the circle of light with a bundle in his hands. "I brought you some clothes, Ms. Callahan."

"Thank you, Mr. MacLaren." She gave him a smile, but didn't reach for the clothes. "Do you mind if I move somewhere darker to change? I feel rather exposed."

"Of course." MacLaren handed the clothes to Aiden and turned his back.

She took them, gave Aiden a smile, and limped out of the bright circle of light.

Aiden stepped up to MacLaren. "What happened? I thought you'd followed me inside. Where were you?"

MacLaren turned his head and fixed Aiden with softly glowing eyes, eyes he'd seen in the darkness just before a huge wolf took Corsica down. "Calling the cavalry." MacLaren smirked.

For a moment, the world shifted sideways as Aiden's gift tried to fill his head with MacLaren's stats. But the only things that came to him were the scents of pine and snowy wind, sounds of a wolf howling in the distance, and a single phrase. *Not human.*

Aiden swallowed hard. He remembered the moment MacLaren had come to collect the card and flowers at the coffee shop. He'd known the man was different, but now he suspected he tended to turn fuzzy and howl when the urge moved him.

Aiden cleared his throat and held out his hand to shake. "Thank you, Mr. MacLaren."

MacLaren reached out, palm down and twisting at the last moment to grasp Aiden's hand. "You're welcome. And my friends call me Alex."

"Alex." Aiden nodded. "Thank you. I couldn't have done anything without you."

Alex winked. "You distracted him. That was enough. Is Ms. Callahan going to be okay?"

"Yes, I think I will. Thank you for coming for me, Mr. MacLaren."

They both turned to find her dressed in jeans and a long, hooded sweatshirt. She'd pulled her hair back from her face, showing off the black eye, but she moved a little better than she had, and Aiden's throat closed at her beauty and strength. This was the woman he'd wanted since he was a gangly, geeky kid. He wouldn't let her go.

"Alex, please. You look better than when we first arrived. But I'm pretty sure the paramedics will want to check you out." Alex smiled but didn't get close to Moira. He shot a look at Aiden and winked. "Let's go out and meet them. The police will want to investigate and get all the forensic evidence they can. No reason for us to muck it up."

"Are you ready?" Aiden gathered Moira to his side.

"Oh yeah, let's get the flock out of here."

Alex laughed and led the way through the darkness to the door. They pushed out into the rainy evening just as the yard in front of the shed filled up with emergency vehicles and flashing lights. An ambulance, a fire engine, one highway patrol SUV, and two police cruisers from the Cloudburst PD pulled up in an array of emergency personnel. Lt. Fitzroy jumped from one cruiser while the paramedics rushed toward them with a stretcher.

"Any injuries?" One paramedic stopped in front of them.

"A few. She needs to be checked out." Aiden gestured to Moira.

"Can you walk, ma'am?" The paramedic held out her hand.

"Yes, but I could use some help." She accepted the woman's hand and gave Aiden a smile. "I'm going to go rest for a bit."

"Okay. I'll stay here and answer questions."

She nodded and followed the paramedics to the ambulance. Aiden turned his attention to Fitzroy and Alex.

"Any other injuries that need to be checked out?" Fitzroy scanned Aiden's body.

"Nope. Just some bumps and bruises. But there's a body on the floor inside." Aiden waived at the door.

"Corsica?" Fitzroy's gaze sharpened.

Aiden nodded. "Yup."

"Did you kill him?"

Aiden shook his head. "No. Not sure what the true cause of death was, but you'll understand when you see the body. I...got nothin'."

Fitzroy raised an eyebrow. "You were there when he died and you don't know the cause of death?"

Aiden shrugged. "Yeah. It's not something I can explain. I didn't touch him, though. Something else definitely got him." He shot a look at Alex and the other man winked, but didn't smile. Aiden swallowed hard. *Holy shit, that guy's the wolf.*

"All right. I'll get to that soon. Just take me through what happened today, we'll go from there."

Aiden nodded and recounted the events leading up to them finding the equipment shed. He described everything, including how his buddy Sean tracked Corsica's cell phone, and the efforts he'd made to distract him, but he left out the giant wolf who'd come in at the end. *Goddess knows I don't need to sound crazy to the police.* Fitzroy asked a few clarifying questions to make sure he had the details right before someone called him into the shed.

"Sounds like they found something interesting." Fitzroy raised his eyebrows and disappeared through the door.

Aiden met Alex's gaze, wanting to ask about the wolf, but the glowing irises in Alex's eyes made him swallow his questions. *You already know the answer. No need to belabor it.*

"Do you have any idea how Corsica died?"

Alex shook his head. "Honestly, no. I expected him to bleed out. The desiccation was different."

"Yeah." Aiden coughed an incredulous laugh. "Definitely different. Thanks for the backup and calling the cavalry."

"You're welcome. I'm glad we got here when we did." Alex stretched his neck and groaned. "Chewed bones, I'm tired. I hope Fitzroy lets us go soon. I'd like to cuddle with my mate." He tilted his head. "I suggest you do the same."

"My mate?"

Alex clapped him on the shoulder and grinned. "I expect a wedding invitation. Just sayin'."

Aiden gaped after him as he headed into the shed to talk to Fitzroy.

CHAPTER TWENTY

Moira sat in her bed with her knees drawn up to her chest. It was closing in on midnight, and though she was tired, her mind wouldn't let her settle down. The paramedics had checked her over, taking in the injuries they could see. All she had were a few bruises on her sides and face. When they'd insisted she go to the ER, she'd shaken her head and refused treatment. They weren't pleased, but she stood firm on her decision.

I should be more beaten up. Despite her memory, she didn't feel like she'd been tortured. *Must have something to do with that blast of energy at the end.*

It had sustained her enough to make her statements to the police and the long ride home to Cloudburst. Alex and Aiden had taken her to his truck at Willow Park then bid them farewell. There was an understanding between both men she couldn't quite figure out, but they man-hugged at the end and Alex drove off. Aiden took her immediately home, promising to get her Jeep the next day.

She'd taken a shower and climbed into bed while Aiden made phone calls to everyone to let them know she was all right. *That's a relative term.* He also informed her family she wouldn't be attending the Memorial Day party.

She suspected they weren't pleased to hear it from anyone but her, but at the moment, she didn't give a shit.

"Can't sleep?"

Aiden appeared at the bedroom door with a tray holding cheese, crackers, and tomatoes, and a steaming teapot.

She shook her head. "Mind won't settle down."

He nodded as he stepped across the threshold. "I thought you might like some tea and food."

She grunted a laugh. "You can't sleep, either?"

He shrugged with a smirk and settled beside her on the bed. "Too keyed up."

"Yeah, me, too."

He handed her a mug of sweet, spicy tea, and assembled little piles of crackers, tomatoes and cheese. "Here, eat a little and then we'll go to bed."

"I don't know if I can sleep." She took the tray and a mug, grateful to have them in her hands.

"Then we'll just talk. Eventually we'll get tired." He sat back with his own plate and mug.

"Okay." She nodded and sipped her tea. "What do you want to talk about?" She waited him out, her gut tight with worry.

This is where he tells me he's thought it over and he wants to let me down gently.

"I wanted to talk to you about us." He set his mug down and leaned back against the headboard. "I've thought it over and—"

"You don't think you can stay. Right?" She steeled herself for the inevitable crash.

"What? No way in hell, Moira. You got it backwards." He grasped her hand and pulled it to his chest. "No, I've thought it over and I want to stay here, with you, in this apartment above the coffee shop, forever. I don't want to leave. Will you let me stay with you?"

She blinked and tried to let her mind catch up to actual

his words rather than the ones she'd expected him to say.

"You want to stay with me here? What about your business with your friend Sean?"

He waved his hand. "I can do it from anywhere. That's the beauty of digital accounting and cyber security. It doesn't matter where I'm based as long as I have access to the accounts. Sean doesn't need me physically present." He leaned forward. "So, what do you say? Will you let me stay?"

She blinked and swallowed a few times. She wanted him to stay so badly her heart hurt. *But I'm so broken.*

"I don't know if that's a good idea."

His smile dropped away and unease slid through his expression. "Why not?"

She shrugged with one shoulder. "Corsica fucked me up, Aiden. I don't know if I can be intimate ever again, much less anytime soon."

He nodded. "Does that mean you want to be left alone?"

Did it? Did she want to live by herself with nothing but casual contact with friends and family? Her guts clenched and panic welled up.

"No, I don't want to be alone. I don't want you to leave, but I don't know if I can give you any intimacy."

"So, you're pushing me away to protect me?"

When he said it like that, it sounded stupid. She shrugged with a grimace. "Isn't that what you did all those years ago?"

He didn't laugh. Pain wreathed his eyes and lips.

"How about you and I work this out together?" He took a deep breath and raised his chin to meet her gaze squarely. "I know your hard limits. I know your safeword, and I love you as you are, even after this event. Do you have faith in me? Do you trust me to take care of you the way you want and deserve?"

She thought back to all the times she'd been with him,

even in the equipment shed when he'd stood between her and whatever made Corsica scream. And now when he sat beside her waiting for her to think everything through. Did she trust him?

Implicitly.

"Yes, I trust you."

He nodded, his blue eyes warming slowly. "Will you trust me to take care of you and to be patient with you when you get scared? Will you trust me to protect you, defend you, strengthen you, and back you up when you need it, even against your family and friends?"

She studied his handsome face with his thick black brows and his cerulean eyes, and her heart knew him to be honest and true. A protector and defender rather than a marauder.

"Yes, I will trust you to do those things."

Some of the tension left his shoulders as he took her tea and set it aside before he grasped both her hands. "Can you trust me to love you with all my heart, pleasure you with my body, and cherish you with my soul for all the rest of my life?"

Though they sounded like marriage vows, she didn't doubt his need to say them. She'd needed to hear them and feel the energy in the room as he said them. He meant what he said, but he needed her answer.

"Yes, I can trust you."

"And will you trust yourself to love me in return?"

She opened her mouth to reply, but nothing came out. Could she do that? Could she push past the fear and uncertainty of the past to love him the way he deserved? Could she trust herself enough to work through the traumatic events of the evening to give Aiden her whole heart?

The answer was simple and had been there all along. "Yes."

The smile curling his lips warmed her more than the

tea. "Then we'll be okay. We'll work through it all together."

"So, you won't leave?"

He shook his head. "I'm not leaving Cloudburst unless you come with me. You're my heart, my Lady Cloudburst, and my north star." He gave her a small smile. "Besides, it'll be much easier to plan a wedding here than if we moved somewhere else."

She blinked. "A wedding? What wedding?"

"Our wedding." He gave her a soft smile. "This is my second chance with you, and I'm not giving it up for anything. You're my heart, Moira. I can't leave it behind or walk away."

Tears started in her eyes. "I love you, Aiden. Thank you for believing in me."

He settled back against the headboard and gathered her into his arms. Just his touch calmed her down and settled her mind.

"I love you too, my beauty. I'll always believe in you."

Her heart warmed, but one question remained. "Aiden?"

"Yes."

"Did I really see and hear a wolf in that shed tonight?"

He chuckled. "Yes, you did."

She swallowed hard. "Did it kill Lenny?"

He nodded. "Yes, it did."

"Do you think we'll ever see it again?"

He tilted his head so he could meet her gaze. "I don't know, but I can tell you this much. He won't hurt us."

"How do you know that?"

"Because he's a protector of Cloudburst and he knows us now. He protected us from Corsica, and he acknowledged me, knows our scents. I don't know if we'll ever see him again, but he'll have our backs if we do."

She narrowed her eyes. "You seem very sure about that."

Aiden nodded. "I am. As sure as I am about my love for you." He squeezed her again. "Will you marry me, Moira?"

"You're sure?"

"I'm sure."

She took a deep breath. "Yes, I will."

He sighed with what sounded like relief. "Thank the Goddess."

Moira laughed as she settled down to sleep. *Thank the Goddess indeed.*

THE END

THE BELTANE WITCH
CLOUDBURST COLORADO, BOOK 2
SNEEK PEEK

Magic, mayhem, and motherhood… a witch's work is never done, but Sabrina draws the line at the Fae.

After almost two decades as a practicing witch in Cloudburst, Colorado, Sabrina Foxglove is done with men, magic, and the fertility rituals of High Beltane. She's dealt with all three before and ended up with a young daughter and no partner. Twice. She's looking forward to a magic-free May Day, with nothing more exciting than making brownies for a kindergarten class and decorating a May Pole. She definitely doesn't have time for a handsome, Fae-touched man.

After almost two centuries as the human chamberlain to the Fae's Summer Court, Darius Winterbourne is a man accustomed to getting his way. So when the Summer Queen tasks him with finding a witch to perform the annual rituals and strengthen the ancient warding magicks, he figures it should be easy. He doesn't expect Sabrina's hardheaded refusal, her untrained abilities, or his attraction to her. With less than a week to Beltane, he must gain Sabrina's trust before he loses his home, his position…and his heart.

COURTING THE DRAGON WIDOW
CLOUDBURST COLORADO, BOOK 6
SNEEK PEEK

Everyone has demons, but Lissandra's date might have it worse than most…

Lissandra Charforest is finally stepping back into the dating game after three decades of widowhood. Accepting a blind date, she travels to a small town in upstate New York to meet an eligible dragon bachelor. Too bad the guy seems determined to stand her up.

Denarrion Goldencoat wouldn't have agreed to a blind date with the Widow from Colorado if his father hadn't insisted. Happy being the perennial bachelor, he has no desire to settle down on one woman, much less one with kids already. Until he falls into the reservoir with her.

But everything's not as it seems. Beneath the quaint façade of Redfield, darkness and decay lurks to ensnare the unwary. When Lissandra discovers she's been lured to Redfield to kill a demon under the pretense of a courtship, she almost walks away. But the truth jeopardizes the life of her True Bonded mate, leaving her with one choice: Destroy the demon or die trying.

OTHER BOOKS BY SIOBHAN MUIR

Her Devoted Vampire
Queen Bitch of the Callowwood Pack
Second Chance Succubus
Darwin's Evolution
Wildfire's Heart

Bad Boys of Beta Squad Series
Bronco's Rough Ride
The Navy's Ghost
Rimshot's Hard Target
Bam-Bam's Inked Hart

Cloudburst Colorado Series
A Hell Hound's Fire
The Beltane Witch
Christmas I.C.E. Magic
Cloudburst Ice Magic
Cloudburst Coffee & Spa
Courting the Dragon Widow

Rifts Series
Take the Reins
A Centaur's Solstice Wish
In Death's Shadow

The Ivory Road
A Walk in the Sand
Outback Dreams

Triple Star Ranch Series
Rope a Falling Star
Star Light, Star Bright

Warbler Peninsula Series
Order of the Dragon
The Valkyrie's Sword
Burning Yuletide

Coming Soon
My Forever Cocky Biker Rebellion Encounter
Deli's Take Out (Bad Boys of Beta Squad #4)
Star Spangled Banner (Triple Star Ranch #3)

ABOUT THE AUTHOR

Siobhan Muir lives in Cheyenne, Wyoming, with her husband, two daughters, and a vegetarian cat she swears is a shape-shifter, though he's never shifted when she can see him. When not writing, she can be found looking down a microscope at fossil fox teeth, pursuing her other love, paleontology. An avid reader of science fiction/fantasy, her husband gave her a paranormal romance for Christmas one year, and she was hooked for good.

In previous lives, Siobhan has been an actor at the Colorado Renaissance Festival, a field geologist in the Aleutian Islands, and restored inter-planetary imagery at the USGS. She's hiked to the top of Mount St. Helens and to the bottom of Meteor Crater.

Siobhan writes kick-ass adventure with hot sex for men and women to enjoy. She believes in happily ever after, redemption, and communication, all of which you will find in her paranormal romance stories.

Connect with Siobhan online at:
https://www.siobhanmuir.com
https://www.facebook.com/siobhan.muir.35
https://twitter.com/SiobhanMuir
https://www.siobhanmuir.com/siobhans-blog
https://pinterest.com/siobhanmuir.35